PACT OF THE KEEPS:

DARKWING KEEP:

RETURN OF THE CLOUD GIANTS

SECOND BOOK IN THE
"PACT OF THE KEEPS" SERIES

AUTHORS: BK STAPLES & THEO MOON

DEDICATION

We would like to dedicate this book to anyone who has dreams and has the courage to chase them. To anyone that fights injustice in the world. Most importantly, to those that see family as the people connected by love and not only blood.

ACKNOWLEDGMENTS

RD Shull (Gavin Brokinhorn) assisted in the editing.

Brian Lee (Shamash) was also a tremendous help with early editing and constant re-reading and ideas. Also, our systems and communications coordinator.

Each person behind the characters gave me the backstory or history. We then incorporated it into the story and tried to capture each personality.

www.StaplesMoonBooks.com

StaplesMoonBooks@gmail.com

Introduction

A story about an eclectic family of friends' survival. Their trials and tribulations. Their fight to rid the continent of Alahora of a recent rash of dangerous enemies and monsters. They are a variety of races and beliefs, with their family histories being equally exciting and, in some cases, unimaginable to most.

Now that the team has saved the Blackwing Keep and Prayla from a Dark Wizard and his minions, the team must work together to find Lord Darkwing of Darkwing Keep. But unfortunately, their work is cut out for them because no one seems to know where the Cloud Giants reside.

Hasstad keep
FRANKEN
CRAONIA
Craonia Desert
King Wizards Keep
Oceanfalt
Fort Tristan
Starkening Keep
Emberfroat
Voskaola Mountains
VOSKAOLA
Deerbrook
Blackening Keep
PRAYLA
Ocean City
Tentathon
Prayla Town
OSCAIN
O'Malley Keep
Saldalt
Stagbrook
Jennat's Cave
Westsan Ocean
Dark Wizard
Leviathan Cave
Alahora

Map Legend
Dragon Temple
Cloud Giant Temple
Leviathan Fight
Keeps
Towns/City
Unknown Cave
Dragons
Dragon Temple
Stoania
Dragons Rest
Ning Grove
Fídernunf Keep
Riverbank
Styrt Marsh
Darkforest
Cliffshade Keep
Cliffshade Port
Cliffside
Astya
Nimbien Ocean
0   25mi   50mi

Table Of Contents

PROLOGUE
THE FIVE RACES OF GIANTS

Before the time of the modern races, Dragons and Giants ruled the world. There were five races of Giants: Frost, Cloud, Earth, Sea, and Magma. The Dragons and Giants had strong alliances and worked to keep each other safe from the foul Titans of the Dark Gods. The Titans' only purpose was to destroy any living creature and claim the world for their creators.

Many battles were fought against the Titans, and thousands of Giants and hundreds of Dragons lost their lives. With all their combined might, they could not defeat the Titans. In the last year of the Third Age of Giants, the Dragons of the world came together to use magic to create a weapon to use against the Titans. Their friends, the Giants, only stood a chance if the Dragons could unlock their inherent godly power. On top of the tallest mountain in their realm, the Dragons created a forge. They called the mountain Anvilhorn. This is where the

Dragons created the individual amulets for each race of the Giants.

Each amulet required seven Dragons of the same element to sacrifice themselves for the amulet to become imbued with the godly power they contained within. The Dragons presented the Kings of each race of the Giants with an amulet that enhanced their specific element. Now that the races of Giants had these weapons, they were able to defeat or imprison the Dark God's Titans. However, with most creatures that obtain awesome power, the Giants started to abuse the amulets. The world's Dragons were almost destroyed when they tried to retrieve the amulets. The Dragons were only able to retrieve two amulets: the Sea amulet and the Magma amulet. Many Dragons died, and those two races of Giants were destroyed beyond revival. Now only three races of Giants remained. The Dragons feared extinction, so they called for a truce with the remaining races of Giants. This is a crucial Peace Pact that remains to this day amongst the survivors.

The Frost, Cloud, and Earth Giants kept their respective amulets safeguarded for over a thousand years. Then at the turn of the new age, the Cloud Giants feared the emergence of the modern races and wanted all the amulets for themselves. They wanted to rule the lesser races with a firm hand. The

CHAPTER 1
THE AMULET

Slawomir slowly creeps up behind a rock and sees a huge, blue-skinned baby girl giggling, with short blonde hair and big ice blue eyes, grabbing at a dire bear trying to escape its cave. The child has no idea how dangerous her newfound toy is. He notches his bow with two arrows, a skill he learned long ago. If he hits, just right, one will go in the eye and the other in the neck. Either way, the attention of the dire bear will be off the girl. He lets the arrows fly, and as the dire bear turns on him, it starts to charge. With one arrow in the right eye and another in his neck, Slawomir lets loose two more. His aim is so good at this point in his life; the dire bear is now blinded, running simply on smell, roaring as loud as it can in anger. However, it is starting to slow and stumble.

The toddler girl is crying only because she is too young to realize the danger. All she knows is the toy is running away from her. Slawomir notches another arrow and lets it loose towards the dire bear's chest. As it flies, he drops the bow and pulls his sword. The arrow hits its mark so that the dire bear stumbles, falling on its chest, driving the arrow deeper. The dire bear slides to a stop. Slawomir checks the bear to ensure he is dead and does not suddenly attack again.

Slawomir puts his sword in its sheath and heads to the girl to calm her. As she sees him, her sobs start to stop, and she hiccups. This child is as big as he is, so he's wondering when her Giant parents will be showing up. They made enough racket to wake the dead between her and the dire bear. He wonders how far she wandered from her family.

He starts talking to her, and she coos; she giggles again in no time. But, of course, he's realized now that she is too young to talk, so there is no way to find out her name or anything.

He then feels the ground shake a bit, and he looks around. The little girl squeals, "Momma," as she reaches up to the woman that just walked up.

The female Earth Giant, he supposes for her size, is slender with long brown hair, green eyes, and tanned skin. She is dressed like a hunter, but her outfit is made of the finest silks. She is wearing thigh-high boots that would have taken at least four cattle each to make.

Slawomir looks at the Earth Giant, "Good Day, Ma'am. Your youngin here was trying to play with that dire bear over there. I will just take care of the dire bear." Then he starts to walk away.

The female Giant puts a foot in front of Slawomir, "Sir," she says in a loud but motherly voice. "Please give us a minute of your time." A male Giant walks up behind her, and she explains what Slawomir just told her.

This male Giant is glistening as if covered in frost. His skin is blue like the girls, but his hair is a bit redder. His tunic is white silk with blue pants. His boots are just standard boots, but his feet are so big it must have taken four cattle each to make.

He looks at Slawomir and then the dire bear. "Sir, I am King Iglis Frozenbolt. May I ask your name?"

Slawomir is dumbfounded. He is face to face with a Frost Giant King and Earth Giant Queen. But wait, that means the little girl is a Princess. "My name is Slawomir Darkwing, and it is a pleasure to meet you. I was hunting in the area when I heard this youngin of yours giggling. I think she thought that dire bear was a new play toy."

The little Princess giggles at Slawomir and pokes him in the tummy. Since now is not the time to play, she wants to play; her mother picks her up. "We owe him a tremendous debt for saving our little Princess, my husband."

"Slawomir, will you follow us to our camp. I will help you clean the dire bear, as I am sure you want the pelt and meat. I will take it with us." Iglis picks up the dire bear under his arm and starts to walk away. Slawomir must jog to keep up.

Soon they walk into a camp with about thirty Giants. Slawomir feels like the smallest man on the planet walking through this camp. The King hands the dire bear to one of his men, asks him to butcher it, and then points to Slawomir.

He continues to walk through the camp to a huge opulent tent. As they walk into the tent, King Iglis offers Slawomir a seat. Slawomir feels like a child climbing up into the chair, but he's tired from trying to keep up with them.

"Slawomir, that was no small dire bear, and even though the Princess is almost the same size, she is not of an age to protect herself. Nevertheless, my wife and I are so thankful for your intervention and protection of our daughter." The Queen comes from another room in the tent. "I am sorry, I did not introduce my wife, Queen Afa."

Slawomir slides off the chair and bows, "Pleased to meet you, your Majesty." Then climbs back into the chair. He can see the amusement in the King's face, not mean by any means, more appreciation of Slawomir's efforts to be respectful in the presence of royalty.

The King stands and walks to a workbench; he slides an ornate amulet from his neck and picks up a smaller child-sized one from the bench. He holds both in his hands and begins an incantation. His hand begins to glow blue and shake. He places the larger ornate amulet back around his neck and opens his hand as he leans over towards Slawomir.

The King shows him the amulet, "This will be one of the few times you should see this. I enchanted it just for you, but you will only use it in a time of dire need because touching it will freeze whoever takes it in their hand." There is a bright glow in the palm of his hand as the King puts the amulet in a wooden box. The King opens the box once more and shows it to Slawomir. "This is very powerful and will give the user the power of a Frost Giant for a short amount of time. However, it will also freeze them after use until removed with a tool and put back in the box. It is a one-time use but will still freeze anyone who touches it instantly after use. Do you understand?"

Slawomir thought for a second, "So if I need to use it against a Dragon, let's say; I will have your power for a short amount of time. Once that time runs out, it will freeze me solid until someone scoots it back in the box without touching it. Then if anyone after that touches it, they will just freeze instantly forever, is how I understand it."

The King nods and smiles, "Yes, you understand it perfectly. However, it would help if you kept this a secret because some will seek it for their own nefarious wants, needs, and power. So, this is my boon to you and your family; protect it and use it well."

Slawomir stands, "Thank you, your Majesty. It is a great honor."

"It is our honor because not every stranger in the forest would have faced down a dire bear just to save a child, especially alone. You have a special kind heart. Now let's have a meal before you leave; by then, Drift will have your dire bear meat and hide ready to travel."

After the meal, they walk out to see a stretcher rigged for Slawomir to pull the dire bear meat and hide home. Slawomir is a well-muscled man, but he is a bit concerned if he could pull this by himself. Drifter chuckles, "Little friend, I have enchanted it to make it lighter for you to get home; I figured you lived nearby, so you have two days."

Slawomir laughs, "My concern must have been written all over my face because I knew that it was at least a thousand-pound dire bear. I thank you for the assistance; it is greatly appreciated."

The King and Queen wish him safe travels, and the Princess giggles with a bit of a wave goodbye.

As Slawomir pulled the stretcher up to the house, he called for his wife and children. They gathered around as he uncovered the dire bear meat. "We need to get this prepared and preserved as soon as possible. After that, I will put the hide on the tanning rack. Hurry, Hurry. I have a story to tell you at dinner tonight."

Slawomir's wife, Evonnia, cut a chunk of meat off the dire bear to make stew. He can smell the bread baking. "Husband of mine, how did you get this dire bear cleaned and skinned, let alone dragging it home alone?"

With a smile on his face, Slawomir says, "That is the story I will tell at dinner, but at the moment, we don't want any of this to go to waste."

Drifter had done them a big favor by butchering it in the proper cuts, which allowed for appropriate preserving with no extra time. Finally, some of it was put in the smoker, and the fires stoked. The rest was salted and put in the underground cold room.

It took the rest of the afternoon to get the meat stored and the hide on the tanning rack with the first process done. Then, finally, the family gathers at the dinner table to hear their father tell of his adventure that day. He tells the entire story before putting the box with the amulet on the table. "This box is never to be opened or shown to anyone except in a time of great need." Slawomir opens the box. "No one is ever to touch this amulet unless we need to fight a Dragon that is a danger to our community or something worse than a Dragon. This amulet will freeze the person using it once the threat is passed. Someone must use a stick and slide it back into the box to save the person that uses it. You must always remember this, pass it down to each generation, and the rules are never to be broken. This is also never to be revealed to anyone outside of the family, not anyone. Do I make myself clear?"

As he looks from his wife to each child, they nod in earnest.

Over the years, the family would notice clouds roll through that were not natural. They would hover over the community and then move off. The family's Patriarch would keep everyone acting natural, knowing it was something drawn to the magic but not finding it. There were several close calls with strangers, including Cloud Giants, demanding that whatever was magical in the area be handed over. The Darkwing family always played ignorant to anything magic in the area, and of course, the community had no idea what the strangers were demanding.

When Skrymir Darkwing was the head of the household, a plague hit the community. So many people died, families were decimated. Survivors were moving away because the pain was too deep. Skrymir was sad and very angry at the world because he had lost everyone. His wife, his kids, his aunts and uncles, cousins were all gone, leaving him the last of the line. Because so many had died and moved away, keeping the magic amulet hidden was going to be more challenging.

It didn't take long for the odd clouds to pass through again, only this time they stopped right over Skrymir's house. He is furious, feeling harassed for no reason. Then a thought hits him like a rock. What if these beings caused the plague just to get to the amulet? He stomps over to the fireplace and pulls out the box. He will never allow them to have the amulet. He hears thumps outside his door as if something had just landed on the ground. Skrymir puts the amulet over his head and opens the door. He catches the sight of four Cloud Giants heading towards him. Not knowing how to use the amulet, Skrymir pushes his chest forward, hoping for something to will happen. Unfortunately, the Cloud Giants are still heading for him; the amulet senses a wave of fear and begins to vibrate. Darkwing yells, "Freeze these Giants!" A blue beam shoots from the amulet freezing each Giant in place.

He knows that more will come and realizes no one is around to help him remove the amulet, so he heads for a cave in the nearby forest. He knows he cannot allow them to take him when the amulet is frozen to his body. So, he runs as far into the cave as possible before he freezes solid, unaware of the events about to affect the entire region.

Earth and Frost Giants decided that they wanted to live peaceful lives and allow the newer races to develop on their own.

Not long after, the Cloud Giants engaged the Earth Giants in a bloody and torturous battle that lasted five years. In the end, the Cloud Giants defeated the Earth Giants. However, in secret, the Queen of the Earth Giants was able to be smuggled out of the realm and take refuge with the Frost Giants. The King of the Frost Giants and the Queen of the Earth Giants, sharing a common bond, fell in love and married. Now the Frost Giants had two Amulets of Power, and the Cloud Giants would not risk an encounter with them.

Today there is a tense peace between the Giant races, but the Cloud Giants grow ever greedier and will use any means necessary to get another amulet and become the greater power in the world. They have waited for their chance as the modern races of the world have grown stronger and mastered magic. With the help of sinister forces, they may be able to get what they desire most. Only time will tell.

CHAPTER 2
THE GREAT ERUPTION

Shortly after, Skrymir Darkwing disappears deep into the cave; the Cloud Giant King and his Cloud Giant Queen find his men frozen solid at the house door. He is enraged that his men are now permanently frozen; he rips the roof off the house, searching for the person bearing the amulet. But, instead, he sees the empty amulet box on the house floor and nothing else. He knows the amulet has now been used, and the user has left the area. His anger gets the better of him, and his magic starts to build to epic proportions. He digs deep for the old magic; the wind for miles around is churning, the ground is shaking to the point of creating huge rifts. Finally, the Cloud Giant King yells out in a thunderous voice, "Skrymir Darkwing, I know you have that amulet. Give it to me, and you may yet live!"

The Cloud Queen is just as angry as her plans have been thwarted as well as her husbands. She realizes she has the perfect weapon to exact her revenge. Years ago, she had a Dark Wizard, proficient in the ways of Rune magic, create a staff made from the heart of a Stone Dragon that would allow her to manipulate the earth and rock.

Reaching down deep, she focuses all her magic on the staff and starts raising the ground into the sky. Whoever has the amulet will be crushed by rock slabs jutting out of the earth, rockslides, trees toppling over as the mountain grows. As the mountain gets taller and more expansive, she cannot stop the power surging through the staff. The higher the peaks ascend, the more power the staff needs. She soon realizes the staff is taking her life essence and power. She looks at the staff and sees her arm turning to stone; the effect moves towards her body. She calls to her King, but as he tries to pry it from her hand, the staff knocks him several yards back away from her. As he reaches her again, she lets out a scream of anguish as her body turns to stone, cracks, and turns to dust. The staff falls to the ground and explodes, knocking out the Cloud Giant King. Cloud Giant soldiers rush to his aid and take him back to their kingdom.

Skrymir runs using the glow of the amulet to find his way to the back of the cave. Even this far back in the cave, he can hear the howl of the wind outside of the cave. A booming voice rattles him to his bones; it's as if the Cloud Giant is next to him. The Cloud Giant calls for him to give up the amulet in exchange for his life. The voice echoes over and over in his skull. Moments later, the ground starts to rumble and heave as the cave begins to collapse. Ice begins to envelop him, and he is stuck in place. Before he loses consciousness, he can see more ice buildup around him. He wonders if the amulet is protecting him from the falling rocks and debris. Finally, the earth opens up beneath him, and Skrymir falls into a deep crevasse as the mountain grows.

The mountain that was just a hill before now stretches from the ocean in the west to halfway across the continent. Many people and towns have disappeared due to the upheaval of the land. The Dwarves of the region had caverns and cities under the hills of Voskaola for thousands of years. They had to run to the surface as their underground world collapsed around them.

When the dust settled, the people who survived found that the plains, where they once had farms and ranches, had been destroyed by the formation of a gigantic mountain, and must rebuild. As it is called, the Great Eruption closed off most of the trade routes to the northern territory of Craonia and Oceanfalls. Over the next few years, the towns of Emberfrost and Deerbreach popped up in the mountains. Emberfrost is on the backside of the mountain. The community does mining due to all the metals that have been found after the creation of the mountain. Deerbreach is along the trade routes giving people a warm bed as they cross the mountain. The top of the mountain has developed a permafrost, thick ice caps across the entire top of the mountain.

Under the mountain, the Dwarves had to rebuild. Some were mad because they lost thousands of years of history and work. But most looked at it as a way to now expand up, out, and down. Building a giant Dwarven Empire that can be grander than ever before in their history. So, over the next sixty years, they created new grand halls, living quarters, dining halls, smith workshops, and storage rooms. They were digging ever deeper and expanding outward into the middle of the mountain.

A group of Dwarves working in the lower-level mines came upon a cavity in the ground that looked like a chunk of ice was stuck in it. Unfortunately, the ice block had to be removed as it did not fit their plans. It took them some time to remove it, and they were shocked to see a body inside it once they pulled the ice block up. Finding this body in ice was perplexing to the Dwarves. So, they took it to one of their mages. Myles Axiom, an old Dwarven mage, who was astonished at their find. He believes he knows who this is and why he was deep in the mountain. Many years ago, after the Great Eruption, the Cloud Giants were looking for someone they never found. They believed he had something they wanted, and it took a long time before they gave up. They terrorized everyone they came across throughout the mountain region. If this is the man they wanted, there might be a way to revive him. So, he had the men drag him to a smith shop and leave him by the forge fire. Of course, the smith was not happy, but he would not argue with the old mage.

After several hours the mage knew something was different with this ice because the ice block sitting near the forge should have completely melted. However, not even a quarter of it had melted; this puzzled the mage. So, the Dwarf asked the smiths if they could get the forge hotter. They looked at him as if he was crazy but started moving all metal items away from the forge and did what he asked. They noticed that the ice was still not melting.

Everyone left the room as it was too hot for any man to be in the room for long. That's when it came to the mage that this must be of a magical nature; therefore, only magic would be able to undo it. Not knowing the source of the magical ice, he would have to devise another way to release the occupant. After going back to his room and searching through old tomes, he came across a spell that just might work. He returns to the forge, and with a flick of the wrist, he extinguishes the forge flame. He walks up to the block of ice and begins the spell. The occupant begins to shimmer and then disappears. Next to the mage, a ball of light appears and begins to elongate. Poof! The occupant appears and falls to the ground. The teleportation spell the mage had found worked like a charm. The mage quickly realizes that the amulet around the man's neck must be the cause of the freezing, so he uses a simple levitation spell to move it from the man's neck. The man begins to wake.

Skrymir's eyes begin to open and take in his surroundings. "Where am I?"

The old mage looks at Skrymir, "Son, you are in the Durmond Dwarven Hearth Home under the

Voskaola Mountain that the Cloud Giants created. I assume you are the one they were angry at and tried to find or destroy in creating the mountain. What is your name? I am Myles Axiom."

Sitting up, Skrymir answers, "I am Skrymir Darkwing, a farmer. I will say, be sure to put that amulet in a box for safekeeping; it will freeze anyone who touches it now."

The mage looks around the forge, searching for a box to deposit the amulet. Finding one, Myles puts the amulet in the box and seals it. "Skrymir, let's get you a room, some food, and clean, dry clothes of some sort. Being Dwarves, I am not sure what we have for you in the way of clothes, but we will make something work till yours can be cleaned."

Skrymir can barely stand, weak from being in the ice. "May I ask if you have any idea of how long I was trapped in the ice?"

As Myles helps to steady Skrymir, "The Great Eruption was about sixty years ago, so I would imagine about that long."

"The Frost Giant Amulet must have protected me as well as freezing me."

Myles laughs, "I had a hell of a time getting you out of the ice. You were by the forge for almost a full day, and you were not melting. We had to heat the forges to extraordinary levels, which still didn't work. Our smiths are a bit angry that they lost a full day's work, but they will get over it. I believe that you are the reason we have a much larger Hearth Home than we could have dreamed of before."

Myles decided to share his rooms with Skrymir to keep an eye on him. The old mage was curious about the amulet. He realized quickly that Skrymir was clueless about the properties of the amulet.

Skrymir ate and slept a lot for the first couple of days as his body healed from the years of captivity. Then, Myles told him about the Great Eruption, which seemed to be caused due to his hiding from the Cloud Giants. He described that many had died, and new farms, ranches, and even towns were rebuilt. Skrymir felt guilty that his actions caused so much destruction and mayhem, but he knew deep inside, that at the time, there had been no other choice. He knew he could not let them find him or the amulet.

After a few weeks of living in the Dwarven City, Skrymir was tasked with helping in the gardens. Overlooking the gardens was a vast aqueduct area where the children liked to play. One day as he was walking around the gardens, he witnessed a child Dwarf falling off the ledge of the aqueduct. He runs and reaches out his hands to catch the child but knows he won't quite make it. Then, with his hands stretched, he sees a beam of ice shoot out, creating two thick rods mid-air that catches the child. He was worried that the ice would harm the child; he quickly grabbed him and put him on the ground. The rods fall to the ground and roll away.

Skrymir checks the child, "Are you ok? You aren't hurt, are you?"

The child giggles, "Can we do that again? That was fun."

Skrymir relaxes, "I don't think that would be a good idea, as I don't know how that happened to begin with."

A female Dwarf comes running over. "Oh, thank the Gods. I thought for sure Ruskin was going to break his neck. Thank you for saving my boy."

Skrymir replies, "It was nothing, ma'am; after all, boys will be boys."

After the woman and child leave, shock starts to set in. A hundred thoughts flood his mind making him dizzy. He needs to find Myles now. He was not a magic-user; he was a farmer. How was this even possible? What has happened to him during his "hibernation"? He heads back to his room.

It didn't take long for Myles to come hurrying into the room. Apparently, the story of Skrymir saving the child had spread like Dragonfire.

"Skrymir, I need to know if you were a magic-user before all this."

"Myles, I was a farmer. I am in total disbelief as to what happened out there. What has happened to me? What else can I do? Am I now a danger to others?"

Myles chuckles, "I suspect the amulet has changed you in many ways, and we need to find out just what you can do now. As for being a danger to others, yes, you could be however, after today, I think your enemies should run, and your friends will be safe. If you were dangerous, you would have encased the boy in ice instead of just catching him."

Skrymir replies, "My thoughts were to catch him before he hit the ground. But his mother was right; he would have bounced and may have broken his neck."

Myles nods, "I had my suspicions this entire time. I was just waiting to see if something manifested from you. Sixty years encased in ice and still alive, well, it's just about impossible. We need to check the Amulet to see what happened."

Myles goes over and retrieves the box and breaks the seal on it. He opens the box and sees the amulet still in the same state that it was when he put it in there. Having a hunch, he reaches in and grabs the amulet out of curiosity. Nothing happens and he turns his head to Skrymir with a puzzled look on his face, "I thought you said this would freeze anyone who touched it?"

Skrymir walks over to Myles and takes the amulet from his hand, "That was what I was told by my father and when I went into the cave and grabbed it, it froze me."

Myles scratches his beard and looks at the amulet, "It would seem that the amulet has no more power. That would explain why you have the powers that you have. They must have moved into you."

Over the next few months, the two would spend hours testing his abilities. At one point, they found he could produce never-melting ice cubes for drinks. Although Myles found this amusing, Skrymir found it a parlor trick. As his powers developed, he discovered the ability to wield lightning and blue-flamed fire that he could mix with his ice abilities. So, when he was bored and Myles asked for ice in his drink, he would sometimes add a little lightning to give the old man's heart a jolt. Likewise, the blue fire came in handy to light and warm the room and only consumed objects when he wanted them to.

Myles had him practicing the same combinations repeatedly, but he would ask for a variation every once in a while. The variations quite often brought out something new, shocking them both, sometimes quite literally.

Myles explained, "I know you are bored doing the same things repeatedly, but it is also an exercise in control. The more you use it, the more you control it and repeat the same power on command. When we add other variations, we learn more of your capabilities, thus expanding your knowledge and how to master it."

Skrymir replies, "I get it, I do, but I was not raised with this kind of thinking. It's like I died and was reborn someone else."

"In a way, Skrymir, you were. No one else would have survived being in ice. If it was not for the amulet giving you its power, I am sure it would have been a corpse I buried instead of a new magic-user I am training. It is quite an exciting turn of events when you think about it." Myles thinks a minute and asks, "Shall we try something new? You can encase things in ice, but can you undo it?"

Myles puts a chair in the middle of the room. He nods to Skrymir to freeze the chair. The chair becomes encased in ice. Myles nods again, "Now reverse your thoughts." He watches Skrymir concentrate on the chair. It didn't take long before the ice disappeared from the chair. "Good, now we know you can reverse the freeze. This means that even if you accidentally freeze someone or something, you can fix it, just don't leave someone frozen for too long."

Skrymir took another couple of months to train with the mage. He did things that would help the Dwarves with daily living. He converted four storage rooms into ice rooms, giving them a place to store meat all year, simply by coating the walls in ice. He and Myles watched to see if the ice would melt if he stayed away, and it never even gave a sign of starting to melt. He also made several crates of ice cubes because the Dwarves had gotten used to cold drinks all the time. Skrymir felt these were a few ways to repay them for their kindness and hospitality while he recovered. To him, it was nothing but, to the Dwarves, it was life-changing.

Finally, one day he decided it was time to leave, to find a new life for himself. He learned that everything he knew from his past was gone. When he had gone hunting a few times with the dwarves, he had figured out that his farm was somewhere under the mountain now. He had no prayer of even finding a few memories or heirlooms, except the amulet that had been his family's pride for generations. At this time, he takes the amulet from the box and puts it on, he vows never to take it off again.

CHAPTER 3
CAPTURED

High above the lands, Darkwing keeps struggling against the sphere that seems to have robbed him of his ability to use his powers. The last he knew; he was on Martyn's back. Whatever dislodged him struck him hard. Now he can only see flashes of light as the orb he is in flies to its destination. He keeps trying to reach out telepathically to Martyn or any flying beast that will listen, but he is sure his owls cannot keep up with the orb. Finally, after a short time, the orb comes to an abrupt stop, and Darkwing is slammed to one side. Now he can hear loud footsteps outside the churning cloud sphere. Voices begin to break through the silence but can't be understood. Then a familiar voice breaks through. "Skrymir, you have something I want."

"Yeah, I have something, but you won't want it. I can show you why you don't want it if you like. I am happy to oblige."

Four tendrils of light pierce the sphere and wrap around his arms and legs, rendering him unable to move. Next, the cloud walls of the sphere start to dissipate, revealing his captors. A Cloud Giant stands over him, and he is surrounded by four figures in dark robes holding the ends of each tendril of light. The sunlight shimmers on the Cloud Giants' bright alabaster skin, only dimmed by the wisps of mist that swirl around him.

Skrymir looks at his bonds, "How am I supposed to show you if you're going to keep me tied up?"

The Cloud Giant drops to one knee as a mystical wind spins around Skrymir, lifting him to eye level with the Giant King. The tendrils of light lengthen to accommodate the distance. "If I were to let you go, you would attack, and then I would have to destroy you. I, unfortunately, need you alive for the time being. I waited for the right time to take you. I have been watching you for years, and thanks to Evad, I know that you possess the essence of the Frost Amulet. Iglis was a fool to share that power with a lesser race. No matter now, I have a way to extract what I want.

Skrymir tries to struggle against the power of the wind and the light tendrils. It is of no use. He is stuck for the moment.

The Cloud Giant chuckles, "You can try all you want, but you are no match for the strength of King Cirus. My little Dark Wizards discovered a way to render your magical abilities inept, and I could crush you in an instant with my wind. If I didn't need you alive, I would gladly do it to avenge the death of my wife."

Skrymir stares down the Cloud Giant, "Good to know I am that important to you. My condolences about your wife, vengeance can be a double-edged sword, but it will be over my cold dead body that you ever get this power."

King Cirus states, "You might just get your wish at the end, but there is no easy way out for you now."

The King moves back, revealing a pillory-type trap. One that will keep his hands trapped above his shoulders and hold him around the neck. The four Dark Wizards pull him forward and secure him in the pillory. He again tries to break his way out, but to no avail.

Darkwing thinks to himself, 'They must have built it like Ghod's magical cuffs. Well, they will have to let me down at some point; I will just have to bide my time and hope the team gets here fast, that is if they can find me.'

King Cirus orders, "You four, go start preparing for the extraction."

One of the Dark Wizards states, "Sire, it will still take some time before we can start the extraction, as we are still searching for the Key."

King Cirus replies, "We have plenty of time to find the Key, the extraction ritual has to be perfect, and he is not going anywhere. Contact the other Dark Wizard leaders and ask where they are at in their search."

Skrymir is taking in his surroundings to familiarize himself to see if he can escape. He is currently held in a courtyard surrounded by individual conical mud homes. The homes look like they were whipped up from the ground with the wind. He cannot even twist around to see behind him, but the massive mud home in front of him must belong to the King.

Deep in the forest of Stonia, many miles north of Neg Grove, is an ancient Dragon Temple overgrown with greenery. It was used to worship and record the Dragon's histories and lineage in ancient times. Within the temple, reliefs are believed to depict a possible map of their homes in an ancient Dragon language. Several Dark Wizards are working by candlelight, copying the language, copying the map, and attempting to decipher the reliefs. However, their main focus is the history of when the Dragons created the Amulets of Power for the five races of Giants.

Their work is labor-intensive, with all the copying and the search to find the code that is the Key to everything recorded here.

The Dark Wizard Feron walks into the temple and proceeds to the chamber he has set up for himself, where he sees a Seeking Shard glowing. He moves to the Shard and waves a hand over it to receive the message.

"Leader Feron, King Cirus wants to know what progress has been made in finding the Key and deciphering the reliefs. We have Skrymir Darkwing captured and subdued. Time is of the essence now."

Feron replies, *"We are very close; I feel we will have it any day now. My spies have heard of an ancient tablet that comes directly from Anvilhorn. I will soon have it in my possession."* Waving his hand again sends the return message.

Now to send Evad a message. He waves his hand, and he closes his eyes, says the incantation aloud, "Seeking Shard of old, to and fro you go, take this message to Evad Chaos, to only him be told." The Shard Glows, *"You said you would have that Dragon by now. We need it as soon as possible; otherwise, King Cirus is going to blow our skins off."* Waving his hand again sends the message. He mutters to himself, "That half-pint Dark Wizard better be successful, or we are all doomed." Sauntering into the room where his minions are copying the reliefs, he bellows, "I want progress now! Slouchers will be dealt with harshly, so get moving! Where is the Spymaster?"

A tall, gangly Dark Elf slowly turns to look at Leader Feron. Then, he slowly makes his way across the room, "Yes, Master?"

Feron leans in and speaks quietly, "Have your spies obtained the Ancient Dragon Tablet?"

The Spymaster whispers, "The last I knew; they were trying to find a way into King Windu's collection room. From what we know, he has traps upon traps. Unfortunately, we have lost one spy already. So, we have hired a specialist to get us in."

Meh-Kola sits at a table in the back corner of a less than reputable tavern. She has a contact that she is supposed to meet for an assignment. She hopes it's an assassination, but based on their city, she figures she will be stealing something special. Whatever the job is, it must be something that no other race can successfully pull off. She fights the urge to preen while she waits. She has her wings to the wall, so they are not noticeable. After all, a Fenton is rare on this continent.

To most people, she looks just like any ordinary house cat. It is the wings and way of speaking that would give her away. She has bright ice blue eyes, short dark gray fur with vertical black stripes. Behind her shoulder blades are two black leathery wings. Her wings are onyx black and soft as fresh cow leather. She has a small row of black spikes following the length of her spine to her long Dragon-like tail. Her coloring helps her stay hidden in the shadows.

Meh-Kola notices a dumpy-looking man in a dark cloak come into the tavern. He lowers his hood and moves to the back of the room. He sits down at her table, "Shoo, kitty, shoo. I am meeting somebody here."

She says with a purr to her voice, "Oh great, he's insulting One now. Shoo, idiot, shoo; One is supposed to be meeting someone intelligent here."

Big and dumpy recoils in shock, stammering, "Uh, uh, I beg your pardon. I – I – was not informed I was meeting a cat."

"Well, One is not a cat, you oaf. One is a Fenton from Omoth and very dangerous, so you might want to stop insulting One soon, or you will find your eyes scratched out, and One will be gone. So, this is your last warning." Each word vibrates with a growling purr.

He decides to stop talking and hands Meh-Kola a sealed letter. She takes it and leaves the tavern, heading out of the alley, disappearing into the shadows. She opens the letter:

MK,

King Windu has an octagonal Dragon Tablet in his collection. We would like you to retrieve it for us. Unfortunately, his collection is in a heavily protected vault. You will receive payment once you deliver it to us outside the city at the Pigeon Perch Inn.

For the King

Meh-Kola burns the note, so there is no trace of it for someone to find. She does not need to check out the Castle beforehand. She can see traps, smell magic, and possesses a feline intuition. It's now time to head for the Castle by flying over the city. There is a sliver of a moon, so she shouldn't be seen. Finally, she sees an open window and quietly lands on the sill. Meh-Kola sniffs the air; the hall seems clear, so she lowers herself to the floor. Folding her wings tight to her back, she makes her way to the stairs leading down to the main level of the Castle. There are guards at the bottom of each flight of stairs. She decides to just glide down to the first floor, staying in the shadows against the wall. Landing silently, she ducks into a hallway that leads past the kitchen.

She can smell food and bread baking from the door to the left. The door to the right smells like books. She eyes the door at the end of the hall; it smells like magic. Approaching the door, she licks it. Just as she thought, a simple lock spell, they wouldn't suspect that someone with her unique ability would come around. She looks through the keyhole and blinks to the other side of the door. There is a dank smell below as she stands at the top of a staircase. She flies down the stairs, just in case one of the stairs has a trap. Most traps are set for those who must walk, so she can usually bypass them. However, she finds a trap at head or waist level on every flight of stairs, so she is still cautious.

After the seventh flight, there's another door with stronger magic. There's no keyhole to blink through this time, and anyone who would touch this door would become paralyzed instantly. Luckily, there is a small gap at the bottom of the door that she can see just enough to blink through. As she reappears on the other side, she hears a click that signals a trap; a dart flies into the door behind her. She wonders how the King gets through here to add to his collection. She knows there will be more traps as she gets closer to the vault.

She takes a few minutes to examine the hallway forward. Most are not looking for a flying thief, so she decides to stay as close to the ceiling as possible. Flying slowly, she spots a false floor, and as she looks closer, she sees a false ceiling. She thinks to herself, 'great, floor and ceiling spikes'. If she triggers this one, it is bound to set off an alarm of some sort. Then again, maybe not, as they would just find a corpse stuck in the spikes. If she triggers it and blinks through, they won't find anything. She finds various triggers along the wall and is amazed to see a light beams that just must be broken. She decides to fly under this one so that her wings don't accidentally knock off dust from the roof. She notices another beam about ankle level on the way through, so if he doesn't get you going in, he will get you leaving. What does this man have in this vault that requires this much security? She is almost to the door and smells a magic trap at the door. This one is the most powerful so far. However, the design flaw is that they didn't cover the keyhole. She lines herself up with the keyhole and blinks into the next room away from the door. If she was a wizard or warlock, she could just disarm the trap, so her blink works well for her.

As she looks around, she is amazed at the items the King has collected. She can smell several different and dangerous magic's in this one room. He has a treasure that a Dragon would envy. She sees the tablet propped up against rolled-up rugs lying on the ground. Putting the tablet in her unique magically stretchable bag that can hide many items larger than her, she looks around to see if anything interests her. Noticing more traps around the room she stays away from the rarer items. She grabs a handful of gold coins as a tip and blinks past the trap at the door again. Now that she knows the path, she is out of the Castle in minutes and headed to the Inn. She thinks to herself that she may have to visit that vault again.

She heads out of the city towards the rendezvous to meet with the next oaf that the Dark Wizards Guild sends her way. They are trying to conceal their identity, but she knows who they are. It's a short flight to the Inn and the night is clear and crisp. The days and nights are complete opposites in this part of the continent, blazing hot in the day and chilly at night. A sweet memory of her home in the Omoth Jungle flashes through her mind as she reaches the Inn.

Meh-Kola lands in a tree outside of the Pigeon Perch Inn. She sees a familiar warhorse tied at the post. She wonders if that is Runt's mount and what he would be doing at the Inn. She lowers down to look through the windows of the Inn. She sees a man with a black cape sitting at a table at the back of the room. Runt is at the bar; he is not relaxed having a drink; he is tense and pretending to drink. Well, since the cloaked man doesn't seem to know who he is meeting, she thinks she will talk to Runt first. Runt is from the Assassin's Guild, and she's a member. He is a tall Wood Elf with dark skin, long dark black hair, and coppery eyes. Being a Wood Elf, he can fade into any forest and disappear, which enhances his rogue and assassin abilities.

Most people believe that his name comes from something to do with his size; however, his actual name is Runtombulis. So, as most can imagine, he goes by Runt.

Meh-Kola goes into a full feline mode, sauntering in tail swishing, hips swinging, and sits down next to Runt. "Hello, old friend." She purrs in a low tone. "What brings you to this dump of an Inn?"

Runt looks at the Fenton, "I might ask you the same thing. I have heard of heists that told me you were around, and I know you will do just about anything for gold, but I wondered if I would run into you."

Meh-Kola purrs, "One goes where the wind or jobs takes One. It's because there are so few of us here on this continent that One lays low. One is a prize to some and worry when you hear about all the Dragonkin that keep disappearing that One might be of similar value."

Runt replies, "That's why I am here, following up on a job I had a few months back."

Meh-Kola puts a hand on Runt's back to keep up the show. "What do you know about ugly over there? One has noticed you were ready to pounce."

Runt does a low growl, "I don't pounce; that is one of your moves. He insulted my horse, and I am not in the mood for fools."

"Well, my friend, One must ask a favor. Leave the matter be. He owes One gold, and One can't have you harm him before he pays One."

Runt pays for his drink and looks at Meh-Kola, "Ok, but you will owe me for this; It's always gold before fun to you." Then, he stands and leaves the Inn.

Something tells Meh-Kola she hasn't seen the last of Runt. Shrugging her shoulders, she gets up, walks to the corner table, jumps into the chair, and sits.

The cloaked man is waving his hand at her, "Shoo, kitty, shoo. I am waiting for someone important."

With a growling purr, she says, "One doesn't know how any of you get anything done as you all seem to be a bunch of idiots. The last idiot almost got his eyes scratched out. After that, he got smart and quit talking. Do you have Ones' payment?"

He looks at her in disbelief but decides to keep quiet. Instead, he puts a bag of money on the table.

She growls again, "One guesses that you take me for an amateur, so One will take the artifact elsewhere." She starts to get up when she hears another bag land on the table. She pauses for a second and starts to take a step, and a third bag hits the table. "That is more like it." Meh-Kola sits back down at the table. Then, reaching to her waist, she pulls out the tablet under the top of the table.

The man's eyes bulge as he is going to ask where she had it hidden when he thought better of it. Then, Meh-Kola takes the three bags and puts them in her coin pouch, again under the table.

As she stands again, she looks at the man, "One would say it was a pleasure doing business with you, but your almost fatal mistake was trying to swindle One. So, One will be contacting your boss. If he ever wants One's services again, he will not send idiots like the two he sent tonight." She strides out the door and flies off on her long journey to the Assassin's Guild Headquarters.

The cloaked man comes out of the Inn. He climbs into the saddle of his horse and heads east towards the ancient Dragon Temple in Stonia, north of Neg Grove.

CHAPTER 4
GATHERING INTEL

It has been two days since Darkwing was kidnapped and whisked away to a place that only the Gods know where. Ishvet and Ordyn had found a few passages about the Cloud Giants and the Rise of the Voskaola Mountain in a tome, the day they returned from the battle. They have been living in the library ever since, trying to find more information. They did find some information on Cloud Giants, but it mainly referenced their powers and natural abilities, nothing about where they lived. Nothing they have read about the Great Eruption has been enlightening, except that the Cloud Giant King Cirus had a wife who died by catastrophic magic siphoning while the mountain rose. So, they believe the King has more than one reason to want Darkwing.

Mandrake and Vicar have been sending messages to Skip, who is still on the continent of Omoth in the port city of Vaile. So far, there has not been a lot of progress, but he thinks he can get word to the Frost Giants. They have told him to mention Skrymir Darkwing's name in his contact with the Frost Giants. Then, maybe, they will remember and send information or help. No one can remember ever hearing Darkwing's great-great-grandfathers name or if he ever mentioned the name of the Frost King or Earth Queen. That information would be of great help right now.

They also remembered Meh-Kola's an old friend from Omoth but finding her may be challenging. Mandrake seems to remember that she mentioned pulling a heist that involved the Giants before she left Omoth for Alahora. They hope to employ her resourcefulness to get any information to help them. They sent a message to Mystical Messengers because if anyone had a chance to find her, it would be them. They have a vague idea of her stomping grounds, so they sent that information and her description.

Greenbean has taken a big step in her life in an attempt to find out more information about Cloud Giants. However, she wishes she had paid more attention to her studies when she was young. She and Fab Ulous have enlisted the help of Hunter and Warrior to take her to her cousins at the Durmond Dwarven Hearth Home. She remembered that the old Dwarf mage, Myles Axiom, had been there for the Great Eruption and had saved Darkwing from his icy tomb.

When they arrived, she had to convince the sentries that she was the Greenbean from the Stonebritches Clan. Finally, her cousin, Ruskin, recognized her from the stories running through the family. But unfortunately, most thought it was some crazy rumor that got out of hand.

Greenbean was shocked that old Ruskin was the child Darkwing had saved all those years ago. She was even more surprised to find that old Myles was still alive. But, when they got to Myles' quarters, she could tell he was not well. However, he insisted on telling them the story of the Great Eruption, finding, and saving Darkwing, even some about his training. He gave them so much information but unfortunately, he didn't know where to find the Cloud Giants. No one at the Dwarven Hearth knew that most important information. Ruskin told them he would have it researched in their histories and send word if they found anything.

Greenbean and Fabby were back at Blackwing Keep by nightfall of the second day.

Akita spent the first day helping Shamash with Keep business. She checked on the status of the jail build, Ghod's work with upgrading the soldier's weapons, and a hundred other minor details. But unfortunately, she still had a Keep and a realm to run, no matter how urgently she wanted to help find her friend. She checked with Sham to see how Ben was doing and was pleased to hear he had great promise with the mounts. Greta let her know that the women loved his grandfather, and he was helping teach them about more than just weaving baskets.

Akita waits for Ordyn and Ishvet to complete the interrogation of the Dark Wizards' apprentices. On her way to see Annut, she wondered just how much these guys would know and if any of them were more than just worker bees. Her other thought was what to do with them once they had all the answers they could get. They couldn't set them free, couldn't let them use their magic on anything. But they did aid in the destruction of Prayla and were working for the man that ordered her uncle's death.

Akita lands on the ledge outside Annut's cave; she opens the door, steps in, and closes it behind her. Then, lighting a flame in her palm, she heads for Annut's eggs. She hears them restless in their shells as she walks through the cave. As she enters the cavern, she warmly greets each of the babies.

"Annut, my friend, we need to talk. I need to ask what you know about the Cloud Giants. I know you have been around for hundreds of years, so you know about the Great Eruption. Everyone is trying to find any information we can to get Darkwing back."

"Akita, the Giants and Dragons have a pact that goes back to the third age. We ruled together until the Titans became a major threat, then we bled together to defeat them. The Dragons made considerable sacrifices to create weapons for the Giants against the Titans. With the Titans defeated, some Giants started abusing their power. It was so bad that two races of Giants are no more, the Sea and Magma Giants, for instance. As a result, thousands of Giants and hundreds of Dragons perished. So, we had to agree to a Peace Pact to save us all, and the Dragons went into hiding. The

Dragons felt they had sacrificed too much at that point."

Akita inquires, "What were the weapons that were made?"

"The amulet that Frostbite wears was a Lesser Amulet of Power compared to the amulets made by the Dragons for the Giants. The Dragons used ancient magic back then, but it cannot be replicated, as there are not enough Dragons alive to do it."

Akita thinks a minute, "I understand the Peace Pact and the Amulets of Power. I know the Frost Giants and Earth Giants are united. I know that for many years the Cloud Giants have been hunting down Darkwing's amulet. But unfortunately, I don't know where to find any of these groups of Giants. Do you know or do any of the other Dragons know where the Cloud Giants live?"

"My friend, I will send word, asking each Dragon I speak to, to ask the question to the others. Hmmm. I was just wondering." Annut pauses to think, tapping a claw on the cave floor. "Ok, I will trust you and your team with this information. In the far north of Stonia, there is an ancient Dragon Temple. I have never been there myself, and I don't think anyone else has in thousands of years. It was said to have Dragon lineage and history carved into the walls. I also do not know if there is anything related to Giants there. It would probably be overgrown and hard to find, but you could try there. I know one thing. King Cirus of the Cloud Giants is dangerous and smart. He won't hurt Frostbite until whatever he has planned is complete. If it is King Cirus that has him."

Akita has another essential question. "This is going to take time to find Darkwing and free him. Before that, it may take us to Stonia and King Windu's Castle in Oceanfalls, and of course, to wherever the Cloud Giants have him. So, when are your eggs due to hatch? I do not want to be away or have you away when they hatch."

Annut chuckles in her deep Dragon way, "We have a little more time. One of the little ones wants you to find Frostbite for him first."

Akita thanks Annut for the information, "I will let you know when we start so you can listen in. We are meeting tonight to share all our information." Then, she says goodbye to the babies, heads out of the cave, and back to the Keep.

Ishvet and Ordyn step up to the first dungeon cell, with an apprentice hiding in the corner. The guard unlocks the gate and lets the two in but closes it behind them. There is a slight whimper from the prisoner.

Ishvet puts a hand on the prisoner, "What is your name?"

The prisoner chooses not to answer the question.

Ordyn crosses his arms and states loudly for all to hear, "Look, we can be nice, or we can be mean. Just know that your interrogator's families were killed because of your actions and your master's actions. So, your master is dead as well. So, we will have no issue taking you out here and now."

Ishvet cringes, "You really scared this one; he just messed himself." Moving arm's length away from him. "I will ask you again; what is your name?"

Whimpy answers, "Kor is my name. I was just his punching bag and gopher. I was too afraid to leave; as you know, he was dangerous." Ishvets ring did not glow.

Ordyn folds his arms and looks down at him, "What do you know about other Dark Wizards in the area?"

Kor looks at his feet, "I don't know about others in the area, but he had a Seeking Shard and was messaging somewhere in Stonia and someone on another continent or island or something." But, again, the ring did not glow.

Ishvet asks, "Can you give us a list of names?"

Kor nods, "No, Sir, I can't." He points in the direction of the other cells, still nodding to Ishvet.

Ishvet points to the other cells slowly while looking at Kor, trying to get him to let them know who they should question next. Kor nods at the third cell.

Ishvet and Ordyn walk out of the cell and wait for the guard to lock it. Then, they go to the cell that Kor indicated. The guard opens the cell door for them to enter.

Again, Ishvet puts a hand on the prisoner, "What is your name?"

With a growl, he states, "Get your grimy hand off me, you damn lizard."

Ordyn stands over him, staring down at the prisoner. "Ishvet, I think we have another fool for the ice block."

Ishvet applies pressure on the man's shoulder, "What is your name?"

This time they are met with silence.

Ordyn addresses Ishvet, "This one must be guilty of everything that his master was, therefore subject to the death sentence."

The prisoner remains stubborn, glaring at Ishvet and Ordyn, speaking loudly. "Unlike Kor, you will not get any information from me. I will deal with Kor later." There is a whimper across the jail.

Ordyn and Ishvet go to the next two cells to find the same stubborn attitude. As they walk into the last cell, the man faces the ground. Ishvet asks, "What is your name?"

"I am Tonda, and I am a friend of Kor." The ring does not glow. "The other three stubborn ones were our master's pets. They fought for his favor and did his important requests. So, I wouldn't put them on ice until you can get more out of them. Kor and I were like maids. We fetched his food, drink, emptied his chamber pot, mopped floors." Still, the ring did not glow.

Ordyn asks, "Do you or Kor have magic? If so, how much would you say?"

Tonda answers, "I think we would be considered intermediate wizards when compared to him, maybe. But we have nothing else to judge it against."

Ishvet and Ordyn look at each other and nod. Then, Ishvet states, "Thank you for your answers. We know you both were truthful. We will return to talk to you again."

As they leave the dungeon, Ishvet says to Ordyn, "We need to move Kor and Tonda. They will be in grave danger if the other three somehow get those cuffs off."

Ordyn agrees, "I think we should talk to Akita. We need to see if there is another way to suppress powers. They might be of use in other ways. In the meantime, let's have the guards move them to the storage rooms that we used when we needed more cells."

They head to Shamash's office to find Olek.

Rogue has been home for a couple of days now, pouring through his private library, trying to find anything on the Cloud Giants and Frost Giants. But unfortunately, he cannot remember ever doing a job for or against them in his long, illustrious career as an assassin and rogue. Still, he searches because Akita needs any information he can find. So, he's thinking he will have better luck visiting his old contacts to see if he can find a lead that way.

He's been thinking about the situation that he is in with Akita and the Blackbrew twins. If they did their due diligence when they left the Castle years ago, they talked to the guards, so who knows what description they have of the people going through the gates that night. After working with them and the team this last couple of weeks, he knows they will have been investigating this over the years. He knows this is his own fault because he didn't finish the job. He could have waited a day longer to be sure they were back at the Castle, but alas, he didn't, and now he has clean up to do.

While gathering a few supplies, he decides to drop in on his Assassin Guild. He hasn't been there in years, but he figures he can get some information there that might help him. At worst, he finds a patsy to send the twins after.

He leaves a note for his sister Midge and heads out to saddle Ransom. In no time, he is headed to a little village in the area of Neg Grove.

Gavin has been outside the cave for several days now. The Wyvern seems to leave her cave twice a day. The first day he was there, he watched her leave and tracked how long she was gone. The next time she left, he snuck to the mouth of the cave, careful not to touch anything. Peering in, he found a clutch of four eggs. After that, he eased his way out and back to his hiding spot. When the Wyvern returned, she went into the cave and peeked out again. Gavin could see she was sniffing the air and searching for something around the mouth of her cave.

On the second day, Momma Wyvern left for her morning hunt. Gavin and Blitz are set to spend another day hoping to speak telepathically to the Wyvern. Gavin hears a branch break, and it is a good size branch, by the sound it made. Blitz starts to sneak out to circle around the left of the sound. Gavin crouches, looking to see what is lurking behind the tall brush. Before he can see it, he can smell it. Blitz tells Gavin he sees what looks like a young cave troll, which can be more dangerous than a full-grown adult because they are as dumb as they are strong. Even a young troll can be ten-plus feet in height and beefy. This one is no exception; it's at least nine feet tall and muscular with long dark hair, greenish-brown skin, a large, elongated nose, small dark eyes, and a dirty ragged loincloth. It's headed straight for the cave entrance. The one thing they know is they cannot let the troll near the cave entrance, and they don't want other trolls coming to investigate anytime soon.

Gavin sends his magic through the ground, emerging roots to wrap around the troll's legs. The troll is caught off guard and is growling, trying to pull the roots away and snap them loose. Blitz runs in and bites at his hands, distracting the troll, while Gavin maneuvers around to let loose one of his power shots, rain of arrows, at the troll. Then, Blitz tells Gavin he is out of range, and Gavin lets it loose. The troll shrieks in pain as forty arrows rain down on him, piercing his body all at once. Gavin notches another arrow and sends it into the troll's heart. With this, the troll falls to the ground. Blitz moves in to make sure the troll is dead and then lets Gavin know. Gavin starts to figure out what to do with the body.

At that moment, the Momma Wyvern flies in and examines the situation, flying in a circle around the body. Then, landing beside it, she uses her hind leg to dig a big hole in the ground. Once the hole is big enough, she uses her claws to get the body into it. Then, she starts covering the body again. Gavin is impressed but doesn't move, and Blitz also just watches yet stays still.

Gavin looks at the momma and says aloud, "Your eggs are safe for now; however, we might want to move them if the family of that troll comes."

She looks at him, turns her head, and then looks at the cave. Then, she looks back to Gavin, expecting him to say more.

Gavin decides to throw out an idea to see how she reacts. "I know you can't safely move all the eggs at once by yourself. I can use a few of my blankets to rig up a soft, warm pouch to hold the eggs. You will be able to carry them far away." She looks at him and nods a little. "My last suggestion, if you will trust me, is that we will move you to my family farm, as my father has created Wyvern dens just for this purpose. We will help protect your eggs, and you can live there too. My friend has two Wyverns, Hunter, and Warrior, who will be glad to have you as a friend. Of course, I would have to ride you to show you the way, so we don't have to make so many stops."

Blitz nips at Gavin's ankles, a bit irritated with the idea. "Now Blitz, relax, you know this is what we do now for Akita. Don't be a brat, you are my baby." Blitz, then knocks into Gavin's leg almost knocking him down, with a low growl. "What don't you like the word Baby? Make up my mind, what do you want?"

The Momma Wyvern walks to the cave and looks at her eggs as if she is thinking about his offer. Gavin realizes that she may be worried about a trap. She is worried if her babies, when hatched, would be safe or slaves.

Gavin steps up next to the Momma, "I need to call you something until you can tell me your name. Until then, because you are a beautiful Sky-Blue Wyvern with White horns and trim, we should call you Skylar. You and your babies will be honored guests and hopefully be our friends. Maybe, my friend, Annut, can teach you to talk to me if we don't figure it out along the way. But then, you need to meet Akita; she will explain everything that should put your mind at ease."

Skylar swings her head to Gavin, gently nudging him. Then lays down with her wings around her eggs. Gavin isn't sure what her answer is. Was that a yes to make the pouch or a gentle nudge to get out of her cave? Nevertheless, Gavin decides to make the pouch and see how she reacts. He looks over his shoulder as he leaves the cave and says, "We may have a day before they come searching for a missing troll and find a fresh grave that leads to this cave."

Gavin goes to his hiding place and rolls out his blankets, looking at them. As he's sitting there, he wishes Annut wasn't so far away and that he had some way of getting a message to her. He would tell her that he needed assistance to get a Wyvern to talk to him and needed more blankets. He grabs a snack out of his bags to munch on while he thinks.

A strange voice enters his head; it gurgles strangely, "Who is this that can talk like Dragons? Who is this that knows Annut – The Fast, and wishes to speak with her? Identify yourself before I send her to kill you."

Gavin jumps, thinking to himself, 'that was not Annut.' "Is this another Dragon or a Wyvern?"

The voice seems to respond, "I am asking the questions here, and I expect an answer now."

'By the Gods, it is another Dragon.' Finally, he decides to answer its questions. "I am Gavin, and I have met Annut. She is the friend of my Ruler, High Duchess Akita Blackwing. Annut is our friend; she has helped us destroy two Leviathans. If you can reach Annut from here, she knows I am on a mission to find Wyverns and invite them to our realm. I need someone from the Keep to assist me."

The voice growls, "So you say stranger, but why should I take your word for it. You must answer this, what is Annut's most precious treasure?"

Gavin chuckles, "Oh, I know, but not many others do, and we do not want the world to know. So, therefore, I will answer you in a riddle. "Giant Oysters would be jealous of her treasure but not in a million years could they bring the same joy. However, isn't it enough that I can speak to you. I mean, how many other people have you spoken to in your life."

The voice speaks again, "You make good points. I will contact Annut and let her know where you are. But, if danger comes your way, I will not be able to assist you. I cannot risk being discovered."

Gavin heads out to find the troll tracks and hide them, so his clan doesn't track him to this area. Grabbing a bunch of branches with leaves, he erases the troll's tracks for several miles. How fortunate that the troll walked in a circle at some point; it will help confuse anyone looking for him.

When he returns to Skylar, he tells her about his conversation and that he hid the trail the troll took to get to her cave. "If you wouldn't mind, Skylar, I would like to move my things here just inside the cave so that Blitz and I can better help you protect your eggs."

Skylar looks at him again and gives a gentle nod. So, he quickly moves his things, keeping distance from the eggs and yet still being where he can easily be of assistance.

Skrymir struggles against his magical bonds. He can still feel his magical power inside, but he can't get it to come out. He doesn't know how many days it's been since he was knocked off of Martyn and brought here, but it seems like a fading memory now. He needs to escape because he knows that he will be destroyed when they have what King Cirus wants.

The Dark Wizard lackeys have been giving him water and cold oatmeal once a day when the sun is the highest in the sky. He's tried talking to them, but they won't respond. He thought that maybe he could make a deal with one to aid in his escape, but no takers yet. Once again, they come with water and oats. Just enough to keep him alive. What is this the third time? So, has it been three days?

A different Cloud Giant approaches after being fed and watered like chained livestock. The Giant kneels and whispers to Skrymir. "Not all of us agree with King Cirus; when you give him what he wants, we will try to help you."

Skrymir looks up, "You really think that is going to work on me? I know how to play good soldier, bad soldier. It's not happening to me. Tell your king he's not getting what I was given."

The Cloud Giant stands and walks away. Skrymir again struggles against his pillory, and he can feel something different now. Small crystals of frost begin emanating from his wrists into the pillory. The magic bonds must be weakening against his struggles. Maybe he can freeze and break them before they come back to feed him tomorrow?

CHAPTER 5
SHARING INTEL

Akita is headed to the dining room when Annut contacts her. "I just had a message from an old friend that hides except when feeding. He says he has word from Gavin and that he needs help moving a Wyvern mom and her eggs as soon as possible. He needs something to carry the eggs."

"Oh my, well, I can send Hunter and Warrior to them. Tell them where they need to go." So, Akita flies by Greenbean on her way through the hall to find Sham. Then, she finds him and Ben with the twins' warhorses.

Sham sees Lady Blackwing flying towards him, "Lady Blackwing, what can I help you with?"

"Sham sends Ben for as many sheep's wool blankets or piles of sheep's wool as he can carry. Then, have him bring them to the cage. Next, you grab several ropes and follow me."

Akita goes to the cage and starts helping Sham weave the ropes through the cage bars. "We don't want any big holes. We need to make it so that a Wyvern egg cannot slip through."

Ben comes running back with wool blankets and bundles of wool. "Put them in the cage, Ben, and go get more. I want this thing half full. Tell any two guards you see along the way that I said to help you bring me wool blankets. Run!" Ben takes off running through the Keep.

Akita jumps in the cage to lay out the blankets and spread the wool over them. "I'll be right back, Sham." Akita flies out to Hunter and Warrior.

Akita fills her pets in, "Boy's, I need you to take one of the cages to Gavin. He will place Wyvern eggs in it to be carried back to his family's farm. Apparently, they are in danger, so fly as fast as you can. The mother is there too, so make her feel comfortable, reassure her she is safe with us."

Warrior replies, "Not to worry; we just wonder where her mate is. Does she not talk to Gavin?"

"I don't know, Warrior. Gavin was talking to a Dragon we didn't know about. But unfortunately, that Dragon has gone back into hiding. We will have the cage ready in a few minutes. Let's go."

Akita flies back to the cage to check the ropes and rearrange the wool. "Sham, one more rope in that corner, please."

Ben and the guards run up with a wagon full of unprocessed wool and help Akita load it into the cage. The cage is now a huge nest for the Wyvern eggs and ready for flight.

"Warrior, Hunter, Tell Gavin we will meet you all in about eleven hours at his dad's farm. Fly." Warrior takes the cage, and they take off toward Salthall.

"Thank you, Sham, and Ben. Unfortunately, I must get back to the dining hall. Have a good evening." Akita flies into the grand hall to the dining room.

She lands next to her chair and has a seat. "Well, the good news is Gavin found a clutch and mother Wyvern. So, Hunter and Warrior are taking him to one of the cages padded with wool to carry the eggs to his dad's farm. The interesting news is another Dragon relayed his message to Annut; she says he is in hiding and prefers not to get involved; it is too risky for him."

Greenbean asks, "Where is Gavin that he has another Dragon near him?"

Akita replied, "Gavin is on the Oscain and Stonia border. So, basically, near Grace's backyard."

Grace looks up, "News to me. I just hope no one else knows about him at this point."

Akita looks at the group, "So, let's go around the table and see what information we have to work with." She looks to her right at Greenbean.

Greenbean and Fab Ulous tell them the story of Myles Axiom's experience of the Great Eruption as well saving and training Darkwing. "We are confused how the Cloud Giants have suppressed his magic when it is not like any of the other's magic in this room," Fabby says in passing.

Mandrake explains that Skip is trying to get a message to the Frost Giants to see what he can find out and if they can help. But unfortunately, they have not heard from Meh-Kola yet.

Ghod explains that he is almost done with the upgraded weapons for the army. "Fabby has a point. I am not sure if my cuffs would work on him. Darkwing's magic comes from a different place than other beings I've dealt with. The runes I put into the cuffs can muffle a magic user's aura; therefore, they cannot cast magic. Darkwing gained his magic ability from a relic, and it doesn't come from a magical aura. So, not knowing what they are using to suppress his magic, he might be able to find a way around the suppression."

Akita looks to Ghod, "We can only hope he can find a way to free himself, but I think we can all agree he will need all of us to escape. So, Ishvet and Ordyn, what did you find in the library or from our prisoners?"

Ishvet explains, "Out of the five Dark Wizard fledglings, we have two that are cooperating. The other three seem to be of higher ranks and won't talk. We will be using harsher techniques to acquire information from them in the near future. However, our main focus is locating Darkwing and getting him back as soon as possible."

Ordyn holds up the book, "The Great Eruption book has nothing different from what Greenbean just told us, and her story is from the person that lived it. As for the Frost Giant book, it only gives theories, but Skip should find King Iglis, I believe. According to the book, he was the King at the time and probably still is."

Vicar replies, "Yes, we have needed names. Does anyone know Darkwing's great-great-grandfather's name? We have given Skip the only name we do have, Skrymir Darkwing."

Fab Ulous speaks up. "Myles at one point said a name, but I thought he was just having a memory issue. Instead of saying Skrymir, he said Slawomir;

maybe that wasn't a slip of thought. It's worth a try, Vicar."

Mandrake and Vicar look at each other, nod, then nod to Fabby.

Akita looks at Vivian, "Vivian, Annut tells me there is an ancient overgrown Dragon Temple in the northwest area of Stonia. Do you know anything about it?"

Vivian answers, "I know where it is. There is a town and Paladin training area in the vicinity. I went there once as I was hoping to find a Dragon tending the temple. Unfortunately, it is overgrown, but the right magic could clear it quickly, or a small team of soldiers would take a few weeks."

Akita's interest is piqued, "Do you think we could ask your father to have some soldiers fly over and check it out?"

Vivian nods, "We have Griffin patrols, so yeah, I can send him a message. First, I will ask him if he knows anything about Cloud Giants. Then, I will send him a small summary of what is going on and that we would appreciate an answer fast."

Akita looks to Shamash, "Can you assist her in getting the message out? Also, what is the latest on getting a Seeking Shard here at the Keep?"

Shamash replies, "Our little messenger, Alican, will be here soon, so if everyone has the messages at my office, we will get them out. She comes here twice a day normally. As for the Seeking Shard, I am trying to find one, but it's not like a store in every town sells them. However, I am awaiting word from Mystical Messengers to see where we can get one."

Akita looks to her newest friend, "Wulf Wari, I hope you are finding your stay and time to heal here comfortable. Unfortunately, I have not had a chance to sit down and get to know you better, but I think you can ascertain that we have a serious issue going on. I would be grateful if you had any information on any of the subjects you have heard us talk about, the Great Eruption, Frost Giants, Cloud Giants, or even where to find Wyverns."

Wulf Wari rubs his chin while thinking, "Sorry, I am still getting used to names, but" he points at Mandrake and Vicar, "their friend is on the right track to contacting the Frost Giants. King Iglis is known to be fair, and his wife, Queen Afa, is known for helping farmers with their crops."

Mandrake asks, "Do you know the Frost Giants? Because I was thinking a message from a friend would probably get through versus a message from a stranger looking for information."

Wulf replies, "I have met the King a couple of times. Let's sit down and put the message together and send it to me, as I don't know all the details. The whirlwind path that the Gods have me on seems righteous. My next stop was in Oscain, but that can wait until I have helped you in whatever way I can."

Akita looks at the group, "When I went to visit Annut, she told me about the history between the Dragons and the five races of Giants. They were in an alliance to fight the Titans. Most of us learned that growing up. Some may not know that the Dragons sacrificed a lot to create the Amulets of Power for each race of Giant. As we know, power can corrupt even those with the best intentions. After the Titans were defeated, some Giant rulers abused their power, so the Dragons tried to retrieve the amulets. The battles with the Sea and Magma Giants were so horrific that those races no longer exist, and that's why Dragons are so scarce.

The Cloud Giants are the issue now. They want all the amulets for themselves as they look at the youngest races of the world as a threat. The Cloud Giants are why there is only one Earth Giant left, Queen Afa. The amulet Darkwing wears was created from King Iglis' Frost Giant Amulet. The Cloud Giants hunted the Darkwing family and caused the Great Eruption to use it to get the last two amulets. The sad part is that we still don't know where the Cloud Giants are with all this information."

Shamash stands up, "Wulf, Mandrake, Vicar, and Vivian, let's go get those messages written and sent off. I am hoping to have a word about the Seeking Shard as well. Good evening, everyone." The five leave the room.

Ordyn addresses Akita, "So you know, we have separated the two Dark Wizards to one of the rooms created for the traitors. We didn't want the three 'tough guys' somehow getting to the two that were more cooperative. They are 'supposedly' making lists of anything they know. I don't trust them either, but I suggest we protect them for as long as they cooperate. The other three can rot in their cells until we are ready to dispose of them. We are headed to see what information they have given us."

Akita agrees, "Excellent idea. My question is, are the other three worth our time? Can we work on one that will break faster than the others? Or, if we break the toughest one, will one of the other two start talking?"

Ordyn does his Dragonkin smile, "That is what we will be finding out, depending on time and when we leave to rescue Darkwing. They might have to wait a while in that cold dark dungeon." Ordyn chuckles. "I really don't like being mean and vicious, but when they resort to putting down my race, well, then all bets are off. With that said, the majority of the population of this world are not like these three Dark Wizards, the Major or the Lieutenant. It's a small minority of people that have to act stupid when you think about it."

"You are so right, Ordyn. Let me know what you find. I am going to take a long hot, soaking bath, as I have a feeling, we are going to get busy soon." Patting Ordyn and Ishvet on the shoulder, she heads out of the room.

Gavin and Blitz have kept watch for many hours. The mother Wyvern has not left the cave since the Troll incident.

Warrior reaches out to Gavin as soon as they are in the vicinity, "Gavin, where are you? We are here, it's Hunter and Warrior, but we can't figure out where you are."

Gavin stands quickly and moves out of the cave, looking into the sky. "I don't see you yet." Gavin flies into the air, straight up from the cave entrance. He spots them in the distance. "Turn to your right and fly straight to me."

"We see you; we are trying to talk to the mother. Be there soon."

Gavin lands and starts packing up his few belongings. The mother stands and walks out of the cave, keeping her back to the eggs in a defensive stance.

Gavin walks up to her, "Skylar, you and your babies are ok. Hunter and Warrior are here to help." He looks around to ensure she doesn't see or hear something other than the Wyverns.

Warrior sets the cage down in front of the cave as Hunter dives past. Warrior follows, as does the mother. Gavin grabs his bow and knocks an arrow but stays in front of the cave. He sees the Wyverns flaming at a target just out of his vision range.

Gavin reaches out to Warrior, "What are you attacking?"

Warrior answers, "Giant Spider. Almost dead. We didn't need it coming to the cave while helping to load eggs."

Gavin sees three more spouts of flame, one from each Wyvern. Then, they spin around and head back to the cave.

Warrior explains to Gavin, "She now understands fully what you were trying to make her understand. Her mate left many weeks ago, and she doesn't know if he is coming back. She likes the name you chose to use, but her name is Alura."

"Nice to meet you, Alura. Can we start moving your eggs to a safe home now? Giant spiders and trolls in one day make me a bit nervous, only because we had a Basilisk show up at Blackwing Keep not long ago. It's dead, but they like eggs, as you know."

Hunter answers, "Yes, you can move them now. She has decided we are safe."

Gavin unties a few ropes to allow him to slide the eggs into the cage easily. He moves to the eggs, looks at Alura, then slowly picks one up. "Good thing these aren't Dragon eggs, or I wouldn't be picking them up." He waddles one over to the cage and gently sets it on the wool padding. Then climbs in and moves it to the far side of the cage. Alura nods approval. He repeats this until all the eggs are in the cage then reties the ropes to cover the openings.

Gavin looks at Blitz, "I know you aren't going to like this because you hate it when I have to carry you anywhere while flying, but I need you to help keep the eggs warm and warn me if they move at all."

Blitz glares at him and stomps his paws but relents and jumps into the cage.

Gavin then looks at Alura, "Do you want to carry the cage, or should Warrior since he is used to it?"

Warrior answers, "She will carry the cage; I will carry you unless you want to ride Hunter. I have explained to her the balancing."

"I don't suppose there is any chance of you teaching her to talk to me. Or does Annut have to be here?"

Hunter replies, "We are trying to teach her, but I think her fear for her babies is what's on her mind. Either way, Annut will be there with Akita when we get to your dad's farm."

Gavin, after putting his things in the cage, he climbs up to ride Warrior, "Let's go!

Akita is startled from a deep sleep by a loud crash in her room. She jumps up, grabbing her sword as she gets in a defensive position. Shamash pushes through her bedroom door. "Holy smokes, Shamash, you scared me and almost got yourself killed."

Huffing and puffing from the long run to her room Shamash finally gets words out, "Akita, the craziest thing just happened! [deep breath] a quill I received a month ago stood up on my desk and started writing a message to you. [another deep breath] I can't remember who sent it to me, but the message is from King Windu. He says he knows where the Cloud Giants live, but we will need many preparations to get there. So, he says to come to Port Tristan, and he will meet you there. [large exhale] Shamash plops into the chair next to Akitas writing desk and melts into an exhausted lump.

Vicar steps into the room from where he was sleeping on the couch, "I was going to stop him, but the look on his face said not to. It says something when Shamash comes running through a room with eyes as big as dinner plates. So, I'll get everyone up, and we can meet in the Great Hall to decide who's going."

Akita lowers her sword, "Great, just give me a moment to get changed. We need to act on this quickly." She then goes over to Shamash, "Should I let you rest, or will you be meeting us in the Great Hall?"

Shamash looks up, "Yes, yes, but you should have seen it, Akita; it stood up on its own. I thought I had a ghost! Then it wrote your name! I was about to run screaming from my office when I saw that it said Cloud Giants."

Akita ponders aloud, "Well, that is convenient that King Windu can send us a message like that, but I wonder if it works in reverse. I need to let him know that we will be there when my boys return from their mission. Shamash, meet me in your office; I will be there in a minute."

Shamash struggles and finally gets himself out of the chair to slowly head to his office. Akita quickly dresses. She flies down the hall and the stairs passing several startled and sleepy people. Finally, she catches up to Shamash at his office door.

Shamash goes to his desk, pointing at the quill, "That's the quill. But I tell you, it writes on its own. So, I am not touching it; you can if you want to."

Akita takes another piece of parchment and slowly picks up the quill. "I am going to see if this works in reverse." She uses the quill to write:

King Windu,

We received your message. You scared my Cleric half to death. We will leave Prayla's Port tomorrow. Is there anything specific we should know or bring?

Akita

She takes another fresh sheet of parchment and lays the quill on it. Shamash and Akita watch the quill for several minutes. Akita was beginning to think it was a one-way message. Slowly the quill starts to vibrate and slide towards the top of the parchment. Once it's at the top, it stands abruptly, and Shamash practically jumps out of his skin.

Akita Giggles, "We are definitely packing this for the trip." Akita watches the quill move across the page on its own. It is a sight to behold. Akita could understand how this would have been distressing for someone who didn't know it was coming. However, it was actually quite beautiful how the quill danced across the parchment, like a tiny dancer.

Akita,

Sorry, Shamash; you would think he would be used to magical items. Unfortunately, it will take me two days to get there due to my schedule. So, I am not sure what you will need at this moment.

King Windu

Akita picks up the quill and the notes to take them to the Great Hall. "Shamash, let's go fill everyone in so they can pack and get the ship ready to sail." Shamash nods and follows Akita out of the office.

As they enter the great hall, you would expect to see half-asleep people, but all seem wide awake as they all turn in anticipation.

Akita sighs, "We have word from King Windu. He wants us to meet him at Port Tristan, as he knows where the Cloud Giants can be found. Grace, can we get your assistance to get the team to Port Tristan? I will follow with Gavin on Hunter and Warrior."

Grace replies, "We can start loading up now. I will roust my crew and have them go straight to the ship. You all follow as soon as you can. I can take the horses and that lion, but anything bigger will have to fly anyway."

Shamash and Akita await more comments from Grace about the cost of the ship and the crew.

Grace continues, "We will have to wait for morning to get provisions, like food and water, for mounts and people."

Akita nods, "Is there anything else we will need?"

"No, I think I have the rest covered."

Akita looks to Mandrake, "In the morning, please make arrangements for the food and water for all. If you think of anything else, make sure you have it. I will catch up to you all."

Akita looks to Vivian and Wulf. "If you need supplies for travel, get them from the storerooms below: bedrolls, gear, and anything else you might need. Any of us can tell you where to find it or take you to it at this point.

Akita looks specifically at Wulf, "When the Dark Wizard took you, did you have a sword on you or blade of some sort?"

Wulf answers, "No, actually, I assumed my magic would cover my needs here."

Ghod steps up next to Wulf, "I've been woken up, so someone better make use of it. Come with me to the forge. I might have something already made that will benefit you." Ghod turns to leave, and Akita shoos Wulf after him.

Akita searches for Greta, "Greta is Vivian's armor fixed and polished?

Greta steps up, "Yes, Akita, the armorers finished it just today. I will have it to her before she leaves the Keep."

Akita states, "Let's go get our friend." So, everyone splits off in all directions to get packed. "Shamash, at dawn, I will have Annut take me to the farm, but I am not asking her to go with us to the Cloud Giants. I don't know how long we will be gone, and she has her eggs to tend. So, I am going to get some more sleep; the others can sleep on the ship."

"Safe travels; I am going to bed. Send me messages as you can." Shamash heads to his room.

CHAPTER 6
KING WINDU

As the sun comes up, Mandrake and Grace are securing provisions for the ship. They should be underway in a couple of hours.

Akita flies to Annut's cave, but she flies around through the front cave entrance this time. Again, it's something no one would have dreamed of doing before. As she lands, Annut is backing up from tending the eggs.

"Akita, I was awoken this morning when you nearly jumped out of your skin from a dead sleep. Shamash made quite an entrance; apparently, Vicar didn't even get him stopped."

"Yes, Shamash was overly excited and, shall we say, freaked out at the same time. But then you know I need to go welcome the new mother and eggs at Gavin's farm. Would you be so kind as to take me? Also, can you contact Hunter or Warrior from here? Gavin's fox Blitz needs to head as fast as he can to Grace's ship. He can't be running over or around the Voskaola mountains to get to us, and I don't think riding with Gavin on Hunter would be good."

Annut kneels so that Akita can climb on. "I will also tell Mandrake to await the fox. There should be plenty of time." Annut effortlessly steps out of the cave, dropping fast until her wings unfurl to glide out over the ocean and back to the port. "Mandrake says they will wait, and Blitz is on his way. We will be at the farm in a few minutes."

As they fly over the city, Akita sees Blitz running through the back alleys of Prayla, headed to the ship. Looking back inland, she sees a large patch of sky blue in the middle of a meadow next to a farm structure. "Annut, that sky blue object over there must be the mother Wyvern."

"Yes, she is a bit panicked, so I am already talking to her. Her name is Alura." Annut starts to land next to Alura. Gavin is waving, and his dad is in awe over the fact that Annut just landed at his farm. Unfortunately, he will have to go round up his cattle again, but he would have to do that with the arrival of the three Wyverns anyway.

Akita slides down Annut's leg and heads to Alura. "Oh, you are a pretty lady; nice to meet you, Alura; I am Akita." Alura gives a gentle nod. "I take it she is not communicating yet. It might take some time; I can imagine this is all a bit of a shock to her. Alura, I am just going to have a look at your eggs. I found Hunter and Warrior already hatched but orphaned years ago." She notices these are more like traditional eggs when compared to Annut's round pearl-like spheres. She reaches out to touch one; there is an ever so slight vibration but not as animated as the Dragon eggs.

Akita states, "Alura, I am thinking you laid these eggs recently and that we still have quite a while until they hatch."

Blue looks at Akita, "How do you know that it will be a while before they hatch?"

Akita replies, "Eggs close to hatching give off an energy and will almost talk to you. The closer to hatching, the louder they get. These are just slightly vibrating when you touch them."

Alura nods. Annut answers to all, "She only laid them a few weeks ago. Her mate, who would have helped guard them, disappeared. She is worried but is also grateful for the help. She didn't want to lose her first clutch to trolls or anything else."

Akita walks up to Alura and rubs her snout and cheeks, "You no longer have to worry about losing your eggs to enemies. We will do all we can to help you. However, Blue and his wife Rose will help you, and Annut will check on you. If you are going to hunt, please go away from the farms. Gavin and I have to take Hunter and Warrior with us to save a friend."

Gavin looks at Akita, "What is going on? I was wondering why Blitz was summoned to Grace's ship."

Akita responds, "Just before we fought the Dark Wizards, the Cloud Giants kidnapped Darkwing right off the back of Martyn. We have spent the last few days trying to find out where the Cloud Giants are. Last night we got word from King Windu to meet at Port Tristan. Everyone is on the ship except us because the Wyverns are too big for the ship. We will meet them there."

Gavin looks shocked. "Never a dull moment with you is there?" He chuckles. "But, how in the name of the Gods, did he not Perma-freeze them before they took him away."

"Gavin, all we can figure is that they suppressed his powers like Ghod's cuffs due to the Dark Wizards. So, I will fill you in on all that happened on our way to the port. But, first, I must stop at the Keep and grab my packed bags. If you need anything, we can get it from the storage rooms." She climbs up onto Warrior. "And we are getting their saddles for this trip."

Gavin grabs his bags and climbs up onto Hunter. "Sounds good to me. Whenever you're ready."

"Alura, relax, we will see you soon. Annut, thank you as always for your assistance. As for you, Blue, good farming." Warrior and Akita launch with Hunter and Gavin right behind her, headed for Blackwing Keep. They see that the ship is still in the harbor as they fly by the town.

Grabbing the items needed for the trip, Akita and Gavin are ready to fly in just a few minutes. As they fly over the sea, Akita has Warrior tell Mandrake they are going over the mountain and stopping at Darkwing Keep. With that, Warrior and Hunter spin around and head towards the mountain.

Flying straight up and over the mountain is the coldest and fastest trip. Gavin and Akita are hunkered down against the bodies of Hunter and Warrior as they fly up the mountain because the Wyvern bodies radiate heat. It's been several hours of flying, and Akita knows they are almost to the

Darkwing Keep. She's not sure if there is any information to be found at the Keep, but it's worth a try. She can at least check on Martyn and Mylar to reassure everyone that they are going after Darkwing.

As they fly over a ridge, the Keep comes into view. But, unless you know what you are looking for, you might not notice it. So, Akita has the Wyverns fly to the Aviary, where the Owl Rocs live. Many of the Owl Rocs get nervous until Martyn takes control when they land. Akita slides off Warrior and heads to Martyn and Mylar.

Martyn starts talking so fast, "We couldn't catch him, we couldn't stop them, we couldn't do anything. So, we lost our friend."

Akita shushes the Owl Roc, "Quiet, Martyn. We know we tried to catch up too. We are on our way to rescue him. I am glad you are here where you are safe. I need to talk to Stan, so you guys just relax, and we will bring Darkwing back as soon as we can."

Akita hugs both birds and heads inside the Keep. It always amazes her how warm and cozy this place is when you consider it is all stone and ice. In the great room, there is a nice blue fire burning. Stan is coming through the room and jumps when he sees Akita.

"Oh! Hello, Lady Blackwing. I suppose you are here looking for Darkwing. But unfortunately, he is not here, and we don't know why. The Owl Rocs came back without him, and we are at a loss." Stan blurts out.

Akita tells him to sit down; Gavin is standing by the fire warming up. "Stan, the Cloud Giants kidnapped Darkwing out from under all of us. Martyn and the other two tried to chase and stop them from taking him, but we could not stop it as it happened so fast. However, we now have a lead as to where he might be, and we are headed to rescue him now."

Stan's eyes are wide as he thinks about the consequences of what Lady Blackwing just told him. "What do you need from here? Although I know all he had from his past life was the amulet."

Akita asks, "Does he have a library? Do you know if he keeps a journal?"

Stan stands, "Follow me to his study. He has so many documents and books. We don't touch it, as he says we will mess up his filing system, whatever that means. If there is a system to it, I don't see it."

They walk down a short hallway to a closed ice door. Stan unlocks it with a wave of his hand. They see ice bookshelves, ice tables, and a considerable ice desk when they walk in. Stan walks in and starts the fire to warm up the room.

Akita and Gavin start looking through all the parchment lying around. She finds many notes on the Giants themselves but has yet to have spotted anything directly relating to the Cloud Giants. She opens a few desk drawers and finds a few quills, ink bottles, and parchment. One drawer is locked.

Akita asks, "Stan can you open the drawer here?"

Stan walks over and looks. "I am afraid that is one of the few locks I don't have the spell to."

It looks like a wizard lock, but she tries a few of her spells anyway. Nothing works. Looking around the desk some more, "I bet his most important information is in that drawer. If Stan can't open it and I certainly can't open it, then we are probably done here. Gavin, do you see anything that might help on that table?"

Gavin shakes his head, "If we had more time, there is so much Giant lore here we might learn something. But unfortunately, I think that would take weeks to decipher and read."

Akita sighs, "So we will have to rely on the information we have and King Windu. Just know we are going to rescue him. Keep the Owl Rocs calm. We will bring him back here as soon as possible. Gavin, let's go."

Gavin states, "I was just getting the chill out of my bones. How does anyone live in this damnable cold full time?" Stan chuckles as he watches them walk away.

Akita replies, "At least Hunter and Warrior are like flying heaters. It's more the breathing I worry about, as I get tired faster here."

They leave the Aviary flying down the backside of the mountain. They should be past Emberfrost in a few hours and be in Port Tristan just before nightfall.

As Grace's ship, the Sea Horse, pulls out of the harbor, Wulf calls Mandrake and Ordyn to the stern. Fabby and Vicar join them.

Wulf asks Mandrake, "Can you generate a cold air vortex in your hand?"

Mandrake looks at Wulf, "You mean like a tornado of cold air?"

"Yes, exactly. If we can make this work, Ordyn, you might have to help Grace hold the steering straight."

Intrigued, Mandrake starts a one-foot-tall vortex spinning in his hand. Then, with Mandrake's vortex turning clockwise, Wulf creates a hot air vortex spinning counterclockwise in his hand. "Now, at this size, it won't be as powerful, but I can demonstrate my idea before putting it into practice. As you know, when the hot air of the atmosphere meets the cold air, it creates a tornado. So, I thought we could create a strong wind to push the ship along faster. But we cannot go too fast, or it might break up the ship." He moves his hand near Mandrakes. "Notice the wind pushing out in front of us."

Everyone waves their hands in front of the vortexes. Mandrake responds, "This might work, but how tall do they have to be to affect the speed of the ship and for how long?"

Vicar looks at Fabby and states, "We might be able to buff each of you so that they don't have to be too big, but as Mandrake asked, for how long?"

Wulf scratches his chin, "In theory, if we can hold it for an hour, then the ship will coast for quite a bit at that speed, giving us a chance to rest. Then, of course, it depends on the waves, but since we will be going primarily parallel to the coast, it should be quite easy."

Grace adds, "If I keep us out in smooth water, that will shave a ton of time off our trip. Right now, we are looking at a full day to get to the far side of the Voskaola mountain range."

Mandrake looks at the team, "Let's give it a try; what do we have to lose? Let's see if we can hold it for a bit longer than an hour."

Wulf tests the air in front of the current vortexes. "Vicar, Fabby, add your buffs slowly, as Mandrake and I will go up to three feet, slowly."

As the buffs are added and the vortexes grow, everyone can see the ship picking up speed. Grace has Ordyn hold the steering wheel straight as she goes portside to inspect her ship. The ship moves by the shore much faster than prevailing winds would have provided.

As Grace comes up the stairs, "I think I would stop increasing the power there. Let's see how close we are to passing the mountains at about noon."

Wulf nods in agreement, "Now, can we hold this strength for an hour or more?"

Mandrake replies, "As long as our clerics are good, I should be fine. I would like some water, though."

Grace signals one of her ship hands to bring water and takes over steering again. "There is quite a pull on the steering but being out here on smoother water helps. I wouldn't want to do this closer to shore."

Not quite two hours later, they stopped the tornado power to see how far the boat would still coast at high speeds.

Grace takes her spyglass and surveys the coast. "Well, your efforts are more than paying off. There is the center of the mountain range, so we should hit the far side by noon if we can keep up this speed. Feed these people; we need to keep their strength up."

They sit down for some good ole stew and catch a quick nap. Most have been up half the night just helping to get the ship ready to set sail.

Ordyn, Greenbean, and Ishvet are on the main deck practicing their craft while sailors dodge around, taking care of their duties.

The speed of the ship kept up much longer than anyone expected. Finally, after about an hour, Wulf, Mandrake, Fabby, and Vicar started again with the vortexes. As the ship picked up speed again, Grace used her spyglass to see if Emberfrost was viewable. She thinks she could make out the smoke from chimneys as they passed the mountain ridge. Next, she checked the sky for Akita and Gavin on the Wyverns.

Grace announces, "If we keep this pace up, we should be in Port Tristan by nightfall. I didn't see the Wyverns, but they could be on the far side of Emberfrost, and I can usually only see the smoke from their fires when we go by."

Akita and Gavin meet the ship at the pier. Hunter and Warrior are relaxing just outside of town. As Akita walks up, she sees Grace arguing with the Port Master.

Grace states, "I am here on official business, for the High Duchess Lady Blackwing. We were told to meet King Windu here, and you're telling me I cannot tie up to the pier."

"Captain O'Malley, I am afraid your reputation proceeds you. Is Lady Blackwing here to vouch for you?"

Grace retorts, "If you would give me a minute before automatically presuming the worst, I will find her. I have done nothing wrong in this port, so I must confess I have no idea what you are so up in arms about."

Akita steps up behind Grace putting hands on her shoulders, "I am the High Duchess Lady Akita Blackwing. Captain O'Malley is assisting us on a mission of great importance." Akita looks at Grace before making her following statement as if you better play nice. "I will vouch for her and take note that from now on if she says she is my emissary, let her through. With that said, if there are any issues, you contact me, and we will straighten it out."

The Port Master bows, "Yes, Lady Blackwing, as with Captain O'Malley, your reputation proceeds you as well. Anything we can do to help."

Akita does a head bow, "You can tell me where I would find King Windu when he is in Port Tristan. I have only met with him when he is in Oceanfalls."

The Port Master turns and points down the beach, "He will be at his retreat house; just follow the beach to the edge of town."

Akita replies, "Thank you." Then, she turns to her friends, "I would leave the mounts on the ship. I think Hunter and Warrior are actually out near King Windu's home."

She heads down the beach, watching the fishermen working on their nets as the sun sets. The sky shifts from a fiery yellow and orange to cool pinks, purples, and darker blues. Port Tristan is a bustling port with a large market, where you will find almost anything you could be looking for. Along the beach is where the fishermen reside. Their mud-brick homes are built with thick walls for the desert to keep night's cool air inside all day. The thick walls hold the heat from the cooking fires in the winter to keep everyone warm. They are more efficient than the stone bricks of her Keep in some ways. It is a quaint little seaside village, and one of the safest, because of King Windu's ways. You didn't use to be able to say that any place north of the Voskaola mountains was safe, so he must be doing something right.

It didn't take her long to spot the guards outside of a gigantic villa on the beach. High walls rise from deep in the water up and around the housing structures, giving a private beach for evening swims and dinner parties.

Akita and her group walk right up to the guards at the main entrance. Before they can do more than get in a defensive stance, she holds up her hands, "I am High Duchess Lady Blackwing, and I was told King Windu would be awaiting our arrival."

Another guard of higher rank steps out of the gate and bows, "Good evening, High Duchess Lady Blackwing. We have been expecting your arrival, and King Windu should be here in a few minutes, as he got held up by one thing or another. So, we are pleased to welcome you and your friends. We have a light dinner waiting in the dining room." Then, with a flourish and another bow, he signals them to enter the mansion.

Akita does a head bow, "Thank you; it has been quite a trip, the hospitality is greatly appreciated."

They are led to a formal dining room set up with a buffet of meats, cheeses, exotic fruits, vegetables, and bread. They each grab a plate with tasty morsels of food and move to a table where wine is served.

Akita tells them about stopping at Darkwing Keep. She knows he has to have information there but fears it's locked in the drawer in his desk. She tells Ordyn and Ishvet about all the tomes and books on Giants of all kinds. "There has to be something there that can help us. If I find out the information we need is in that drawer, I'm going to slap him upside the head."

Mandrake chuckles, "Maybe I should have a look at that drawer. Wizard magic might be all you need."

Akita agrees, "Well, if the information King Windu gives us doesn't work, then you and I will make a trip up that mountain. If I must, I will build a forge around it."

Greenbean giggles, "A teleportation spell might work; that is what Myles used on Darkwing. Although he had the ice half-melted, I don't think we want to melt Darkwing's desk."

King Windu walks into the room, "Greetings, Lady Akita Blackwing. Greetings to you all."

Anyone who saw King Windu would instantly know that he was someone of great importance. His onyx black hair and beard are meticulously groomed. He is a portly Dwarf and wears a Sultan's desert robe with gold embroidery and green accents. Gold rings adorn each of his ten fingers, and an ornate jeweled broach hangs from a thick gold chain to the middle of his chest.

Akita stands, "Hello, King Windu, old friend." She introduces her friends and notices when he stops at Grace. "Captain O'Malley was very instrumental in the last battle and destroying Evad Chaos and the Dark Wizard's cave."

King Windu gives a bow nod and kisses the back of all the ladies' hands, including Greenbean and Vivian. He sits down at the head of the table as his servants set a plate in front of him. Another steps forward and takes a small bite of each item on his plate. After a few minutes, everyone sits, and the King eats. Akita would have found this eccentric any other time, but she completely understands after what just happened to her uncle.

The King sits back, "So one of the crew, the Frozen One, has been kidnapped by the Cloud Giants. I am aware of history because it is prudent for me to know the histories of items as a collector. The Cloud Giants have been a menace to everyone for centuries. I have a proposition for you."

Akita looks at King Windu, "Well, we need to rescue Lord Darkwing, so what is your proposition?" Like dealing with Grace, you have to be careful when you request anything from King Windu. Akita knows that the Cloud Giants have something he wants for his collection, or he wouldn't be so eager to help.

King Windu scratches his beard, "I have occasionally dealt with the Cloud Giants, specifically King Cirus. I have a way to get to their island unscathed, but there is a price to be paid. King Cirus has a wind flute that I want for my collection.

I have tried many times to get him to part with it. I even sent a rather exotic thief one time, but she returned empty-handed. So, if you agree to get this for me when you rescue Lord Darkwing, I will give you the key to enter their waters.

Akita looks to her crew, "We'll have to discuss this; we didn't come here to steal anything from the Cloud Giants; we only want to rescue our friend."

Mandrake and Vicar look at each other, eyes wide and full of wonder. The words "exotic thief" has piqued their interests. They wonder if this could be the thief and assassin that they know. The twin thing is at full speed, and they nod their heads in agreement. They will pull King Windu aside later and ask him about the thief he sent.

Ishvet stands, "King Windu, is this the only bargain you will strike with us? Will you not agree to other terms?" Ishvet sits back down.

Grace interjects, "I know from experience that there is always another angle. However, if I had to guess, you have set your mind to this flute, and nothing will dissuade you from obtaining it."

King Windu chuckles, "Yes, Grace O'Malley, the pirate, thief, and smuggler are right. I have my mind set, and it's the only thing that I believe is of the same value as what I am about to give you."

Grace leans forward in her seat and begins to rebuke King Windu for his sly jabs at her recent past. Akita puts up a hand quickly to stop her from making the situation worse. Grace sits back and crosses her arms in defiance. However, she knows that she is working towards changing others' ideas about her. She stays silent.

Akita sighs in exasperation, "Fine, we will make the trade. We cannot waste any more time. Darkwing is depending on us to come get him, or he would have already found his way back to us." Akita looks directly into King Windu's eyes, "Hear me, King Windu, if you think for one minute that you will double-cross us in any form or fashion, I will have my friend Annut-the Fast burn everything you own to the ground!" Akita stands, pressing her arms locked and palms down on the table, and leans in. "Are we clear?"

King Windu's face lights up, "Great! It is agreed upon then. I will give you the sail, and you will get me the wind flute. So, you can rest assured, High Duchess Lady Akita Blackwing, that there will be no double-cross. I want the flute as much as you want your friend back." Akita thinks to herself, 'I highly doubt that.'

King Windu leans back, "Now that we have that business out of the way, please enjoy the hospitality of my wealth. Rooms have been made up for you to rest in, and the sail will be affixed to the Sea Horse in the morning. It will allow you to pass through their magical barrier into their waters."

Everyone except Mandrake and Vicar turns their attention to their plates. They stand in unison and move towards King Windu. They stand at the edge of the table and address him. Vicar starts first "King Windu, may we have a moment of your time?" Mandrake finishes, "To discuss a sensitive matter?"

King Windu stands, "Please follow me into the study."

Mandrake and Vicar follow King Windu into the study. The space is quite unusual. There are stuffed animal heads hung on the walls and tropical plants strewn throughout. The walls are some type of exotic wood carved in a jungle motif. In the center is a long ornate table surrounded by leather chairs. Behind that is a very well-stocked wet bar with various colored bottles and glassware. King Windu motions for them to sit in the two closest leather chairs. He then walks up to the bar and asks them if they would like a drink. They both decline as he pours himself a full glass of some type of wine. King Windu then sits at the head of the table. He motions for his taster to come into the room. After the wine proves to be good, the taster quickly leaves.

King Windu starts, "So, you have something to discuss?"

Vicar begins, "You mentioned earlier that you hired a thief to procure the wind flute from the Cloud Giants." Mandrake takes his turn, "We have a friend that fits that description. She has the skill set that would have been warranted for a special job like that." Vicar pipes up, "Her name is Meh-Kola. Is that name familiar to you?"

Kind Windu leans forward, picks up his glass of wine, and inhales the aroma. He then takes a small sip and returns the glass to the table. "I'm not in the habit of revealing my secrets for free. However, I know something from both of your pasts that not many people know. I know where you have escaped from and the reason why. Both of you may have some information that I seek concerning the incident that brought you to Alahora. So, I will tell you that Meh-Kola was indeed hired to steal the wind flute. Now to get to the information that I want. The assailant that killed the Queen, your father, and all the people in the Castle, do you have any leads or descriptions of them?"

Vicar and Mandrake look at each other, then nod their heads. Vicar states, "You are very well informed and ask the right questions at the right time." Mandrake adds, "We know very little about the assassin that killed everyone in the Castle. What we do know is that the gate guard stopped a rider before we arrived home that night." Vicar explains, "The person was a cloaked rider with a jeweled tobacco pouch and a matching jeweled dagger. I feel like we have been close to catching that rider many times." Mandrake finishes, "We are missing a vital piece of the puzzle. The one-piece that connects everything and leads to the person who committed these crimes. All the other information that we have gathered tells us that this cloaked figure boarded a ship and came to Alahora."

King Windu grits his teeth, "This cloaked figure fits the description of someone that I have run into before. They attempted the same scenario at my Castle shortly before yours and then vanished. So only the taster perished from the poison in my case. I have also been searching for this person ever since. One thing I do know that you don't is that this person is a male Elf. Everything else fits the description you both gave." King Windu leans forward again, "I have my cleverest people investigating the incident, and I have learned another piece of the puzzle. The assassin comes from the area of Darkforest."

Mandrake and Vicar spin their heads quickly to see each other's faces. They have just been given the final piece of their puzzle, and all is coming into focus. They agree not to give away their suspicions to King Windu and return to the conversation as if nothing has changed.

Mandrake turns back to King Windu, "Thanks for the information, but back to Meh-Kola." Vicar nods, "Yes, do you know where we can find her?

King Windu sits back in his chair, "I have an idea. She works in conjunction with an Assassin's Guild. They have ways to contact her. I will get a message sent to them to pass on to her. If she is in this region, it shouldn't take much time for her to contact you."

Vicar and Mandrake stand in unison and excuse themselves from the study. They return to the formal dining room, where the rest of the team is just finishing their meals.

Akita looks at them both and tilts her head as they enter the room, "Do you have something to tell me?"

Vicar puts his right hand up to signal that it's not the right time, and Mandrake shakes his head no.

To that, Akita stands and addresses the group, "We all need our strength for tomorrow morning, so let's get some sleep."

Everyone else stands up from the table and begins to move towards the sleeping quarters provided by King Windu. Grace states that she will be sleeping on the ship and wants to oversee the installation of this sail that King Windu has given them. The house staff shows all of them to their rooms, and they all try to sleep before the impending battle.

Skrymir Darkwing is still trying to concentrate all his strength into freezing the pillory he is trapped in. No one has noticed the frost accumulation on the metal hinges. Before long, it may be just enough to break them, and he can attempt his escape. He doesn't know where he is at, but he can figure that out when he gets free.

A Dark Wizard walks by Skrymir, headed for King Cirus' hut. Skrymir wishes he could freeze the man in his tracks.

The Dark Wizard starts reporting to the Cloud Giant King upon entering the hut. "King Cirus, we have received some terrible news. Evad Chaos has been killed and his cave destroyed. Everything he had stored is buried, and he never got control of the Red Dragon, Annut – The Fast. This is quite a setback towards finding the Key; however," the Dark Wizard quickly finishes with the good news, "the Dragon Tablet has been delivered to our operative and is on its way to the Ancient Dragon Temple."

King Cirus asks, "Is that all you have to say?"

The Dark Wizard responds, "Yes, Sir. But unfortunately, that is all the information we have at the moment."

The King lets loose a deafening roar. "If you want something done right, you have to do it yourself." Then, with a flick of the King's hand, a strong gust of wind seemingly out of nowhere, the Dark Wizard is blown out of the hut and out to sea.

Darkwing heard everything and chuckles. as the Dark Wizard flew over his head and disappeared. Then, thinking to himself, that is one less Dark Wizard I have to worry about. I hope they get the King angry more often. They successfully killed Evad Chaos, but what is this about a Dragon Tablet and Temple, I wonder.

King Cirus steps out of his hut with his amulet glowing and bellowing so that everyone can hear him on every breeze and gust of wind. "If anyone brings me more bad news, you will join that idgit floating in the sea as fish food."

The King looks at Skrymir, "Evad Chaos was of no consequence to my plans. I have you now; that is all I really need." King Cirus turns and goes back into his hut.

Darkwing mumbles under his breath, "Yeah, okay, for the moment, you overgrown bag of wind." He goes back to concentrating on the pillory and hears a faint crack in one of the hinges.

The morning sun rises above the mountains and peers into the Chateaus eastern-facing windows. It creates small rays of light that dance upon Akita's face as she opens her eyes for the day. If it weren't for the fact that they were going to battle shortly, she would think this would be a great day. But instead, she rolls out of bed and begins putting on her leather armor. There's a faint knock on the door. Akita steps to the door and opens it a crack. A small housemaid slips a tightly rolled scroll through the crack. The maid whispers, "King Windu asked me to inform you that this is the last bit of information he will be able to provide." With that said, she turned and hurried down the hall out of Akitas' sight.

Akita unrolls the scroll and sees King Windu's familiar handwriting.

Akita,

The Cloud Giant King possesses a very powerful amulet that can control the weather and the wind. Beware attacking from the sky if at all possible. Furthermore, the flute that I need is in the grand temple. It would be best if you had someone to sneak in as you are battling. Good Luck!

K.W.

Akita gathers her belongings and heads to the dining room, where the rest of the team has started to assemble. Vicar and Mandrake are in the back corner discussing something. Ishvet and Ordyn are sharpening their blades at the table. Vivian is explaining to Wulf and Gavin how she meditates right before a battle to improve her dexterity. Greenbean and Fab Ulous gather gear and discuss their great night's sleep. Finally, she sees the house staff bringing in plates full of bacon and sausage, shortcakes, fresh fruit, and huge decanters of coffee.

Akita announces, "We only have a short time before we head to the Cloud Giants Island. I'm not exactly sure what type of opposition we will face when we land at the dock. King Windu has informed me that the Cloud Giant King has an amulet that helps him control the weather and the wind. For this reason, I suggest that we leave behind Hunter and Warrior. Ishvet, have you and Rani fought without flying?"

Ishvet replies, "A couple of times, she doesn't need to fly to use her heat vision."

Akita Continues, "Mandrake and Vicar, do you have any spells that would counteract the weather or wind?

Mandrake speaks up first, "I have defensive spells that would shield us from the lightning, and I can create ice shields to partially protect us from the wind. However, they will not last long if the Cloud Giant King is as powerful as I believe him to be."

Wulf thinks for a moment, "Well, beyond the basic defense spell we all know, I can use psychic magic to confuse the Giants or make them see their worst fears. That may be enough to keep them from casting at us."

Akita then turns and looks at Vivian, "Vivian, when we saw you fighting the basilisk, you were using a shield of light. Would lightning or wind be able to get through that?"

Vivian looks around at the group, "I know I can deflect lightning, but I'm not sure about wind magic. If it were dark magic, I would say yes. However, from what I understand, this is ancient magic. That is a whole other level."

Ishvet looks towards Ordyn and then interjects, "Before you even ask Akita, Ordyn and I are not lightning or windproof."

Ordyn nods in agreement to Ishvet, "We have been testing Ishvets' blue streak ability, and I think he may be able to get in a few hits with his sword before any Giant could see him."

Akita then turns to Greenbean and Fabby, "Fabby, I want you to stay near the shore in the event we have enemies circle around to the ship. Greenbean, you stay close to me, and I'll use my defensive spells for us."

Akita then address the whole group, "Grace will also stay with the ship, and her crew will make sure we have an escape route after we get Darkwing. Now, Gavin, I have an important task for you. I need you to sneak into the temple and get the flute that King Windu wants. You'll have to use your skills to stay undetected. I don't want them to find out that it is gone before we get off the island. Lastly, we will leave the horses behind with the Wyverns since they will have a hard time combating the wind. So, let's grab our gear and get to the ship. I want to have Darkwing home for dinner."

CHAPTER 7
THE RESCUE

Akita walks to the ship to talk with Grace, "What can you see that makes this sail so unique? Or does it look like the rest?

Grace looks towards the pier. "After we replaced one of the other sails on the forward mast, you could see it shimmer as if lightly sprinkled with gold. The question is will it do what he says it will do? The man that helped put the sail up said it is only an hour-long trip."

"I guess we will know soon enough. I wish we had a way to make the entire ship invisible, but that would drain anyone's magical strength for the rest of the day. So, I say let's charge in like we own the place, to a point."

Grace giggles, "You mean stealthily like we own the place. However, know this, if you come to the dock and I am not there, don't panic because I will return. I have to protect the ship if any of us are getting back to the mainland."

Akita nods as the team walks up the gangway onto the ship. Mandrake and Vicar follow with a local stable hand to take the horses to his boarding stable until they return.

Akita calls Warrior, "Are you close enough to hear me?" She waits for an answer. Unfortunately, the Wyverns believe they are going with her, so they scare everyone on the piers by flying over while looking for a place to land. They land in the middle of the street as Akita flies over to talk to her boys. Only then did the townspeople calm down. "My boys, I need you to stay nearby but not near the town where anyone can try to capture you or harm you. You are not allowed to roast anyone other than bandits and thieves."

Warrior questions, "We are not going with you? We are all set to help you battle these Giants."

Akita replies, "None of the flying mounts are going except Rani, as she can be stealthy and fight from the ground. We cannot risk you all flying in and the Cloud Giant blowing you into a mountain or something and breaking a wing or worse."

Hunter pouts, "You make it sound like we are hatchlings. We have been great in fights."

Akita smiles and rubs his snout, "Yes, you have, but we are not sure what we are up against with these Cloud Giants. So, we will need to hide and stay out of sight. You two are not exactly small and stealthy."

Warrior states, "We will stay close to the beach, farther away from town, so if you call us, we might be able to hear you."

Akita hugs both of them, "Thank you, boys, for understanding. We will return as fast as we can."

The Wyverns take off with their wing gusts dusting everyone in the sand. Akita flies back to the ship.

Akita's team is on deck in groups talking amongst themselves. Next, Akita meets Grace at the Captain's Helm. "Are we ready?"

Grace nods and starts yelling orders at her crew. It took about five minutes, and the ship moved out to sea. As the ship turned, the unique sail glowed brighter. Grace decides to test a theory and turns the ship to starboard. The sail glow dims, so she turns back to her original course, and the sail glows brightly again.

Grace looks at Akita, "The sail seems to know where we are going; it glows brighter when I turn towards open water and dims if I try to follow the shore."

Akita agrees, "I noticed that too. So hopefully, it's a good omen."

The voyage doesn't take very long. The ship seems to be moving almost as fast as when Mandrake and Wulf were creating the wind. Only an hour has passed since they left the docks, but they have traveled over one hundred nautical miles by Grace's calculations. Finally, they approach a towering wall of mist. It spans in either direction as far as the eye can see, and the top reaches far into the clouds. The reflection of the sail can be seen on the massive wall as they near it. The mist opens for them when they are close to touching the wall, revealing a long corridor just big enough for the ship to sail through.

Akita nervously looks at Grace, "I hope this works both ways. I would hate to imagine that we free Darkwing only to be trapped by this mist afterward."

Grace swallows hard and looks up at the shimmering sail, "We will do everything we can on the ship to protect the sail as I think it is our only means of escape."

The ship nears the end of the long corridor, and light can be seen at the end. As the ship emerges, an enormous island can be seen directly in front of them. The ship is still being pulled towards the island. Several large figures can be seen on the shore closest to the dock area. The figures seem to be as tall as the trees and, in some cases, taller. The ship begins to slow down, and the air becomes thick with anticipation. Everyone is nervously waiting for the first strikes of battle. The team crowds the gangway waiting for the ship to completely stop. Akita, Ordyn, and Wulf begin to flap their wings to clear the ship and land on the dock.

Akita says in as calm of a voice as she can muster, "Do your best to subdue the Giants. Unfortunately, it may be too difficult to kill them. Our main priority is to get Darkwing and leave. Gavin, you know what to do. Hopefully, you are back to the ship before we are."

The ship stops, and the gangway goes down. Akita, Ordyn, and Wulf are at the dock before the others can make their way down. Gavin flies up and disappears, headed in the direction of a large temple. At the end of the dock area is a road leading up to a plateau; the team will follow it up as quickly as they can. As they make their way up the road, Rani leaps from the ship and lands right behind them. Ishvet grabs Rani's saddle and mounts. Moments later, dark clouds instantly form above them. The sun is blocked from the sky, and they can barely see each other. Thunder begins reverberating off the mountain in front of them, and lightning streaks across the sky. Directly in front of them, they feel the ground vibrate as if something heavy has fallen. Lightning strikes ahead, revealing a Cloud Giant. In its hand is a long white blade seemingly made of mist and in its other hand is a shield of cloud. Akita, Mandrake, and Wulf step in front of the group and begin casting defensive shield spells. Again, lightning strikes, radiating across the shields and into the ground. The group is protected this time.

Two more lightning bolts strike the shields, and the shields are dissipated. Vicar steps behind Mandrake and buffs his power to create a new shield covering the group while Akita and Wulf conjure fireballs to hurl at the Giant. Ishvet and Rani circle around the Giant on the left side while Ordyn runs around on the right. Akita and Wulf begin throwing the fireballs to distract the Giant while the others get into position. The Cloud Giant easily blows the fireballs off course, but it buys the time that Ishvet and Ordyn need. Once behind the Giant, they use their extremely sharp blades to slice the Giant's legs just behind the knees. A loud groan can be heard in between the flashes of lightning and explosions of fireballs. The Giant falls to his knees then bends over, catching himself with his arms. Akita moves in and uses a pain-inflicting spell that causes the

Giant to fall to his side and writhes in pain. Next, Wulf casts a psychic torment spell that causes the Giant to grab his head and scream. Now that the shield is not needed, Mandrake freezes the Giant. This will buy them some time to get to the plateau. As the Giant is frozen, the clouds quickly dissipate and reveal the sunlight.

Akita looks to Mandrake, "Good Lord if it takes that much to subdue just one Giant, what are we going to do?

Mandrake replies, "Maybe we should have snuck into the camp instead of trying to fight."

Vicar adds, "Let's do our best to avoid any more Giants because our power does have limitations."

As the group crests the hill, they can see several Giant huts in a semicircle with a grander hut in the middle. From their position to the grand hut is a wide-open space like a courtyard. Branching off from the semicircle on the right is a road leading to a temple. Behind the village is a massive mountain. It's three times as tall as it is wide. It appears to be a dormant volcano.

Something dark catches Akita's eyes to the left. She throws a fireball as quickly as she can. A black-robed figure jumps out from behind a large water urn. They, in turn, fling a lightning bolt from their fingertips. Mandrake instantly shields Akita from the bolt. Rani lunges forward and uses her heat vision to slice the man in half. His torso topples face down in the dirt in front of where his legs are still standing.

Rani to Ishvet's mind, "Oops, maybe I used too much power."

Ishvet muses, "That was a Dark Wizard, not a Giant. What in Bahamut's name are they doing here?"

Ordyn goes up and quickly investigates the body, "Yep, definitely a Dark Wizard. Glad he's dead. Good work, Rani."

Vivian steps up and puts a hand over the body, "I can sense the dark magic, but it was very little. This person wasn't very powerful. I'm sensing a larger concentration of dark magic coming from the temple."

Vicar looks towards the temple, "I hope Gavin is okay up there."

Mandrake adds, "He definitely wasn't expecting Dark Wizards."

Akita states, "He's a Hunter Ranger of Prayla, he can be invisible in a snap, and no one here can outshoot his bow. So, he will be fine."

As soon as Akita finishes the statement, the wind picks up drastically, and dark clouds begin to form above them. Rani lets out a loud roar that startles everyone not looking in her direction. The team whips around and can see what Rani is roaring at. The biggest Giant they have seen thus far is standing just outside of the grand-looking hut at the apex of the semicircle. Flanking him, one on each side is a Dark Wizard. Behind them, they can see Darkwing for the first time. He's in some type of restraint.

The wind begins to howl and push down on them even harder. Vivian steps to the middle of the group, and Vicar begins to buff her to amplify her paladin light shield. Mandrake tries to weave his shield spell with Vivian's to create an even larger and stronger dome. The shield of light grows and envelops the group just as an enormous bolt of lightning strikes down directly from the dark clouds. The thunder it creates is deafening, and the ground vibrates as the bolt splinters against the shield they have created.

Greenbean yells to Akita, "We can't stay here and allow him to hit us repeatedly! We have to make our move, or we will all be dead!"

Akita looks around, "I know, Greeny! If this wind would let up for a second, and we could bust out of this bubble and surprise them, I think we might have a chance."

Rani screams to Ishvet's mind, "Nooo! I can't take it. It hurts my ears!"

The thunder and lightning are too much for Rani to take, and she darts out of the bubble running directly for the Cloud Giant.

Ishvet yells, "No! Rani!" He runs after her into the wind, and lightning strikes.

Akita yells above the thunder, "Attack now!"

Vivian deflects the last lightning bolt as her shield radiates out a blast of lightning in all directions. Everyone else scatters to the left or right. Akita and Wulf immediately start to throw fire in front of them. Greenbean and Ordyn head directly for the Dark Wizards on the sides of the Giant. They dodge lightning and struggle against the wind as they run. Mandrake throws ice shards at the Giant's legs as Vicar sends orbs of stinging light towards the Giant's face. They are all advancing as quickly as they can.

The Giant steps forward, and the lightning stops, and the wind dies down, "I know who you are. Evad told me all about your so-called triumphs. Come at me with all your might, and it will still not be enough. I am King Cirus. I am a god."

Rani leaps up to go for King Cirus' neck. King Cirus catches her with his right hand and throws her to the ground as hard as possible. She hits the ground causing an indentation and lays there motionless. Ishvet becomes enraged and leaps from the ground as everything around him starts moving in slow motion. He intends to inflict as much damage as he can on the Giant King. Anyone watching would only see a blue streak flying through the air. His sword is positioned straight out in front of him, ready to impale the Giant. As he heads for the heart, the Giant swings his torso to the right and catches Ishvet in his hand. Ishvet slices into the Giant's palm, causing him to lose grip. Ishvet streaks out of his hand down to the rest of the group. Ishvet is astonished that the Cloud Giant King is just as fast as his ability.

Gavin approaches the side of the temple and lands in the brush close to a side entrance. The invisibility ability he has now ceased. In a few moments, he will be able to use it again. He can see through the doorway into an inner chamber. There are cloaked figures walking back and forth, moving vessels and large tablets. He can't see the flute yet. He needs to be as stealthy as possible.

Now that he can become invisible again, he can enter the building. He crouches and moves along the inner walls to the next doorway. He can see another chamber at the back of the inner room. A Dark Wizard is standing in front of it with a key dangling from his cloak belt. If he had to guess, he would say that the flute is behind that door. Gavin pulls his bow and notches an arrow that creates a plume of smoke. He releases, and it flies into a far corner. The Dark Wizards run over to the smoke plume leaving the one with the key alone at the door. He sneaks up to the Dark Wizard with the key, punches him in the back of the head, and removes the key as the Dark Wizard slowly crumples to the ground.

Within a few seconds, Gavin is inside the room and can see the flute. He looks around to see if any traps are noticeable to his keen senses. He sees nothing that would impede his progress. He approaches the flute and picks it up from its stand. He quickly makes his way back to the door. He can't see who's on the other side. He closes his eyes and whispers a short chant. When he opens his eyes, they are completely white. He can now see the life force of everyone beyond the door.

The Dark Wizards are still gathered around the arrow he shot. The door guard is still on the floor. He knows he must move quickly because his invisibility will soon be over, and he'll be seen. As quickly as he can, he opens the door, shuts it behind him, and sprints towards the door leading to the brush he was hiding in earlier. Someone will soon find the Dark Wizard guard on the floor, so he needs to get back to the ship. As he exits the temple, he can hear thunder and see lightning on the plateau. He now knows that everyone up there is engaged in battle. If he can get the flute back to the ship, he may be able to get up there and help.

Ishvet goes to Rani's side and tries to shake her awake. He gets no response. The others run and surround him and Rani to protect them from King Cirus. Vicar bends down and begins healing spells. Ishvet is shaking Rani in desperation. Rani is not moving, and Ishvet can feel broken bones beneath her skin.

Ishvet pleads to Vicar, "Vicar do something! Her bones aren't healing! I can't lose her!"

Vicar looks to Ishvet, closes his eyes, and shakes his head slightly back and forth, "I'm trying everything I know, Ishvet. I think she's gone."

At this time, the Dark Wizards that were on the sides of King Cirus are casting powerful offensive spells towards the group. Akita and Wulf are returning fire with columns of flame, and Mandrake is shielding the group with ice walls. Vivian is shielding herself, Orydn, and Greenbean from the various attacks.

Greenbean turns to Akita, "Akita, we have to retreat. The king is way too powerful for us to take on this way."

Akita growls, "I know!"

Vicar screams to Akita, "Akita! Akita! Something is happening!"

Akita looks down and sees that Ishvet is glowing bluer than she has ever seen. She no more than takes one step towards Ishvet, and he is gone. She reaches her hand out to where he was as she hears guttural screams from behind her. She whips her head around to where the King and two Dark Wizards were standing. The Dark Wizards are gone. The Cloud Giant King steps back and stumbles. Akita can now see the deep gashes in the Giant's shins. To the right of the Giant, she can see the bodies of the Dark Wizards lying on top of each other and Ishvet standing over them.

Akita yells to Ishvet, "Ishvet, we have to go. He's too powerful for us."

Ishvet turns and snaps out of his rage. Standing in front of him is Darkwing, still locked in his pillory. Ishvet has tears running down his face. Ishvet starts to step towards Darkwing, but the king takes a step blocking Ishvet from Darkwing with his massive bleeding leg. Ishvet turns and heads back to the group.

The king says through clenched teeth, "I have had enough of this! If you do not leave immediately, I will destroy you. Darkwing will not be going anywhere at this time. You can have what remains after I am done with him."

Akita runs to Ishvet and puts an arm around him. She pulls him to her, lifts him off the ground, and begins flying, carrying Ishvet towards the ship. Mandrake and Vicar use a levitation spell on Rani's body and run down the hill, following Akita in the air. Vivian and Greenbean also turn and run down the hill, but at a little slower pace in case another danger is following. Wulf and Ordyn also take flight, gliding down the hill. Halfway down, they meet up with Gavin and Akita yells down to Gavin,

"Get back to the ship Gavin. We are leaving immediately!"

Gavin turns and takes flight back to the ship. The others are now right behind him. Gavin lands first, and then Akita is still holding Ishvet. Fabby runs up to them and catches Ishvet as he falls from Akita's arms.

Fabby looks up to Akita, "What's happened?"

Akita ignores him and yells to Grace, "Grace, we need to sail as soon as everyone is aboard. Let's hope the wall lets us out."

Vicar and Mandrake come up the gangway with Rani's body and lay it on the deck. Greenbean and Vivian follow behind. Ordyn and Wulf land near the helm. Before Akita can say anything, Mandrake and Wulf move into position to create a wind if they need to move from the dock. Fabby pulls Ishvet over to Rani's body and lays him next to her. Ishvet rolls towards her, puts his arm under her wing and looks at her face. Tears are streaming down his face, and his sobs are becoming more audible.

The others that are not needed to make the wind, so everyone gathers around both Ishvet and Rani lying on the show deck. They are all tearing up. They don't know what they can do at this point but to close their eyes and say a prayer for Rani. Akita kneels and puts a hand on Rani's hindquarter. The tears are coming even faster now.

The ship begins to move when Grace turns the helm. Mandrake and Wulf only have to produce a slight wind to get the ship moving out of the harbor. The sail the King Windu gave them billows out and shimmers as they head away from the island. Then, just as before, when they are to the wall of mist, it opens and allows them passage. Ishvet's sobs only break the silence on the ship as they move through the corridor and out to sea.

Darkwing listens to the angry ramblings of the King as he yells for his healers. His leg is bleeding on his shoes, clothes, and rugs. His hand is bleeding from Ishvets attack after his dear Rani had been thrown to the ground. Darkwing will never forget the look in Ishvet's eyes, and he cannot wait to Perma Freeze, that Giant.

His friends almost made it to him, and he knows they will be back. They took out at least three more Dark Wizards that he doesn't have to worry about anymore. But he knows he has to keep trying himself. He keeps hearing the pillory weaken, but he also doesn't want to wear himself out just in case he gets a chance to escape due to novice wizards' stupidity.

CHAPTER 8
SAYING GOODBYE

Grace pulls the ship into the harbor. Akita calls everyone to her. "Grace, will you take everyone to Blackwing Keep? I want to have a talk with his highness. Greenbean, will you come with me? That way, you guys can put some wind behind the sails again. Then, we will return home on Hunter and Warrior. Mandrake set up a funeral for Rani and ask Ghod to make a unique marker if you get there before me."

Grace answers, "Not a problem. We can regroup from there and figure out what is next."

"Thank you, your help is very much appreciated."

Greenbean grabs her things, "Let's go verbally abuse a King. That sounds fun and something we haven't done together before."

Akita turns to Gavin, "Do you have the flute? Check on our mother-to-be and meet us back at the Keep once you get there."

Gavin nods and hands Akita the flute. "Yes, I will check on Alura; she has a special place in my heart because she is the first."

Akita takes Ordyn's arm, moving him away from Ishvet. "I cannot imagine his pain. Please watch over him."

Ordyn nods, "I have grown quite fond of this young man; I will keep him safe and fed."

Mandrake looks to Grace, "Give us time to go get our horses, and we will be ready to sail. We shouldn't be long." Vicar goes with Mandrake to the stables.

Akita looks to Grace, "Does the ship need any provisions while you are here?"

Grace replies, "We will be good for several days yet, but thank you for checking."

Akita nods, "Safe Travels. We will get there probably at the same time."

Akita and Greenbean leave the ship headed to the King's retreat house. If Greeny had wings, it would have been a short trip, but Akita figures the walk will do her good to calm down.

"Greeny, I am going to threaten him the loss of his kingdom, again. He withheld the information that the Dark Wizards would be there. I believe he knew because of the last-minute private note I received this morning. A servant in secrecy delivered it. I didn't put it together this morning, but now I suspect he is working with the Dark Wizards when he wants something for his collection. This is not acceptable. If he wants collectibles, he can put together a team to find them legitimately, not with the enemy's help."

Greenbean glances at Akita, "Agreed, and I will follow your lead in dealing with his men. I am sure we can find someone to take over his kingdom if needed." She chuckles.

"Most people are good; however, when they find out that a person of power is working with these evil sects, they put their trust behind the might of good." But Akita sighs, "we just don't need this on top of everything else right now. I despise this part of politics, but we will play this game until a later date."

As they reach the main gate, a guard steps out, bows, and leads them to King Windu. As they head down the halls, she counts the guards that could be seen along the way. She notes ten as they come to a stop at a set of double doors. Akita and Greenbean walk straight up to King Windu as the doors open.

Akita stops right in front of the King, "Clear this room. I want only the three of us here." The guards look at the King and then Akita. "If I was going to attack him, he would be dead already and the ten guards I saw on the way in."

King Windu waves his hand, telling his guards and people to leave the room. He turns and stares down Akita, "Yes, Lady Blackwing."

"I came to you for assistance. I know you did not have to do anything for me; trust me, I understand that. However, I am of the opinion, based on a note handed to me on your behalf by a servant, that you knew there would be Dark Wizards there too. If I find you are working with them, you and I will have significant issues. My team and I will destroy all the Dark Wizards, and anyone affiliated with them. Do we have an understanding?"

King Windu says nothing but nods his head slowly.

Akita states in a firm and dangerous voice. "We have your flute. Unfortunately, although we have it, we lost a valuable friend and Lamassu, Rani, due to having Dark Wizards assist the Cloud Giants, and we almost got to Darkwing. Had we known about the Dark Wizards, I know that we would have handled the situation differently. So, your cryptic note warning me of things that would be common sense tells me you knew more than you were letting on." Akita walks up to him, putting her right hand on his shoulder, and places the flute on his chest. "Are you helping the Dark Wizards?"

King Windu, who can't take his eyes off the flute, states a flat "NO." the ring glows just a little bit and dims. He can't see the ring because it is over the back of his shoulder.

She asks her second question, "Have you utilized them to get your precious collectibles?"

King Windu holds his hands out and shrugs, "I have been known to utilize operatives who might have used them. I cannot be held accountable for their actions; surely, I mean, I can't say for sure who they employed." The ring glows more than before but not with full brightness.

Akita backs away, leaving the flute in his hand. "You are only telling partial truths, King Windu. I will remember this if we have dealings in the future. If I find that you ever betray us, Annut and friends will be visiting." Akita nods to Greenbean, who does a quick flourish with her blade, and they leave the room, heading to the courtyard.

Hunter and Warrior land in the courtyard, awaiting Akita and Greenbean.

As they take off over the ocean, they see the ship making its way to the open sea. Akita decides to fly over the town on their way back to Blackwing Keep. They fly out of the south side of town, head to the mountain, and then back out to sea to follow the ship.

As Hunter and Warrior skim over the desert floor toward the mountain, the sand shifts, and moves as if something is under it. They watch a hole develop in front of them in the sand, so they veer off to the side. As they circle around the hole, the head and wings of a creature Akita had only heard of, emerges. Akita orders her Wyverns to evade the Coatyl, a serpent-type Dragon with wings and no legs. The Coatyl is a good sixty feet long, brown with a tan underbelly; its wings allow him to fly but not for long distances. As he flies up, he tries to snap at Hunter. Greenbean riding on Warrior turn so that he can engulf the creature in flames, turning its attention on them now, as they race by evading another snap of its jaws. Akita notices that it does not use fire or any spitting weapon when attacking, so it's probably young and not developed yet. Hunter and Akita make another run at it, with Akita using her soul siphon spell followed by an immediate fear spell. The serpent recoils back toward the hole it came out of, while Warrior and Greenbean try to blind it with fire. A screech of pain fills the air as

Hunter and Akita dive for its throat, grabbing on and biting down hard while using Hunter's hind legs to rip at the serpent's wings. Its tail is flailing, so Warrior grabs it and bites its body in the midsection. Akita doubles down on the soul siphon spell as they stretch and rip at it. Slowly the serpent weakens and droops to the ground.

Akita and Greenbean fly side by side over the dead body. Then, yelling to Greenbean, "If this was one of King Windu's collectibles or pets, he didn't take very good care of it."

Greenbean nods, "He and his men can clean this mess up; let's go home."

Hunter and Warrior head out to the ocean to catch up with the ship with that statement.

Wulf and Mandrake use their combined magic to propel the ship, and it sails into the Prayla docks in record time. They added a bit more power to the spells so they would get to Blackwing Keep faster. Upon arriving, Mandrake enchants the horses with their ice wings. After mounting, the twins levitate Rani to carry her back to Blackwing Keep from the Prayla docks.

Akita and Greenbean land shortly after the ship docks. Ishvet climbs onto Hunter. Fabby takes a ride with Greenbean.

Gavin says to Akita, "I will head to the Farm and check on the Wyvern and her eggs. Then, I will be at the Keep in time for the ceremony." Gavin and Blitz take off.

Akita nods to Gavin, "Thank you, my friend. Wulf ride with me, and Vivian ride with Fabby and Greenbean. Ordyn, we will meet you there."

Annut flies out to them and escorts them all to the Keep. She felt Ishvet's pain as they sailed past her cave. She is waiting for Akita to land, "If you show me where you want it, I will dig the grave now, before Ishvet has a chance to get out to it."

Akita nods and walks away from the group. "I am going to have Ghod join us. Give me a few minutes." Then, she heads to the smith shop. She finds Ghod working on yet another project.

"Ghod, we need to talk. I know you're busy, but can you take a walk with me?"

Ghod nods and starts to follow, "What has happened? Is Vivian, ok?"

Akita shakes her head, "Vivian is fine; in fact, if we didn't have her, we would have had more casualties. We found Dark Wizards working with the Cloud Giants when we got to the island. When we got to Darkwing, the King of the Cloud Giants stepped out with two Dark Wizards, which divided our attention. He started with lightning and thunder that impacted Rani; she just couldn't take the noise. She flew to attack and got thrown to the ground so hard she was instantly killed. Vivian kept us all safe while Vicar tried to save Rani and the rest of us kept fighting."

They are at the new cemetery when she finishes the short version of the story. Rani is lying on the ground, and Annut is standing nearby. Ghod stands in silence for a minute. "We need a proper monument for this beautiful friend and brave beast. Then I need to know more details about what you experienced so I can work on a weapon or two to assist you when you go back for Darkwing."

Akita agrees, "Yes, that is why I came to you after we landed. Right now, we are not talking about it much in front of Ishvet, as he is crushed by the loss of Rani. With that said, after we have a ceremony here, the rest of us will meet to talk about what to do next. That would probably be a good time to get the details."

On the ocean side of the Keep, they chose a large grassy area with scattered trees that sits near the base of the mountain for a special cemetery. The cemetery was created after the battle against the Dark Wizard Evad and the Dark Wizard Sect. It is meant to memorialize the brave soldiers that have fought against evil under the leadership of Akita Blackwing. There are currently four monuments, one for their friend Jessa and three for the soldiers killed in the battle to take the Grotto. In addition, workers have started building a fence around the site, encompassing a slowly rising hill near the mountain's base. Akita takes note that it is big enough for more mounts if it ever came to that.

Akita says to Annut and Ghod, "I think we will make that hill the sacred place for our beloved mounts. I am not naive enough to believe we won't lose more as we keep fighting these Dark Wizards and dangerous monsters, they seem to want to throw at us." So, she walks to the hill to find the best spot.

Ghod looks around, "I know I do not seem like I would ever have sympathy, apathy, empathy, or any other emotion; believe me, that is by design. If you tell anyone different, I will deny it. But if it were me, I would bury Rani here to look out over the ocean and a clear view of the Keep. As you move closer to the mountain, you only get one or the other view, if that makes sense. She was a protector and would want to watch over us from all directions."

Akita looks at Ghod, "I fully agree with you. However, I have also learned there are many layers to you, and you never cease to amaze me." She looks at Annut. "My boys are lucky they did not go with us to the island, or I am sure we would be burying more if we could have gotten them home. As it is, we had to fight a Coatyl as we left Port Tristan, near the mountain. Then we flew home, following the ship. Your help is greatly appreciated."

Annut speaks to Akita and Ghod, "Rani was a unique beast and very rare. Ishvet is a good man, and I respect him. It is my honor to do this for them." She then takes two claws and carves a deep hole in the ground. "I think this will work with her legs folded up as if she is sleeping."

Akita nods and looks at Rani. Luckily her legs were already curled up from when the twins levitated her and brought her home. "Thank you, Annut. We will be back soon. Ghod, I know you will come up with something amazing."

Annut states, "I am going to lay here in the sun watching the waves with Rani, so she is not alone, and nothing comes near her."

"Thank you, my friend." Akita and Ghod head back to the Keep.

Ghod heads to the forge while Akita heads to find Greta.

Akita finds Greta in the storage rooms. "Greta, I know this is going to be a strange request, but I remember growing up with a massive tapestry of lions hanging in the Grand Hall. Do you know where that is?"

Greta thinks a minute. "Yes, I know the one you mean. Your uncle had it taken down because it reminded him too much of your aunt. It is safely rolled up and stored in the next room."

Akita heads to the room with Greta behind her. "I want to see if it is really as big as I remember or if it was just that big because I was little."

Greta looks at Akita, "What do you have in mind?"

"You probably haven't heard yet, but we did not get Darkwing back, and we lost Rani in the battle to just get to Darkwing. So, I want to see if it is big enough to wrap Rani in for burial. She gave her all in the fight against the Cloud Giant King. Ishvet is crushed, and I want to do something special for the two of them."

Greta suggests, "I will go get a couple of soldiers to take this to the ballroom where we can lay it out."

Akita starts moving boxes and other items that are blocking the corner it is standing in. She hopes it is still in good condition and not thin or dingy in spots. Greta was right; it was her aunt's favorite that hung in the Grand Hall.

Greta returns with two soldiers to take the tapestry up the stairs to the ballroom within a few minutes. They follow the men and then instruct them to lay it down. As Akita starts unrolling it, the soldiers jump in to help. "Greta, this will just about make it, I think. The other thing I would like to do, and I know it is a poor use of resources, but I want a bed of wool in the bottom of the grave."

One of the soldiers speaks up, "Lady Blackwing, I know it is not my place to say anything, but if this is for Rani, the beautiful lioness, then I think it is a grand idea. Most of us are saddened that she lost her life, but we know she fought bravely."

Akita looks to the soldiers, "Gentlemen, I know how my uncle was, and yes, there is a time and a place, but I appreciate your thoughts on the matter. I will only be upset if you step in a conversation with dignitaries because you won't know all I may be doing in the background. So, with that said, can I get you to roll this tapestry back up and take it out to where Rani is waiting, as well as enough wool. I will warn you, Annut is guarding Rani against scavengers and the like, but you can go about business as she won't bother you. She dug the grave so you can see the size while you are there."

Both soldiers say at the same time, "Yes, Ma'am, right away." As they start rolling the tapestry back up.

Greta says, "Lady Blackwing, so you know, word has gotten around to the soldiers and staff as to how approachable you are, and the moral around here is the highest I have ever seen it."

Akita scrunches her face but understands they are in front of the soldiers, so Greta is in character, but it still doesn't sit well with her. Will she ever get used to it? She supposes in time she will; things have just been too busy for weeks now. "Good to know. Things have been so crazy and messed up since I came home. However, I have noticed how smooth things are running. I am going to go take a quick bath and then check on Ishvet."

Akita makes her way around the Keep but cannot find Ishvet. For that matter, she hasn't found anyone. She asks Annut, "Is everyone out there already?"

Annut answers, "One by one, as they have sought out Ishvet, they have found him here, quietly sobbing. The tapestry is beautiful, and he has laid it out beside her."

"Well then, I will stop by and get Ghod. Be there in a few minutes. Oh, and would you let Hunter and Warrior know, as well as the twin's horses."

Akita finds Ghod just leaving the smiths shop with a heavy item wrapped in burlap in a cart. She walks up next to him, and they head to the cemetery.

Ghod gestures to the item in the cart. "It's not much yet but will do temporarily until I can complete a proper marker."

Hunter and Warrior fly over as they walk, as the Warhorses catch up to Akita and follow. The stable hands that were panicking slowed down and followed as well. It is heartening to see the care and love amongst her people, and it's not just restricted to her friends.

As they round the corner of the Keep getting closer to the new cemetery, Akita sees Annut with

Hunter and Warrior on each side of her. Very interesting, as if standing in some sort of formation. Then Mandrake and Vicar's horses, Judgement and Apothecary, take off at a trot; as they get to the Dragons, they too move one to each side. Then she notices Blitz, in the center in front of Annut, sitting tall and handsome.

The soldiers not on duty are standing in the field in formation, awaiting the proceedings—Olek among them, standing in front with General Ambrose.

Akita walks to the head of the grave and looks in. It has been nicely padded on the bottom. Ghod walks up next to her and signals for Olek to join him. Olek marches to Ghod, and they pick up the burlap-wrapped item. Akita moves as they lift it above their heads, letting the item's weight push the two spiked bars into the ground. Ghod tests it, and they push down a little more, making sure it will not come dislodged. Olek goes back to take his place next to the general.

Akita nods to Mandrake and Vicar as they proceed to levitate Rani to the grave. Ishvet follows behind Rani, with the entire team behind him. The twins' step to each side of the grave and slowly lower Rani down. Then six soldiers grab the large tapestry with three on each side. They slowly move it into position over Rani's body and lower it upon her. The tapestry completely covers her body, and the ends are folded down into the grave. The sunlight shimmers on hand-embroidered golden lions on the tapestry giving the illusion that they are playing in a summer field.

Akita amplifies her voice; she notices the rest of the Blackwing Keep cooks, housekeeping, and stable hands. She is so impressed with the love shown by the Keep's people. "We are here today to say goodbye to our friend, Rani. I want to thank all of the people of the Keep who have come to show respect to Ishvet and his best friend in life and battle. Rani was a beautiful, brave lioness devoted to Ishvet and the fight. In her last fight, she valiantly flew directly at danger, allowing us to destroy two Dark Wizards and escape the Cloud Giant King. Ishvet left the Cloud Giant King wounded and bloodied as we all retreated. Darkwing, unfortunately, is still there and trapped for the moment. Nevertheless, Rani saved lives today and gave us a chance to gather vital information to save another life. Looking around at the people gathered today, we can see that Rani had touched many lives."

"Rani, may you fly high with the Gods today and watch over Ishvet in his many endeavors to come."

Akita steps back and nods at Ghod, who slowly pulls the burlap off his creation. Using twisted wrought iron, he had created a Lion Head with wings on each side, and Rani spelled out below the head. It was quite detailed and impressive when you consider Ghod only had a few hours to complete it.

Ghod walks up to Ishvet, "This is a start; when I am done, it will be a monument to behold my friend." He puts a hand on Ishvets shoulder, pauses, and walks back to Akita's side.

Annut, Hunter, Warrior, the Warhorses, and the Fox all move forward to the grave. Annut and the Wyverns raise their heads to the sky and roar in one voice. The Warhorses, Apothecary and Judgement, rear up and whinny, with Blitz sitting up churring and yipping mournfully. All were paying their respects to Rani, then backing up. Everyone is in awe of the mount's display of respect. Annut touches everyone's minds in the cemetery and the Keep and softly begins to sing a beautiful song in the Dragon tongue. No one knows what she is saying, but it is compelling and sorrowful at the same time.

Akita moves to stand by Ishvet, putting an arm around his shoulder, and just be there with him. After Annut finishes the song, there isn't a dry eye that can be seen. Even Ghod's mask has wet spots under his eyes.

Ishvet looks out to sea, "I can't stand to lose anyone else to these evil forces. First my mother, then Jessa, and now Rani. Rani was right in front of me, and even with my mother's power, I couldn't save her. So, Akita, we have to destroy all of them. Promise me that we will."

Akita turns to Ishvet and sees the tears streaming down his bluish Dragonkin face. The light passing through each tear makes them look like tiny blue oceans. Akita squeezes Ishvet's body with her arm around him. She whispers to him in a soft, careful tone, "I promise you."

Ordyn steps up, "We are all with you, Ishvet. It is time this be done, and the evil we can find will be destroyed."

Vicar steps up to the grave, "Ishvet has asked me to say a few words. My heart is heavy in these times. We all have experienced death in some form or fashion over the years, but it is never as painful as when it is family. Not just family in the sense of blood, but the sense of who you have strong bonds with. Rani was Ishvet's family, and she grew to be a part of our family here at Blackwing Keep. We now lay her to rest, to lay and sun herself in the meadows of the Gods. She will forever be in our hearts, and her passing will forever strengthen our love for the ones we call family that are still with us. We will now cover Rani's body with soil that she may nourish the land and give new life to things yet to come. Praise the Gods."

Everyone at the service replies in unison, "Praise the Gods."

Several guards walk up, salute, and then start refilling the grave as the team walks away.

Akita states as she walks with Ishvet, "You need to know that I threatened to burn King Windu's Castle to the ground and gut it if I found that he was working with the Dark Wizards. My ring had a low glow when I questioned him as if he had had some direct business with them. So, when this is over, we will be addressing him and any other leader or ruler that has been working with or doing business with the Dark Wizards. For now, let's get some rest and start planning our next move tomorrow when we are fresh."

CHAPTER 9
REVELATIONS

It's been two and a half days since Akita and the team came to rescue him. Ishvet was so close when the Cloud Giant King stepped between them.

Darkwing has noticed reinforcements of Dark Wizards arriving. Healers have managed to heal the King's wounds left by Ishvet. Darkwing wonders how close Ishvet came to wounding the King that he would bleed out. Probably not that close, but something he knows they will be working on, as the vengeance in Ishvets eyes was unmistakable. Darkwing has built up even more hatred for these Giants after what they did to his family and now Rani. At one point, he thought Ishvet was doomed when the King grabbed him in mid-air. However, had Ishvet been any slower with slicing the King's hand, he might have met the same fate as Rani. The more Darkwing thinks about it, the angrier he gets.

Darkwing had been continuing to try and freeze the pillory. With each crack he heard, he felt he was getting closer to freeing himself. Then four new

Dark Wizards come to lasso Darkwing's hands and feet. Another unlocks the pillory, and Darkwing collapses. "You know it's inhumane to leave someone standing like that for days on end. I suppose you expect me to walk now that you released me." The top of the pillory closes above him, and he hears the locks snap. Thinking to himself, he was almost free.

One of them growls at him, "Shut up and crawl if you have to; we don't care."

Darkwing stretches his arms getting the circulation going again, which is painful as they start tingling and stinging. He rubs his hands together to get the feeling back, while his legs feel like they have sandbags tied to them. As he attempts to stand, he lunges at one of the wizards with a lasso in his hand. He tries to use his magic, but all that happens is a cube of ice falls out of his hand. The Dark Wizards tighten the restraints restricting his movement again with this attack.

Darkwing chuckles, "You can't blame a guy for trying." His smile says I will kill you versus any joy a smile usually shows.

The Dark Wizard that has the leash of light on his right-hand screams, "Shut up, Skrymir! Soon you'll be in the midst of the ritual. We now have everything we need to get that stolen magic out of you!

All the wizards pull on the leashes hard, and Darkwing stumbles forward. They walk him up the path to the temple and take him inside. A large iron "X" lies in the inner chamber on its back. At each end of the four points are restraints. They maneuver Darkwing into position and restrain him at both wrists and ankles. The restraints are enchanted like the previous ones and subdue his magic. A lesser Dark Wizard comes up and gives Darkwing a drink of water from a ladle and feeds him a small biscuit.

A tall Dark Wizard comes up towards Darkwing's legs. This Wizard is dressed a little differently. He has dark maroon robes and large ornate gold bracelets. He looks down at Darkwing, "We can't have you dying of thirst or starvation before the ritual. You must know by now that we want the magic that you absorbed from the amulet that King Idris gave you. That magic is not meant for someone like you. Once we extract it and can study it, King Cirus will put you out of your misery."

Before Darkwing can even respond, the Dark Wizard raises his right hand and turns his wrist. The golden cuff glows, and Darkwing is rendered mute. The Dark Wizard chuckles, "No, please don't say anything. You are so pathetic. I don't know how my son can be friends with you!"

The Dark Wizard pushes back his hood, revealing his face to Darkwing, "You may not know my face, but Sir Ishvet Bluescale would. Yes, I see the cogs moving in your mind. I am King Carthon III of Astya. I am one of the most powerful wizards on the continent."

Rogue sits at a table at the back of the room, watching various guild members come and go. He has spoken to a couple of old friends, trying to glean some information from them, but they are either secretive or don't know what is going on in the area. Most around here have not even heard about Annut yet. However, one did state to watch your back in the north that the Dark Wizards seem to be everywhere. This bit of information has piqued Rogue's interest because he only knew about the Prayla issue. Word has not even spread about the demise of that sect. Rogue wonders if he should place a well-worded rumor to see the reactions.

Two members sit at a table near him; he listens as well as he can to hear their conversation. They seem to be discussing some temple full of Dark Wizards and something about a Dragon.

Rogue leans over and asks, "Have you heard about any Dark Wizards or Dragons on the west coast?"

One of the men looks at Rogue, "I can't say that I have heard anything from the west coast in many years."

Rogue runs a hand through his hair; they must be talking about another Dragon. He nods to the men and walks up to the bar. As he sits down, the door opens, and in comes Meh-Kola. The bartender waves her over to the counter, handing her a drink and a message. She nods her thanks.

She looks at Rogue, "Well, look who is here. So long time no see old friend. What brings you to the guild this night?"

Rogue answers, "Nice to see you again, Meh-Kola, and it has been a while, hasn't it. I thought you had gone home."

Meh-Kola chuckles, "Things are getting interesting around here; One is curious to see where they end."

Rogue scratches his chin, "I guess I have spent too much time retired. What has gotten so interesting?"

Meh-Kola looks at Rogue slyly. "Have you been that underground? One finds that suspect. Don't you know that the Dark Wizards are running rampant in your backyard?"

Rogue shrugs, "I have been raising my pets and hunting, as well as relaxing. I have been reading books and working hard to enjoy life."

"Rogue, my friend, One suggests you consider pulling your head out of retirement. The north and east of this continent are becoming more and more dangerous, even for us assassins."

"Ok, dear, I know you are trying to tell me something without telling me something. But I need something concrete if I am going to consider sticking my nose out of my backyard bliss."

Meh-Kola looks down and reads the message while she thinks about telling Rogue anything and what to tell him. Finally, she looks back at Rogue, "One will tell you something, but One needs information in return. What do you know about Blackwing Keep?"

Rogue gives a sly smile, "Well, the High Duke Edmond Blackwing has passed. I believe I heard he was murdered. However, his niece is now the High Duchess Akita Blackwing, and she has stepped into his shoes as ruler of Prayla and her realm. I take it that message is from someone there?"

Meh-Kola shrugs, "It seems old friends from Ones' home want my expertise in something. So, instead of trusting messages, One is going to head there. You, my friend, should maybe stock up on your secret weapon and check out the Dragon temple, which is north and east of here."

Rogue thinks to himself, the Twins, Mandrake, and Vicar are from the continent of Omoth like the Fenton's are. I wonder why they want Meh-Kola at Blackwing Keep. As he sees Meh-Kola finishing her drink, he states, "Safe travels, my old friend."

Meh-Kola nods, "Safe travels to you, and One is not old, and don't you forget it." She saunters out the door and disappears before the door can fully swing shut.

Rogue pulls out a piece of parchment, and the bartender, who was obviously paying attention, hands him a quill and ink. Rogue rights down a few notes about Dark Wizards and the Dragon Temple and puts the parchment in his pocket after it dried.

He looks around then tells the bartender that he is returning to his table and would like a drink for the road. Rogue gets up and goes to the table in the back, pulls out his tobacco pouch, and starts rolling a cigarette. The bartender approaches and puts the drink down in front of the tobacco pouch, then picks up the candlestick and lights Rogue's cigarette for him. The pouch catches the eye of the bartender, "You know it just came to me that about two days back, two cloaked figures came into the guild asking about any members that had a pouch just like that and a dagger to match."

Rogue looks up, "I don't suppose you remember who these guys were, do you? Maybe, where they came from or who they worked for?"

The bartender leans back and looks up to the ceiling as if thinking, "They said that they were from the desert and that they traveled as fast as possible to get here for their boss. They were the ones that gave me the message for Meh-Kola."

Rogue jumps from his chair, tosses the cigarette into his drink, pushes by the Barkeep, and runs out the door. He goes out to Ransom, thinking if there are Dark Wizards in the area, I will have to loop around and vary my path back to Blackwing Keep. So, they take off in the direction of Darkforest. Rogue attempts to talk to Ransom, "Someone knows who I am. We will only travel by night and hide during the day. I was in there for a long time, so who knows who could have seen me and reported back to someone."

It is about an hour's flight from the assassin's guild to the Stoania and Astya border. Shortly after crossing the border, they turn towards their home. To give the illusion that he was just going back home after visiting friends.

Flying over the dense forest gives an illusion of black waves speeding underneath them while they hover above. The moonlight touches the tips of the trees and shimmers as if the forest is mirroring the stars in the night sky. If Rogue weren't in such a panic, it would have been a beautiful site to enjoy. He gets almost halfway home and turns Ransom northwest. They fly low to the treetops to obscure themselves from being backlit by the moon.

As they continue on their path northwest, the clouds become thicker. In about another twenty minutes of flying, they will be able to turn southwest and fly until first light. Rogue is keeping a close eye on the landscape they are passing above to look for a water source to land by. Ransom would be thirsty by now with all this flying and maneuvering.

Rogue sees a clearing ahead that has a small river running through it, "Ransom, circle around that clearing and then land by the river so we can get a drink."

As soon as Rogue finishes his sentence, he feels the air pressure change above him. It's pushing down upon him forcefully. He looks up and sees an enormous black shadow closing in. The moonlight reveals the outline of massive wings, a long-jagged tail, and a horned head. The Dragon is on top of them in a flash. Rogue's scream splits the silent night as a talon pierces his right shoulder then releases.

Rogue yells to Ransom, "Faster; we can't beat this one alone. So, fly like the wind."

Ransom dives to the right narrowly missed getting singed by flames as soon as these words were spoken, "That's it; keep dodging."

Ransom is flying for her life, but a talon catches a wing as she weaves in and out of treetops.

Rogue looks over his shoulder, "Fly girl, fly, I know you can do this." She dodges to the left, dodging another claw, then to the right, dodging flames yet again.

Rogue leans in low over Ransom's spines, urging her faster. The next clawed attack rips Ransom's left-wing heavily, so she tries to fly lower into the trees, hoping the swipes by the Giant black

Dragon will take out trees instead of hitting her. The Dragon swoops in again, headfirst directly towards Rogue. The Dragon is too fast for Ransom to dodge, and Rogue is caught. The Dragon has Rogue in its mouth. Its teeth are slowly sinking into Rogue's flesh. The Dragon is tumbling forward from the inertia of its dive attack, and Rogue and Ransom are tumbling mid-air with it. The Dragon bites down, and Ransom can hear the crack of bones. Rogue screams in anguish while beating the Dragon's nose with his left arm.

The Dragon releases Rogue from its mouth and steadies its flying before turning away. Ransom catches herself in mid-tumble and levels out. Rogue is slumped over Ransom's back, lightly clinging to her spines. Rogue tries to speak, but all that Ransom can make out is "home" and "Drako." Then there is only the sound of the wind fluttering through Ransom's torn wings.

Ransom keeps weaving in and out of the trees as fast as she can, but her now tattered wings are making it hard to fly. Finally, she screams out to Drako for help that their master has been hurt. She doesn't even notice she has passed the house heading west as she is in a panic. She keeps expecting the black Dragon to finish her off too.

Drako flies in behind her and sees her wings shredded and a long gash to the left of her spine above her right leg. He gently speaks to her to keep flying to Blackwing Keep. No one is home, and we need the help of our masters' friends.

Ransom conveys that she doesn't know how long she will last. Drako assures her that he is there to help, but they can't land; she is too injured. Furthermore, he could not protect her from bandits or Dark Wizards if they landed. Drako maneuvers under her to lift her and carry her, to assist in flying.

Drako quietly mourns the loss of their master. He knows Rogue is slumped over Ransom's ridge horns, the only thing holding him in place, including the saddle ties.

Ishvet and Ordyn have lived in the library for days looking for any hints that might tell them what is needed to go against the Cloud Giants.

Ishvet found an old tome that refers to an ancient Dwarven settlement on the northern side of the Voskaola Mountains. He wonders if they would be able to find the entrance now or if the Great

Eruption has totally destroyed the entrance and the caves themselves.

Ishvet and Ordyn go to the map room to see if a mountain map might have some detail and an older map of the region before the Great Eruption.

They find Akita, Mandrake, and Vicar going over maps of Stoania. Akita and the team are looking for some marker or reference to the ancient Dragon Temple that Annut told her about.

There are maps laid open on every table, and it looks like more tables were brought in. Ishvet states, "It looks like you have been busy. Have you found the temple yet?"

Mandrake answers, "We think we might have a general area." Showing Ishvet and Ordyn the map they have been looking at. "If you use the information Annut gave us, it should be just a little southeast of Dragon Rest and basically north of Neg Grove."

Akita says off-handed, "That's Jessa's neck of the wood's; she might have known something that would have been helpful."

Vicar replies, "Yes, that would have been helpful, but at least we have a place to start looking."

Akita looks to Ishvet, "I take it you need the maps as well."

Ishvet looks around, "We need maps of the north side of the Voskaola mountains. We think a cave there might hold some secrets to the Cloud Giants. If the description is correct, the cave will be at the foot of the mountain below Darkwing Keep. However, this tome was written before the Great Eruption, so we need a newer and an older map."

Vicar walks to a table and starts rolling up maps they don't need anymore. "I think there is a map in this pile that is before the Great Eruption."

Mandrake heads to another table, "I seem to remember one in this pile that is newer." Mandrake is rolling up maps and moving them to the side.

Vicar states, "Mandrake, we should put them back in their slots for next time, not just set them aside."

Mandrake shrugs, "You do you and put them back then." He takes the two maps and lays them over all the maps on the main table.

Ishvet and Ordyn step up to the table. Ordyn starts looking for common towns or markers between the two maps. Ordyn sighs, "I don't think the old map is going to help us much. Nothing is the same on the new map, as the Great Eruption destroyed the towns and farms in the area. I wish we could make the newer map transparent and lay it over the old map."

Ishvet chuckles, "I don't know of a spell for that, do you Akita or Mandrake?"

Vicar has an idea, "Ordyn and Ishvet hold the newer map up over the old map. I want to try something." So, he creates little balls of light and floats them between the two maps. He keeps muting the light until it shows map details through the top map but isn't too bright to hinder. He also moves them more in a circle to highlight the mountain range. "Akita and Mandrake hold up the old map, and I will put lights under that one too. That is the best I can do, as the parchment is a bit thick, but I think it is close to what you were asking."

Ordyn laughs, "That my friend is genius, and we couldn't have used candles without burning the maps, not that I would have thought about that until you did this work of magic."

Ishvet looks at Akita, "I think we have a starting point for the cave as well. The only issue will be if we can find an entrance that the Great Eruption did not cover up and if the Dwarven caves didn't collapse at that time either." He points at a spot on the map. "If we start at Darkwing Keep and go straight down the mountain to this ravine, we might find it."

Akita asks, "We know the Dark Wizards seem to be everywhere, so I don't want to split us up anymore. So where do we go first? The Cave that is closest to us or the ancient Dragon Temple?"

Mandrake says, "For what is it worth, I suggest looking for the cave. If the entrance is gone, then we can mark it off our list. But, on the other hand, if we find the entrance, that is a bonus, with it being close to the Keep, so to speak."

As the others nod in agreement, Akita states, "Let's let the others know, so we can start gathering our supplies. We will want the heavy tents, heavy blankets, coats, hats, mittens, the works because we don't know how far down the other side of the mountain the entrance might be. We also need to figure out the mounts. It might be too long of a flight up to Darkwing Keep for the horses, and you don't want to stop on the way up. Their hooves might freeze just standing there for thirty minutes, not to mention us freezing."

Mandrake replies, "We can wrap the horses' hooves, and I can put up an ice shield around us to keep most of the wind and cold out long enough to recharge them. But is there room in the aviary for the mounts with Darkwing's Owl Roc's?"

Akita nods, "Yes, there is room, and maybe we can get Martyn and Mylar to join us as extra mounts once we get there. This will also allow us to see if his people need any supplies since Darkwing hasn't been around to take care of things."

Vicar asks, "Do we know if Shamash was able to get a Seeking Shard for the Keep? Actually, I will go check with him, as I want to see if Skip has sent us a message about the Frost Giants."

Everyone heads to gather supplies, and Akita starts looking for the others to tell them the plan.

CHAPTER 10
SURPRISES

After a long day of getting supplies ready for the flight over the mountain, Akita went to bed early. Curled up in her big canopy bed, she snuggled up under the blankets while dreaming of talking to Annut. Just a pleasant conversation about what exactly she couldn't tell you. All of a sudden, Annut is yelling at her. She hears her but doesn't quite understand the message. She awakens with a start, and Annut is yelling something about hatchlings.

Akita hears Annut in her head, "Come quick and bring meat; some eggs are hatching." She shakes herself out of her dream world and realizes what Annut is telling her.

Akita jumps to her feet and throws her clothes on, stumbling as she tries to get her boots on, running through her rooms. As she runs through the halls, she's pounding on doors; yelling Dragons are hatching.

Ordyn grabs her around the belly, stopping her as she runs by, "Hold on there, Akita, did you say the Dragons are hatching? No one can understand you with how excited you are."

Akita catches her breath. "Yes, some are hatching. Annut says she needs straw and meat as soon as possible. I'm going to go wake up the stable hands, Sham, Scotch, and Ben, so they can load a wagon and get moving up the hill. Those who want to be there will need help flying up to the ledge; Mandrake and Vicar can double up on the horses. Warrior and Hunter can take four for that short of a trip. I will also go open the back of the cave and meet you there."

Ordyn starts laughing, "Slow down and give people a chance to wipe the sleep out of their eyes. Then, I will spread the word about why you have gone nuts tonight. Go get the stable hands."

Akita flies down the stairs and out the door. She finds Sham asleep in his quarters. "Sham, wake up; some of the eggs are hatching. Get a wagon, meat, and straw. Wake up Scotch and Ben as well. Then, head up the hill as fast as you can."

She calls to Warrior and Hunter, calling to them, "My boys wait in the courtyard, Dragons are hatching, and we need you to carry four at a time to the ledge, if you need to, make a couple of trips, and come back for the others."

Ben comes running up to her. "Lady Blackwing, is it true, baby Dragons are hatching?"

"Yes, Ben. Now go get horses hitched to the wagons and load lots of straw and meat. This is the secret of Blackwing Keep, so keep it to yourself."

Ben looks at Akita, "Yes Ma'am. Just so you know, Grandpa heard you yelling all the way through the building, but then he has excellent hearing."

Akita giggles, "I guess you could say I am excited. This morning is historic. See you up there, so hurry."

Akita sees others streaming out of the Keep. She flies over quickly and does a little dance in the air. Greenbean laughs at her as Fabby smiles. Mandrake calls the horses to him with a whistle as Akita announces, "Anyone not making it on this trip, Warrior and Hunter will come back for you."

She turns to see Shamash running up to Hunter, and she smiles. Mandrake enchants both horses as quickly as possible. Their ice wings will make the trip very short, even with the two riders apiece. With that, she turns and flies towards Annut's cave, with Ordyn following behind her. As she flies up the valley, she notices something really fast running up ahead of her. But of course, Judas would not want to ride any of the mounts, so he's running. She points the little guy out to Ordyn, who nods.

It takes very little time to fly to the ledge. Judas comes to a stop just under it, looking for a way up. He squeals and cusses up a storm as Ordyn grabs him lifting him to the ledge.

Akita is laughing so hard she almost can't speak, "Judas! Calm yourself. There is no other way up here."

Judas grumbles a bit more and straightens his tunic. "Well, a little warning would have been nice."

"But not as much fun, my dear." She turns to the cave wall and opens it, then creates a fire in her hand to light up the cave.

The horses land on the ledge. Vivian, Gavin, Mandrake, and Vicar dismount, and the horses stand to the side. Vicar casts a calming spell. Warrior lands on the ledge allowing Olek, Wulf, Grace, and Greenbean to dismount. Warrior flies down to the ground enabling Hunter to land on the ledge. Fabby, Ixenvorlux, Ishvet, and Shamash dismount.

Shamash tells Akita, "The wagon is loaded full and on the way."

Akita asks, "Warrior, please let me know as soon as the wagon gets here. We will come out to bring them and the supplies up." Then turning to her friends. "Please remember this is to be kept a secret amongst ourselves. We don't tell parents, brothers, sisters, aunts, uncles, cousins, best friends, well you get the idea. Everyone in the Keep will be sworn to secrecy for the time being."

Akita turns to Vicar, "Would you light up the cave and cavern, please."

Vicar summons many glowing balls, sending them down the cave in front of them and leaving one every few feet to keep it lit for the stable hands when they get here and anyone else moving through the caves.

Akita can barely contain herself as she walks quickly to the cavern with the eggs. As she rounds the corner, "Annut, we are here, and the supplies you asked for are on the way."

Annut gives her Dragon chuckle. "I see everyone came for this momentous day."

Akita starts wandering around the room, looking for eggs that are beginning to crack. "But of course, my friend. As you said, it is a momentous day." Those that had been there before are inspecting the shells. The first timers are standing and staring in awe at the six giant pearls.

Akita asks, "Annut, how many will be hatching?"

Annut answers so everyone can hear. "I believe three will be hatching this morning. However, the one that is smitten with Darkwing says he won't hatch until he returns."

Akita looks at the first-timers, "Come and feel the eggs. Oh, and look, this one has fine cracks in it." It is an egg sitting closest to Annut.

Akita is looking around the cavern. "We need a place to put the meat, and we need a trough for water. Gavin, can you gently manipulate rock? Making a ridge along the wall for food and maybe a deeper ridge, as tall as Judas, next to it for water. We don't want to disturb the eggs that aren't hatching."

Gavin replies, "Well, I reckon I can heat the rock to draw it up. I did it years ago without disturbing too much of my area. Let's see if it works here."

As Gavin concentrates on a portion of the floor away from the eggs, there is an audible crack. He immediately stops, turning around to see what just happened.

Akita waves him on as she steps to an egg that now has a sizeable crack in it and is wobbling. To her right, another egg cracks with the tail and neck showing because the shell is covering its head. As she walks around the egg, she sees the hind legs sticking out too. A baby Black Dragon is about to emerge. The third egg nearest Annut snaps quite loudly as wings have popped through the shell. The orange and golden wings give a hint to its color.

Ordyn states, "I don't know what I was expecting, but this is kinda funny. I expected the shells just to burst, but it looks like they are more challenging than I thought."

Gavin continues creating his ridge for the meat trough. He has built up a four-inch ridge that he is now stretching to connect with the wall.

Wulf and Ordyn head for the mouth of the cave to see if the wagon has arrived yet. It's almost there, so they have Sham tie off the wagon as they lift Sham, Scotch, and Ben to the ledge.

Ordyn tells the hands, "You want to hurry; they are breaking through. We can get this stuff when they are fully hatched."

Ordyn and Wulf fly in, and the hands run to keep up.

Olek has made his way over to the Black Dragon. Akita can hear him whispering to the hatchling. "Hey there, little one, keep trying to get that shell off." The Dragon sighs and then sneezes as smoke fills up the shell, rolling over on its back, knocking the shell off his head and cracking the main shell further. The Dragon is black with shadowy gold horns, spines, and belly. He is absolutely incredible in Olek's eyes. It rolls over and starts kicking and biting the rest of the shell.

Akita is giggly with excitement like a child. Then, she hears another crack and sees the dark red body with a golden belly peeking out of the shell. At that moment, the little Dragon headbutts the shell breaking more of it off. If a Dragon could grin, this one does, looking proud of itself for breaking more of the shell.

As another egg cracks more, Akita notices that her friends are circled around the Dragon hatchlings. Annut is sitting so proud watching the antics of her babies. The third egg with the wings out now has its legs poking through and is on his feet, trying to headbutt the shell off. It finally gets frustrated, and it sits down hard, which puts a large crack up the egg.

It only took a few more minutes for all three to find their way out of the shells. As they do, they all look up at Annut, their Mother.

Akita looks at those that fly. "Let's get the straw and the meat up here. These guys are probably hungry."

Gavin, Wulf, Ordyn, and Akita head for the door. "Sham, Scotch, and Ben, as well as anyone else, if you could carry the supplies in from the ledge." Akita notices that Olek is still with the little Black Dragon.

Wulf and Ordyn fly the meat in and dump it in Gavin's newly made meat trough. Next, Mandrake creates a large ice cube in the deeper water trough that Gavin created.

Mandrake looks to Annut, "Would you be so kind as to melt this ice so we can see if we need another to fill it?" Annut nods and breathes hot air on the ice, which causes it to melt by half. She melts the other half, and Mandrake creates another ice block to melt slowly.

The hatchlings are drawn to the fresh meat. They wobble and stumble on their new legs to the food and immediately start chowing down.

Greenbean and Fabby haven't seen Akita so happy in months. Greenbean joins Akita at the hatchling that reminds her of fire. Its body is orange and reddish-orange with yellow gold horns, spines, and accents around the wings. Greenbean looks to Akita, "Akita, my dear, Shemera here says she's delighted to see you finally."

Akita claps, but not for the reason Greenbean is thinking. "Greeny dear, meet your own special Dragon. She spoke to you first and told you, her name. She has claimed you."

Olek overhears Akita, "Lady Blackwing, does that mean Addrit has chosen me? We have had the best chat since the shell fell off his head."

Akita looks at Olek, "Wow, I guess you will lead the Dragon Armada. Congratulations, Olek."

One lone Dragon, a mixture of reds with a gold chest, horns, spines, and wing accents, has yet to have bonded with anyone in the room. Instead, it looks up at Akita and then Annut.

Annut states, "He is confused as to what to do. He is drawn to a person, but because he has had contact with you, Akita, he knows this person is new to the group."

Akita looks around the room, "Well, that would be Ben, Gavin, Vivian, and Wulf. They are the newest people in our group. Gavin and Ben will probably be with Blackwing Keep for a long time, but Vivian has her Keep to take over and rule someday, which might be a good thing for her to have a Dragon. Then we have Wulf; even I am not sure about his plans. Wulf, you have been quiet and seem to be taking all this in."

Wulf looks around at everyone and then at the ground. "Lady Blackwing, yes, I have been observing but not wanting to pry into affairs as a new guest, I have been quiet. I admire the way you all work together, the fellowship, the loyalty, and if I may say so, you are one of the best leaders I have ever met in my life. You lead effortlessly, and you don't "Lord" over your friends or people if that makes any sense at all. Honestly, I have wondered if I could have my belongings shipped here, that is if you will have me, or let me join your plans to destroy the Dark Wizards and such." Wulf jumps and turns to the little Dragon.

Akita laughs, "Let me guess; it just made my mind and your mind up for us."

Wulf smiles, "Yes, My Lady, he did. Choren just asked me to stay and teach him to fight evil."

Mandrake walks up, "Welcome to the family, Wulf. But, of course, we all know Akita and her Dragons, so if the hatchling wants you, you are in;

as we all know, animals are usually a better judge of character than people."

Sham clears his throat to interrupt. "Lady Blackwing, the beds are prepared for the hatchlings, but we need to consider caring for them. If your flyers, especially you, leave then no one can get in the cave."

Akita looks a Sham, "Oh, you are so right. Thank you for bringing this to my attention. I have been so excited it didn't even dawn on me." Akita turns to Annut, "Would you tell Ghod that Warrior is coming to pick him up and that I need him here urgently."

Annut replies, "Done, but he's not happy about it."

Akita tells Warrior to go get Ghod from the Blacksmith's shop.

Akita asks, "Greenbean, Olek, Sham, Scotch, and Wulf, follow me, please."

Wulf looks at Mandrake, "We have to teach her not to say please all the time; after all, she is the leader."

Mandrake chuckles, "We tried that already; she says she can lead without being rude."

Akita stomps her foot, "Will you two stop talking about me as if I'm not here. Shamash, you come too. Actually, everyone follow me; that way, everyone knows what we are going to do about this situation."

They all walk to the ledge, leaving Annut to snuggle with her babies. Akita has never seen even Wyverns with their mothers, so really, the idea of Dragons or Wyvern snuggling is funny.

As they reach the ledge, Warrior arrives with Ghod. "I guess the Dragons have hatched."

Akita nods, "Three of them. So, the issue is we need a locking gate that can be camouflaged as a stone wall. Next, we need keys for Shamash, Wulf, Greenbean, Olek, and myself, with one key for Sham, so the handlers can come with meat until the hatchlings can fly. Once they can fly, we can just herd some cattle up here, so they learn to hunt. Then we need a stairway that can be camouflaged as well. Finally, the gate must be made so that Basilisks cannot get in or anything of that size. Annut can handle anything, but we need this back entrance protected if she is out."

Ghod stands staring at the entrance with his arms folded. "Bob and I can make what you request, but I will need a few days. After that, Warrior and

Hunter will have to carry them up here and help put them in place. May I see the hatchlings?"

Akita smiles, "Of course, you can; besides Greenbean, Olek and Wulf should spend more time with the hatchlings before we go back to the Keep."

Ishvet folds his arms, looking at Akita, "Yeah, push it off on those three; we all know you just aren't ready to leave yet." Then, looking at the group, "She is obsessed with all things Dragon."

Akita starts heading back into the cave. Looking over her shoulder, "That would include Dragonkin, too, you know."

Ishvet retorts, "That's obvious; most of us here are Dragonkin." He chuckles.

Wulf looks at Ishvet, "In my eyes, Dragons are Regal creatures that deserve the utmost respect. I had a familiar back home that I miss terribly; he was a Pseudo Dragon. They are like miniature Dragons that can sit on your shoulder."

Akita stops dead in her tracks and turns, "I have never heard of those; they sound fascinating. We need to talk, that's for sure. I mean, we have needed to talk anyway, but I would like to know more."

Shamash laughs, "Now you have done it, Wulf. Next thing you know, there will be a Pseudo Dragon in the Keep, if not more than one."

Wulf looks sheepish for a second, but in his mind, he entirely agrees that he needs to get to know Akita better. She absolutely fascinates him.

The hatchlings are curled up on their beds when they return to the room. Akita makes a point of communing with the unhatched eggs. Greenbean, Wulf, and Olek have sat down next to their hatchlings, Shemera, Addrit, and Choren.

Gavin, Ghod, and Vivian are discussing the size of the hatchlings and the job ahead of them. Fabby has sat down with Greenbean and Shemera.

Akita notices that Annut has backed out of the cavern. She follows the short way around the wall to Annut's cavern. All the Dragonkin follow her. Ishvet, Shamash, Mandrake, Vicar, Ixenvorlux, and Ordyn all want to pay respects to the Mother of Dragons.

Annut turns her head to face them. Akita sits on her forearm; Vicar attempts a calming spell that causes Annut to put her head down. They all sit around her with a hand on the side of her face or neck. No one speaks; it is just a peaceful and respectful moment in time."

CHAPTER 11
THE RITUAL

Outside the Cloud Giant Temple, all the Dark Wizards and King Cirus await the Dark Wizard Feron. He has deciphered the Dragon language and translated the ritual needed to remove the Frost Giant magic from Skrymir Darkwing. The task was made much easier when the Dark Wizard Sect in Craonia was able to gain control of a Dragon that lives there.

King Cirus announces, "I can sense them approaching now. King Carthon, is everything ready in the temple?"

"Yes, Sire, Skrymir is secured, and the vessel is ready to receive the Frost Giant magic.

King Cirus raises an eyebrow, "It better be. I went to great lengths to capture and subdue him. I need to unlock the secrets of that magic if I'm going to recreate it. My Master Smiths have the new amulets ready for when that time comes. Every one of you Wizards better be at the top of your task, or I will personally rip you apart with the wind! Do I make myself clear?"

All the Dark Wizards look up to King Cirus, nod in agreement, and then bow and walk a few steps back. The Grand Master Dark Wizard King Carthon steps forward, "Sire, all will be done as you have specified. As soon as Leader Feron lands, I will go over his translation and then perform the separation ritual."

King Cirus looks down upon King Carthon with an indifferent stare, then turns around and looks to the sky. A dark, winged shadow can be seen breaking through the cloud barrier that surrounds the island. The Dark Wizards can be heard speaking excitedly amongst themselves. The Dragon gets closer, and they can see that it is a humongous Black Dragon with a silver sheen. The sunlight above sparkles on the tips of its spikes and horns. It is a grand sight to behold. In a small saddle, the Dark Wizard Leader Feron is at the base of the neck, clinging to the spikes in front of him. It is easy to see that his face is devoid of blood and as white as a summer's cloud even from this distance.

The Dragon makes its approach and lands just in front of King Cirus. Dust and debris kick up from the Dragon's enormous wings, and the ground shakes as it finally comes to a stop. The group of

Dark Wizards run up to the Dragon and help Leader Feron down. Leader Feron slides down, hits the ground, and crumbles to his knees, where he then expels his breakfast all over the ground in front of him. The other Dark Wizards help him up in a vain attempt for him to retain a modicum of dignity. King Cirus chuckles deeply and then waves his hand in a gesture to get moving towards the temple.

King Carthon approaches Leader Feron takes his satchel and heads towards the temple. All the Dark Wizards follow, leaving behind Leader Feron to regain his composure. The Dragon stays still during this whole time in its zombie-like state. King Cirus and the Dragon are almost the same size if the Dragon stretches its neck straight up.

King Cirus inquires Leader Feron, "Do you know who this Dragon is?"

Leader Feron looks up, "No, Sire; I only know that Leader Volin found him in some desert ruins in the north of Craonia."

King Cirus leans over and looks directly into the eyes of the Dragon, "Well, I do know him. We fought in the Titan Wars together. His name is Thoraxian - the Shadow. I know he's inside there somewhere."

King Cirus sighs, "I'm sorry, my old friend, but this was necessary. You Dragons hold your secrets so tightly that it forces my hand to break our treaty."

Leader Feron prepares a spell, "Do you wish him to speak Sire? I have the spell ready."

King Cirus puts his hand on top of Thoraxian's head and quietly says "No," and closes his eyes as a deep sadness begins to envelop him. Leader Feron stops his spell and heads toward the temple to catch up to King Carthon. Looking back as he heads to the temple, he can see King Cirus move away from the Dragon and head towards his hut.

King Carthon looks over Leader Feron's translation from the Dragon tablet in the temple. He is beginning to understand some of the techniques that the Dragons used to create the Amulets of Power for the Giant races. Once he has the magic from Skrymir inside the vessel he created, he can study the properties of the magic used to create them.

Leader Feron approaches from behind, "Does everything look in order, my Lord?"

King Carthon continues to read, "It seems adequate, Feron. Did you question the Dragon extensively to make sure that every word was translated correctly?"

Leader Feron chuckles maniacally, "He resisted at first, my Lord, but we eventually made him cooperative."

King Carthon chuckles in allegiance, "Good, good. I will be ready momentarily to perform the separation ritual. Why don't you go check in on our captive?"

Leader Feron slightly bows, turns and walks into the next chamber, where Skrymir is strapped to the "X" shaped restraint. He walks around Skrymir, scrutinizing him up and down. Skrymir has been asleep for several days now. King Carthon thought it would be safer that way until the actual ritual was performed. Leader Feron looks to one of the attendants, "So, this is Skrymir Darkwing, the powerful Ice Wizard from Voskaola? He doesn't look like much to me. Soon he will be just a powerless man, and we can destroy him with a snap of our fingers."

The attendant stares at Leader Feron and smiles. Then the attendant abruptly stands at attention. Leader Feron spins around and sees King Carthon enter the chamber. He then backs away from Skrymir and steps to the side of King Carthon.

King Carthon stops at the side of Skrymir and touches his forehead. Skrymir slowly opens his eyes and looks back and forth at the Dark Wizards surrounding him.

King Carthon leans over, "Skrymir, it is time. Do you have any final words that you would like us to convey for the record in the unfortunate event that the separation doesn't go as planned?" Then he chuckles with a snarl.

Skrymir stares directly at King Carthon, "You don't know who you are dealing with and when my friends find you, you will be sorry that you have turned your back on your son and Alalohra. Do what you must. I don't need my powers to wring your neck."

King Carthon stands back up with a smirk on his face and moves to Skrymir's feet. He then directs Leader Feron to get the vessel and place it on Skrymir's chest. He then places the translated text between Skrymirs' feet and starts speaking an incantation in the Dragon tongue. The lanterns in the chamber begin to dim, and a faint glow can be seen emanating from the hands of King Carthon.

Skrymir starts to feel a tingle in the top of his head and a burning in his chest. The vessel on his chest starts to vibrate. He begins to struggle against his restraints and twist his body, attempting to knock the vessel off his chest. It doesn't work, and he can barely move his body at all. The vessel begins to rise above his chest. He can see the details of the object now. It's made of metal shaped in a teardrop. The metal is carved away in an intricate lattice surrounding a hollow glass bubble. Floating in the middle of the bubble is a small sphere of some unidentifiable crystal.

King Carthon's whole body starts to glow as he repeats the incantation. He rises about four inches off the ground, and his eyes roll back in his head as it tilts back. Skrymir's whole body is tingling and burning now, and the pain is almost unbearable. He clenches his teeth and grunts against the pain. He can feel a different sensation in the pit of his stomach. It's like a ball of cold spinning in place. It seems to be fighting against burning and tingling.

Skrymir can hear King Carthon get louder, and his voice is straining. Something seems to be resisting the separation. Now it feels as if his body is being torn apart at his abdomen. He can no longer resist the pain, and he starts to scream in agony. Skrymir is on the cusp of passing out when a silent calm envelops him. He can hear a strange voice in his mind. It tells him that he is not alone and that he will be okay. He no longer feels the pain from the ritual, and he doesn't know why. The strange voice calls him by name and says that they will be reunited. This doesn't make sense to him.

As quickly as the pain and burning stopped, it started again. He can hear King Carthon yelling the incantation and then stop. Skrymir's body feels limp and heavy. The vessel above his chest now radiates a bright white light that is almost impossible to stare at. The vessel floats towards King Carthon, and he grabs it. As he touches it, the white light dims, and Skrymir can see a pure evil face wide-eyed and smiling sinisterly.

Skrymir is so weak now that he can't even move his lips to form a word. Primitive sounds are the only thing that he can hear coming out of his own mouth. He sees King Carthon turn and walk out of the chamber with all the other Dark Wizards following. The lanterns return to their previous level of illumination. Skrymir closes his eyes, and his mind seems to float away from his body and this moment into a dark abyss.

Akita finally wakes up late in the morning after several of them spent most of the evening with the hatchlings and Annut. She's sitting by the window in the main room enjoying a sweet roll and coffee, just watching the birds and clouds go by. But, as she reflects on the last few weeks, her favorite day was definitely yesterday. It was special to see the hatchlings make their way out of their shells and their genuine happiness to have everyone there to greet them.

There is a knock at the door, and she catches herself from just calling out, 'come in.'. Instead, she walks to the door and finds Wulf on the other side.

She greets Wulf, "What a pleasant surprise, care to join me for coffee and rolls?"

Wulf smiles, "I thought you would never ask." As he enters the room and waits for her to close the door.

She leads him to the table and sits. "To what do I owe this visit?"

Wulf sits down as she pours him some coffee and serves him a roll. "Well, I thought if you weren't busy, this might be a good time to have a get-to-know-you chat."

They enjoy their coffee with the sunlight streaming through the window, sharing stories of their pasts. Before they get too far into their conversation, there is a loud knock on the door, and Shamash comes barreling into the room. Suddenly he comes to a dead stop when he sees Wulf sitting with Akita.

If a Dragonkin could blush, Akita is sure Shamash would be as red as Annut. "Oh, I am so sorry to interrupt. Unfortunately, I will have to, well, never mind that now. Akita, we have a visitor at the gate; she is unique. I was on my way to find Mandrake and Vicar but thought I would come to inform you as well."

Akita is hiding a smile, "It's ok, Shamash, the business of the Keep comes first, right Wulf?"

Wulf nods, "Of course, it does, especially now with all that we have going on."

Shamash breathes easier, "I will go find Mandrake and Vicar now." As he backs out of the room, shutting the door.

Akita looks to Wulf, "Is it wrong that he's mortified and all I want to do is giggle? I know exactly why he knocked and just barged in, as that is the way it always has been. I cannot expect him to think about the new dynamic in the Keep, especially with all that's going on. But he was so cute with his reaction."

Wulf chuckles, "Wrong? No, but telling him he was cute in his embarrassment I would not do. That would add vinegar to the situation, making it much worse than it was."

Akita agrees, "Oh yes, that goes without saying. Let's go see who this unique stranger is at the gate."

As they walk out of her room, she starts flying to the gate without thinking. She is pleasantly surprised when she looks to her right, and Wulf is there. They fly over Mandrake and Vicar, who are halfway down the stairs headed for the door. They both land on the stairs without missing a beat and keep walking with the twins.

Mandrake looks at Vicar, "People say they have to get used to the 'Twin thing' that we do. I think we are all going to have to get used to synchronized flying." The twins start laughing as Wulf looks straight ahead.

Akita chuckles with them, "I do not believe that would be a bad thing. On the contrary, it could be advantageous." Akita catches Wulf relaxing and looking at her in agreement. "So, do you two know who is waiting at the gate for you?"

Vicar clears his throat, "Well if it is who we think it is, she is our version of your friend Rogue."

Mandrake finishes, "If they are a part of the same guild, they might know each other, but we don't know for sure." Finally, the group passed through the Keep door headed to the Gate.

Akita ponders the idea of another Rogue at the Keep. She then vocalizes another thought she was having, "Mandrake or Vicar, do you think we could get your friend Skip to help Wulf with his affairs and getting his stuff shipped to him if he is still so inclined sometime soon? I mean, yesterday, he did express an interest in it, and it would save him a trip."

Mandrake looks to Wulf, "Find us later, and we can help you set it up. Skip is one of our most trusted friends and allies, so you would have no worries."

Wulf never answers Mandrake because he is a little shocked. As they reach the gate, he sees a Fenton awaiting Mandrake and Vicar. It is so rare to see one this far from their home.

Akita steps around Wulf and stops in her tracks, her mouth opens slightly, and she takes a small gasp of air. Meh-Kola is a cat with short dark gray fur with vertical black stripes, flying at the gate. But not just a cat, she has what looks like soft supple black wings like a bat, and a leathery Dragon-like tail with small horns running down her back. She has bright ice blue eyes. If Akita was not seeing it with her own eyes, she would never believe it.

Vicar and Mandrake both throw their arms out, calling their friend, "Meh-Kola!"

In her purring voice, "My dear friends, Mandrake and Vicar, what troubles have you gotten yourselves into this time?"

Vicar laughs as Mandrake answers, "Us get into trouble?... Nah. I just wanted to see if we could find you and reminisce about the past."

Vicar steps in, "But first, we need to introduce you to High Duchess Lady Akita Blackwing of Blackwing Keep. It has been an interesting time since we joined her and her team at Blackwing Keep."

Vicar turns to Akita, "We would like to introduce you to our Fenton friend, Meh-Kola. She is an extremely talented rogue, like your friend Rogue."

Meh-Kola widens her eyes for a split second, and Akita sees it. "Nice to meet you, Meh-Kola, and welcome to Blackwing Keep." Turning to include Wulf, "And this is Wulf Wari, who has recently joined us; I believe he is from Omoth like Mandrake and Vicar."

Meh-Kola turns and nods at Wulf. "Who would have thought One would be greeted here by so many from my homeland. Nice to meet you, High Duchess Lady and Wulfy."

Looking back at the twins, "I have missed our long discussions."

Akita states to the twins, "Find Greta, and she will get Meh-Kola a room. Meet with Wulf and me later in the dining room, as we are going to go check on our other 'guests'. Then Akita and Wulf fly off over the mount pens, dropping over the wall to skim along the ground to the cave.

Vicar leads Meh-Kola to their rooms while Mandrake goes to find Greta.

Pouring Meh-Kola a drink, "So, I hope you had a good trip here. Although we have no idea where you were when you received our message."

Meh-Kola sat in the chair and offered, "One was near Neg Grove when One got your message. Unfortunately, Ones' message also had a bit of a hidden message within it that said to leave the area, so One left immediately."

Vicar nods, "So it took you a couple of days to get here. Do you have any idea as to why the person sending you a message to meet us would warn you to leave the area? We visited King Windu, and things he stated led us to a private conversation. So, we asked him to reach out to you."

Mandrake walks into the room, "Greta will have a room ready for you soon, Meh-Kola. So, what have you two been talking about?"

Vicar answers, "Apparently, our friend King Windu added a hidden message to the one asking her to come to see us. I believe we need to watch him very closely."

Meh-Kola states, "King Windu plays both sides of the line. You can never trust which side he is on or who is doing his bidding."

Mandrake replies, "Yes, we got that impression when we dealt with him. Akita was probably right again with her last words to him."

Meh-Kola purrs, "Something about what you just said leads One to believe that if your new leader finds King Windu on the wrong side of good and evil, she will retaliate. Is One right?"

Vicar sighs, "Meh-Kola, over the past month, our team has destroyed a Dark Wizard sect, and three Leviathans created by the Lead Dark Wizard, Evad Chaos, rescued Wulf from inside one of them, made a pact with a Red Dragon, and lost a battle against the Cloud Giants."

Mandrake adds, "Not to mention, losing several friends along the way. Did you happen to come across Evad Chaos in your line of work?"

Purring again, Meh-Kola states, "One doesn't know him, but One has heard he was one of the stronger evil Dark Wizards. So, then One can say that you and your friends here are set on destroying as many Dark Wizards as you can?"

Mandrake responds, "Eventually, we will get to that. Currently, we need to rescue a friend from the Cloud Giants. When we went to King Windu, he told us that one of his acquaintances that was hired to steal something from the Cloud Giants failed. His description leads us to think it was you, but we know you rarely fail. If it, were you, we would like to know what you were stealing? A wind flute or something else of significance?"

Meh-Kola takes a minute to consider how she wants to answer her friends, if she wants to answer her friends, and if she needs to reconsider her loyalties. Then, she takes a drink of her wine and glances around the room.

At that moment, Meh-Kola's eyes get wide, Mandrake and Vicar jump as Annut's voice sounds off in their heads. "Drako and Ransom are going to crash in the courtyard; Ransom is badly injured and needs help; they have Rogue with them."

Vicar and Mandrake look to Meh-Kola, "We have to go to the courtyard; please join us."

Akita and Wulf come flying into the Keep as others run through the front doors to the courtyard. Looking up, Akita points to the sky and yells, "There they are!"

Gavin looks up and instantly starts his special plant manipulation, making the grass very thick and growing it to the height of the walls. He is trying to provide a soft spot for the Wyverns to crash. Everyone moves back to the stairs, praying that the Wyverns don't hit the walls, causing themselves more damage.

Annut speaks only to Akita, "My friend, I need to inform you that Rogue is dead and still strapped in the saddle on Ransom."

Akita responds softly, "OK, thank you for letting me know. Gavin has made a cushion of grass for them to land. Vicar, Fabby, Shamash,

Ixenvorlux, and Gavin are all here to heal whoever needs it."

Annut states to all, "Drako is exhausted and needs food. Ransom has practically been ripped apart."

Akita amplifies her voice, "Sham and Scotch bring food and water for Drako."

The guards have moved off to the sides of the Keep as they are unsure where the Wyverns will land. The housemaids and kitchen people are looking out the windows of the Keep. Everyone is watching in horror at what is about to unfold right in front of them.

Drako screams to Akita, "Help her!" He fights to land in the courtyard, but his wings give out. He cannot hold all of the weight any longer. He ends up gliding down to the thick grass and slides a good distance until coming to a stop. Ransom slides off his back and skids further before coming to a halt. Ransom is a bloody mess, with wings ripped, gashes in her back and sides. The last thing that is heard is the crack and thump of Rogue's limp body breaking free from the saddle and hitting the ground beside Ransom. He is face down in the grass and not moving.

Gavin releases his power over the grass so it returns to its standard length to make it easier for everyone to render aid. However, he is spent and exhausted for the moment.

Akita is broken, but she always composes herself to take care of business. "Sham and Scotch, after the Clerics get done with Drako, get some food and water in him. The rest work on Ransom; she is close to death." Then Akita starts running to Rogue. Mandrake, Greenbean, Ishvet, and Wulf follow her.

Akita kneels to verify that Rogue is gone. She sees the blood-soaked clothes and the gash down his back, puncture wounds along his sides, then notices the claw puncture in his shoulder. She bows her head, but again only a few tears as she must remain strong for now.

Mandrake rolls Rogue over, noticing the dagger and tobacco pouch. He can hear the words of the guard resonate in his head, 'a jeweled tobaccy pouch and dagger'. The dagger has the gems mentioned by the guard they spoke to as they left their Castle ten years ago, and the tobacco pouch matches too. He removes them from Rogue's waist and stands staring at them. Greenbean checks the inner pockets of his vest and finds a note. Meh-Kola kneels at Rogue's side, puts a paw on his chest, and bows her head.

Akita looks over at Meh-Kola and nods as she slowly stands.

Akita looks over to Ordyn, "Will you please move Rogue's body inside the doorway until we can figure out the next step."

Ordyn nods to Akita then moves over to Rogue's body. He slides one arm under Rogue's neck and one under his legs. He quickly carries him into the Keep and lays him on a bench. Greta meets him there with a black blanket to cover Rogue.

Shamash looks to Akita, "I need my salve for wings from the infirmary for Ransom's wings; they are so destroyed."

Akita nods and flies through the doors and up to the fourth floor. As she enters the infirmary, she notices Wulf is with her.

He stops her and turns her to him. "Do you need a moment before you go back? I can take the salve to Shamash."

Akita shakes her head, but his words let her flood gates open as she starts sobbing. Wulf stands there, not knowing if he should hug her or just let her cry. He feels so bad for her because this was a friend of hers. He finally takes a chance and pulls her to him, holding her until she regains control of her emotions and pulls away.

As she wipes her eyes, "Thank you. I guess with the deaths of my uncle, Jessa, my soldiers, and Rani, losing Rogue was just too much for me to hold in. Then you add how helpless I feel about Darkwing being kidnapped and held by the Cloud Giants, as well as our failure to rescue him the first time when we were so close."

Akita pauses and takes a deep breath, "So let's get this down to Ransom, she is near death, and we can't lose her too."

Again, Wulf nods, and they grab several bottles of the salve. Then, turning toward the door, they fly down and out of the Keeps entrance. After handing all the salve to Shamash and Ixenvorlux, they returned to where Rogue had fallen. Ordyn, Vivian, and Gavin follow Shamash to help apply salve to the Wyverns' wings.

Mandrake looks at Akita, "Akita, I know now is the worst time possible, and I am glad Vicar is busy with Ransom, but I found the assassin who killed our father and everyone in the Castilian Castle, our home."

Akita looks at the items in his hands, and her shoulders sag as she deflates. Mandrake just confirmed to her that her friend Rogue was the assassin.

Meh-Kola flies up, looks at the dagger and pouch, and then looks at Mandrake. "Rogue has had those for a long time. One remembers that he told One it took him a while to procure all the stones and that a friend was killed while getting them."

Greenbean tries to avert the conversation for the moment. "Rogue had a note in his pocket. It seems the Dark Wizards have been at the Dragon Temple. This must refer to the same temple Annut told you about. So, for all the bad he has done, he was at least trying to get this information back to help us. Maybe retirement changed him a bit."

Meh-Kola looks at the group. "One can say he has only been at the Guild a few times in the last ten years. So, One was surprised to see him there three days ago."

Vicar walks up to Akita to update her on how Ransom is doing. He catches something twinkling out of the corner of his eye. He glances at Mandrake's hands and sees him holding the jeweled tobacco pouch and gem-encrusted dagger. Then, without thinking, he let out a huge guttural roar. Everyone around him jumps and swings their heads around. Akita quickly grabs him around the shoulders to let everyone know that it's okay and they can return to their tasks.

Vicar grabs the pouch and frantically searches it. Finally, he finds what he is looking for, a tiny vial of poison. He runs to the blacksmith shop and throws it in the forge without a word. As he comes back, Ghod follows him.

Ghod looks at the ground and the Wyverns, "I just want to know what you threw in the fire because I can't have it affecting the metal of the gate or the stairs."

Mandrake answers, "Let your fires burn a few more minutes, and the remnants of the poison should be gone."

Ghod nods, "I assume we will be having dinner together tonight to discuss this?"

Vicar keeps mumbling while pacing back and forth, every three or four steps stopping and putting his hand to his mouth, "Just one drop, just one drop, just one drop… in the water or food, and all would be dead here. Right under our noses, right under our noses. It had to be destroyed. I couldn't bear living through that again."

Akita absent-mindedly nods to Ghod and Vicar, then walks over to Drako. She needs to know if he knows what happened to them.

Fabby joins Akita, "He is exhausted. I managed to help him with the muscle fatigue and cramping pain he had from carrying them. He needs food, water, and rest."

Akita responds, "That's a relief; I need him to tell me what he knows."

Hunter flies in and lays next to Drako, covering him with a wing and allowing his body warmth to help Drako.

Akita amplifies her voice again. "Olek, we need a team to raise a tarp over Ransom carefully. This is going to be a challenge to find a tarp big enough. Maybe the prison ladies can help sew the tarps together."

Warrior speaks to Akita, "Once the tarp is in place and they have moved away for the evening, I will come to warm her."

Akita replies, "Thank you, my boys, we can't afford to lose her now, and we need to know what Drako knows. Unfortunately, it will be a while before she can tell us what befell them."

Drako slowly opens one eye to look at Akita. His pain and exhaustion were relieved a bit, but the sadness can be seen. He focuses beyond Akita to see Ransom being cared for by many. Then, he focuses back on Akita, "Thank you." He says to her. "My master's last message to me was 'Ransom hurt by Black Dragon, help her.' I flew to find them. We flew two days to get here to you. Ransom told me our master cursed the Dark Wizards before telling her to flee and fly as fast as she could." With that, Drako closes his eye and sleeps.

Akita stands up and begins to feel her blood boil. Her eyes are on fire, and her body looks like a slow-burning log in a hearth. The muscles in her arms and neck are seen flexing under the skin as she squeezes her balled-up fists as tightly as she can. A pained and furious growl is all anyone can hear as she slowly turns to face her friends. She has several minutes to rage, as the grass near the wall she is staring at starts to burn, before Vicar and Fabby put a hand on her shoulder, sending the calming spell through her.

Akita amplifies her voice to just enough for the people in the courtyard to hear, "If I understood Drako correctly, the Dark Wizards have control of a Black Dragon, and it did this to Rogue and Ransom. I will tell you about his exact statements at dinner."

Some are shocked, but it makes perfect sense to others because they know Evad Chaos was after Annut to control her.

Wulf brings Akita a cup of wine and guides her to some chairs that have been set out for people to rest.

Ghod comes back to Akita, "I just wanted to say I am sorry for the loss of your friend. I will start making a marker for him." He then returns to the blacksmith shop.

CHAPTER 12
BACK TO THE PLAN

Shamash, Vicar, and Fabby walk up to Akita pulling up chairs to sit with her. Shamash starts the update, "Ransom's major gashes and cuts are healed. In addition, her wings have mended."

Vicar adds, "She is in shock and has suffered so much trauma we have combined our calming spells so she will sleep for a while. Unfortunately, sliding over her brother's horns did some damage too, but those are now healed."

Shamash continues, "Ixenvorlux will stay with her all night. If Drako hadn't pushed to get her here, we would have lost her for sure; now, she just needs time to get over aches of the body, heart, and mind. So, I instructed Sham and Scotch to make broth and feed it to her every three hours or so to get her strength back."

Akita takes a deep breath. "We need to send a message to his siblings Midge, and Roguette.

Mandrake, we need an ice room to store Rogue until we know the wishes of his sisters."

Mandrake motions to Olek and Ordyn to follow him to the storerooms. They take a couple of guards with them on the way through the door.

Akita states, "It's getting late, we need to discuss all of this, and most of us skipped lunch taking care of Drako and Ransom. So, let's get cleaned up and meet in the dining room for dinner." Then, everyone heads their separate ways.

True to his word, Warrior flies into the courtyard as everyone leaves and gently settles down beside Ransom, putting a wing over her for comfort and warmth.

About thirty minutes later, they start trickling into the dining room. They began with a team of seven, and yet even with one gone and one kidnapped, they now have twelve people on the team.

Akita enters the room alongside Shamash, Ixenvorlux and Wulf. She catches Quinn's eye and nods, letting her know to start serving, as there is no use in waiting. She knows how lucky she is to have these people with her when she looks around the table. Akita notices Meh-Kola is not at dinner.

Walking behind Vicar, "I take it Meh-Kola is having dinner in her room?

Vicar replies, "We told her this is Keep Business."

As plates are being served, Akita says, "So, we were packing to leave to find a mysterious cave, which got postponed." She purposely does not mention the hatchlings. "And then Drako crashes into the courtyard. We know we will eventually have to deal with these Dark Wizard Sects but saving Darkwing is a top priority. After our first attempted rescue, we now know we will have to deal with Dark Wizards and Cloud Giants when we go back for him."

Akita takes a deep breath, "Drako told me about his last contact with Rogue, he was told 'Ransom hurt by Black Dragon, help her.' So, he flew to find them. They flew two days to get to us for healing. Ransom told him their master cursed the Dark Wizards before telling her to flee and fly as fast as she could. I have not asked Annut about this Black Dragon yet, because, well, you saw my reaction."

Mandrake explains, "We purposely tried to contact Meh-Kola, to find out what she knows about the Cloud Giants, as we figured out, she was the one sent on the failed attempt to get the wind flute for

King Windu. So, we are hoping we can get her to enlighten us with some valuable information. We are still waiting for Skip's reply on what he found out from the Frost Giants. Wulf, we will need information from you and a signed letter so he can take care of your business as well. I will say he is seriously considering leaving Omoth as well."

Greenbean looks around the table, "I assume we are still going to go to find that cave soon."

Vicar nods, "We need to, as Ordyn and Ishvet seemed to find a good solid lead."

Vivian responds, "Are you talking about the old Dwarven fortress under the north face of the Voskaola Mountain? If so, I might be able to help with information about that cave." She chuckles. "I have actually studied that part of history pretty extensively."

Akita remarks, "We really need to have more of these conversations; we learn something new every time about someone in our little group here."

Ghod speaks up, "The gate is done, and the stairs will be done tomorrow afternoon, maybe. The only thing we haven't discussed is how to make them look like stone for camouflage. I know we need those in place before you all go gallivanting into a cave on the other side of the mountain."

Wulf answers, "I know several illusion spells that will look and feel real unless you know where the entrance to the stairs is, or the lock on the gate is located."

Akita laughs, "See, the Gods are providing for us even as they place these challenges before us and take friends from us." Then, realizing what she said, she pauses to take a drink. "I know it is wishful thinking to have all this evil thrown at us and not lose anyone, and no time to rest or process. So, forgive me if I sound crazy at the moment."

Ordyn looks around the table, "You know how old I am, so you know I have seen and experienced many things in my life. Most of you also know I have been hunting these Dark Wizards and their minions for years. I like to think of myself as successful in my endeavors as well, but I have to be honest here, we have had more success as a team in the last month than I ever had by myself in the last hundred years. We are doing good work here, although I agree it has been fast and hectic."

Akita states, "Could it have been any other way?"

Ishvet stands abruptly, startling everyone. "Now that I have everyone's attention, I need to say something. So much has happened in the last few months and we have lost so many people and we just Keep going and going. I can't do it anymore. I need a break. I need to stop and remember what I'm fighting for rather than just fighting. Where I am from, we celebrate people's lives not just mourn their deaths. So, I propose that we do that right here and now, before it's too late and there is no one left to celebrate us. That's why I asked Quinn to bring a special cask of Prayla Ale from the cellar."

Quinn walks into the dining room with a tray of mugs and two men carrying a good-sized barrel of ale. After they set the barrel on a side serving table, she fills mugs and hands them out.

Akita turns to Vicar, "Go get Meh-Kola; business is done, no reason why she can't party with the rest of us." Vicar nods and leaves the room.

A few minutes later, Vicar returns with the Fenton, Meh-Kola, and everyone has their first drink.

Ishvet holds up his mug, "Here's to Rani, who gave her life to help us escape King Cirus." Everyone clanks mugs and takes a drink.

Akita stands and holds up her mug, "Here is to the best team, the best friends, and the ones we lost in our fight to destroy evil." Again, everyone clanks mugs and takes a drink.

Vicar stands, holding up his mug, "Life is about the choices you make; we all make different choices at different stages of our lives, and in the end, maybe it is the choices at the end of life that should define us." Everyone drinks. Akita stares at Vicar and nods as she understands his meaning. Meh-Kola takes notice of the exchange.

Greenbean starts chuckling, "Before we came here a month or so ago, I asked Akita if she had any friends that weren't so deadly. She says to me, 'When you meet people under the circumstances that have brought us together, you can't help but to have a dangerous person here and there.' So, when I met Akita, she stood back and watched me slice and dice a few Mountain Trolls.

When she met Fab Ulous, he and I were fighting a camp full of bandits. When she met Darkwing, he tracked two Dark Wizards that had snuck up behind her. He froze them, which startled her, and she tried to burn them, melting the ice only a little bit which intrigued her. So, then we all met Ordyn and Olek as we entered Prayla to fight the Leviathan. Wulf was pulled out of a Leviathan while attacking Evad Chaos. Akita and Ordyn find Vivian fighting a Basilisk on Annut's doorstep. When Judas came to find her in the tavern, she had to protect him from a very grumpy Ghod. So, I guess she is right about most of us. What I don't know is how she met Rogue."

Shamash says, "Well, I don't know about all that; although I have heard the stories, I appreciate all your dangerous friends. She couldn't ask for better friends, in my mind."

Ishvet calls out for more ale, "Akita found me shortly after my father knighted me. I had been searching for my mother's killers in Oscain. She and Skrymir happened upon me as I was fighting some Mountain Trolls that were trying to eat me. Skrymir and I were old friends, so they helped me finish them off with a little fire and ice." He looks over to Akita and winks overtly, and everyone starts chuckling.

Grace chimes in, "Akita and I met under normal circumstances. It was after her uncle sold me her family home. She was so mad at him, and she came to fight me to get it back. We had a good brawl, and I do mean a bruising; she didn't use magic against me, but we ended up laughing. I still don't remember why we were laughing, but she was the only one that treated me with respect for years." Grace pauses a minute and takes a drink, "I remember now; I yelled to her, 'You already have a Keep, what do you need a second one for? All your pretty dresses?' She stopped mid-swing and said, "I don't wear dresses!" We both looked each other up and down, noticing our mutual dislike for dresses, laughing, drinking, talking for hours, and that was that."

Gavin chuckles, "Akita won't remember our first meeting. She was south of Prayla with her bodyguards. I was a gangly teen at the time. Anyway, her guards chased her through a field as she flew away from them. She was vehemently yelling at them that she didn't need any guards and to leave her alone. I flew up to her and got a little too close because she pushed me away with her fingertips, strong enough to spin me away. Well, our little Firestarter here left burn marks on my shirt and my chest. I wore those like a badge of honor when my friends asked me what happened. Mom thought my friends were throwing hot coals at me. I would have been mortified if my parents had found out the truth and came here to confront Akita."

Akita looks at Gavin, "That was you? Didn't your mother teach you to stay away from angry and rebellious women? You're lucky it was just a few hot spots. I like the nickname by the way."

Mandrake looks to Akita, "Right so now he has nicknamed Darkwing to Frostbite and Akita to Firestarter. However, back to Greenbeans statement, just how did you meet Rogue?"

Akita takes a big drink of ale, "Well, I was north of Darkforest, not quite to Myst Marsh. I had found myself a nice little rock cave for shelter for the night. First, of course, I had to kill a twelve-foot serpent who was living in it. I hadn't spotted it, and it tried to wrap itself around me, so I decided it would make a great belt, and that was it."

Greenbean states, "I have seen that belt; it has an amazing pattern."

Ordyn shouts, "More ale before they do a fashion show!"

Ishvet starts laughing, "Took the words right out of my mouth."

Akita laughs, "I had left Warrior and Hunter in Darkforest, so I could practice my magic skills without them trying to protect me. I was in the cave when I found myself surrounded by my worst enemy in the world, Rock Spiders. Rock Spiders camouflage with the walls of the caves and grow up to five feet in diameter if you didn't know. I am casting fire and acid spells at them, trying to back my way out of the cave. I hate spiders, I would rather fight anything else in the world, so I was not being very careful or precise with my spells.

Suddenly there is someone beside me throwing knives and hitting them in the eyes and the underbellies. It was Rogue, apparently, he was flying by on Drako when he saw flashes of light and heard screams coming from a cave below him. I was really grateful he showed up at just the right time. Together we made short work of those eight-legged freaks." A visible chill runs up and down Akita's body.

Shamash laughs, "I am surprised you were even able to cast a spell and not just stand there screaming, kill them!"

Akita keeps talking, "Oh shut up Shamash! Anyway, we went back to my camp, sat down to some snake stew, and Rogue shared bread and cheese. He had even brought a skin of wine. Rogue and I had been friends ever since. So, per usual, I met new friends in what is becoming the normal dangerous way."

Wulf yells out and points behind Akita, "Spider!"

Akita spins around in her chair and tries to stand up and falls backward onto the floor. Everyone breaks out into uncontrollable laughter. She pops back up to her feet and growls as she stares at Wulf. He stares back at her. Then he cocks his head to the side and smiles. She can't hold back anymore and bursts out giggling as Wulf does the same.

Akita, slightly slurring now, she looks at her empty mug, throws it in the air, and hits it with a fireball. The mug goes flying across the dining room and hits the wall shattering into a million pieces. Startled by the power released and what she did, Akita starts laughing hysterically. Her laughter is contagious as others start laughing at her uncontrollable laughter. Then, as she gets a chance to breathe, "I have wanted to do that for so long but knew my Aunt and Uncle would beat me, and you know what? I can do that anytime I want now." She turns and blasts Wulf's mug with a fireball, watching it explode all over the table and Wulf. "Oh sorry, I thought it was a spider!"

Everyone leans back in shock at what Akita just did. They turn to Wulf and see the ale dripping from his horns and chin. Akita puts her hand up to her mouth and fanes a gasp. "Wulf! Why did you jump in front of my fireball?"

Wulf shakes his head and sends ale all over his friends at the table. They are all rolling in laughter again.

Ishvet leans over his mug and puts an arm around it, "Don't you even think about it Akita!"

Mandrake signals Quinn to get Akita and Wulf a new mug of ale. As Quinn heads to the table with the mugs, Mandrake steps out and freezes the floor in front of her. Quinn takes a step and finds herself sliding towards the table, trying not to fall or spill the drinks. Olek steps out, grabs her around the waist, and spins her off the ice. Somehow, they manage to deliver the mugs, without spilling a drop and stay on their feet.

Mandrake and Vicar applaud; Vicar states, "Brother, they outsmarted you this time. No one fell on their butts, and not a drop was spilled."

Mandrake laughs, "But this will take a while to melt, so let's see which drunk forgets and steps on it." Mandrake turns, takes a step, slides a few feet, and lands on his butt.

Vicar starts laughing, and everyone notices Mandrake on the ground. Then, Vicar says, "I guess you were the next drunk."

Quinn is standing nearby with a smirk on her face and her arms crossed as if to say, 'serves you right.' Olek is standing next to her laughing so hard he almost spills his ale.

Greenbean gets up to walk around to Akita. Wulf is watching her as she is distracted by Mandrakes' fall and Olek's laughter. Wulf casts an invisible wall, as Greenbean is looking to the side, and she walks right into it. He dissolves the wall immediately. Greenbean shakes her head and reaches out to see what she ran into. She sweeps her arm back and forth but finds nothing there. She shakes her head and takes another step and smashes her face against some invisible foe again. She steps back and draws her sword, "That's it, where are you? I'll cut you down when I find you!"

Fabby is watching and calls out to Greenbean, "What are you doing with your sword out?"

Greenbean states with a slight growl, "Someone is trying to fight me!"

Fabby chuckles, "Put that thing away before you hurt yourself."

Greenbean puts away the sword and continues on to Akita. No more than two more steps and she bounces her head off the invisible barrier again. Now Wulf and Gavin are laughing and holding their stomachs. She figures out what is going on and takes a step towards them. Wulf looks towards Gavin and Gavin grins. Gavin raises a hand and snaps his fingers and they both disappear.

Greenbeans eyes get wide, and she stops in mid-stride. She grabs the hilt of her sword.

Fabby is laughing so hard he almost falls out of his chair. However, Gavin acts innocent as he leans against the wall, and they reappear. Again, the room erupts in laughter, including the servers.

Ishvet yells, "More Ale!" as he hits the ground. His chair just disappeared out from under him. "Gavin, I'll get you yet."

Gavin laughs, "You have to catch me first."

As Ishvet stands and starts walking fast toward Gavin, he trips and falls on his face with his feet rooted.

Akita laughs so hard, but she knows she needs to get Gavin back. So, with her hands under the table, she directs flames under Gavin's feet.

Gavin starts dancing and yelling, "Ahhh... Hells, fire woman! That's hot!"

Akita looks him dead in the face, "You're not smoldering yet, but I can fix that! Besides, your little trick caused ale abuse!"

Mandrake shouts, "I'll help you, Gavin." As ice bricks appear around each foot.

Gavin replies, "No one spilt any ale. You are seeing things."

Ishvet takes advantage of Gavin being caught off guard and body slams him so that he slides across the room on his ice block feet. Gavin's ale goes flying as he slams against the wall.

Ishvet states, "That was easy! That was ale abuse!"

Gavin replies, "Yeah, you had help."

The entire room erupts in laughter as the staff refill everyone's mugs with ale.

Vicar compliments Gavin, "Those were some good dance moves."

In the meantime, Vicar sends a little light ball bouncing on the top of Ghod's mug of ale, which is annoying to Ghod.

Ghod tries to grab his mug, which slides out of his reach. He glares at Vicar, who is trying not to laugh. Ghod reaches for his mug again, and it moves again. "I knew you could create light, Vicar, but telekinesis is new." Vicar starts laughing as if it is him. Ghod tries one more time for the mug, and it slides just out of his reach. He starts slapping the table around his mug, and Meh-Kola appears from nowhere, giggling, just out of his reach. "Touché little Fenton, Touché." As he chuckles and finally gets a drink of his ale.

Meh-Kola purrs, "One could not leave you out of the fun. One felt you should be laughing too."

Ghod states, "You play a dangerous game, but I must admit it was a good one."

Meh-Kola hisses, "One is danger incarnate for enemies and just a small pest to Ones' friends. But we have much fun."

Ghod notices Vivian slapping herself; then he sees the light is now bouncing off of her, just fast enough that she can't hit it. Now he is laughing as she looks and sounds quite comical.

Vivian doesn't have time to look at Vicar, "Vicar, stop this light, please."

Vicar replies, "Can't do that. Mine went out when Ghod hit the table. Also, I am not the only cleric in the room."

Fabby states, "Don't blame me; I forgot that spell years ago for a more useful damage spell."

Vivian is still smacking anywhere she can reach where the light bounces. "Well, who is doing it then." She has totally forgotten Shamash is a Cleric too.

Shamash is acting innocent as if he is conversing with Olek, who is already three sheets to the wind drunk. But then, he starts laughing and loses concentration for just a second, and she flattens the light into oblivion on her forehead, inadvertently face-palming herself.

Vivian is frustrated and drunk, "Okay you want to see a ball of light? Check this out." Vivian raises her mace into the air and says something under her breath. The purest bright white light fills the room as it radiated from the mace. Everyone is blinded for a few seconds, and they start falling out of their chairs and tripping over each other.

Gavin covers his eyes and yells, "Dang Miss Vivian, I need you when I'm trying to find the outhouse at night." Everyone erupts in laughter again.

Akita yells, slurring every word now, "More Ale! My mug is empty I think I spilled it when Vivian blinded me."

Shamash takes a drink of ale, and when he looks up, he sees Ishvet standing in front of him. "How can I help you, Ishvet?" Then he notices Ishvet standing against the wall a few feet away. He knows he hasn't had that much to drink; "How are there two of Ishvets?" As he looks around, another Ishvet is standing to his right. "I know I am not hallucinating." He states to himself aloud.

Wulf can hear Shamash's confusion. Thank goodness he's sitting behind Shamash because he's lost his poker face, and those around him have taken notice, including Ishvet. Suddenly, another Ishvet pops up next to the real Ishvet.

Shamash stammers, "Now wait a minute, I have purposely stopped at two ales. I am not a lightweight."

Gavin nods to Wulf, and in seconds all illusions and the real Ishvet disappear all at once.

Shamash looks around frantically, worried about his mind at the moment. Then, finally, the real Ishvet pops in right next to Shamash, "You ok ole buddy?"

Shamash jumps out of his skin, "I need to go to bed. The stress must be messing with me."

Akita is laughing very hard, leaning back in her chair and holding her tummy. Then, as she starts to catch her breath and open her eyes again, she lets out an eek! "Well, hey there good lookin!" slurring her words so badly. "When did you sneak into my lap, Wulf?"

Wulf answers from the end of the table. "I haven't moved."

Akita stares at the illusion sitting in her lap, "You have a twin? I only remember one of you. Maybe he should go, and you sit here. Nah… I'm drunk."

Wulf chuckles, "That you are my lady, that you are."

Akita sits up straight and glares around the room, "Don't you "my Lady" me tonight, because tonight I am far from a lady. I want to have fun and ignore the formalities. Do I make myself clear?" She slurs her words, so bad everyone starts laughing.

In one voice, they all say, "Yes, my 'Lady."

Exasperated, Akita starts throwing mini fireballs around the room. Vivian is just sober enough to throw up a shield around the table to protect everyone from Akita.

Akita falls to the floor laughing, praising herself for doing something she always wanted to as a kid when her Aunt and Uncle were being unreasonable. She lays there a minute, staring at the ceiling. "Can someone tell me why the Keep is spinning? Is this a Wulf illusion, the work of some Dark Wizard, or am I just that drunk?"

Again, in one voice, "You are that drunk."

Akita replies, "Ok, as long as it isn't something serious." She stays lying on the floor until she passes out.

Yet again, everyone is laughing.

Mandrake starts to head over to Akita, but he's pretty drunk at this point. As he looks to find Vicar, he takes a step, falls on his face, and slides the rest of the way to Akita.

Vicar laughs, "Well, brother, you got caught in your own ice trap twice tonight. Good job."

Mandrake replies, "That won't stop me from trying again in the future, though."

Gavin looks at Wulf, "Don't worry, guys, Wulf and I will get her up to her room. Greta can take care of the rest."

Wulf steps over and picks Akita up. "Gavin, guide me, so I don't miss a step, as flying is not a good idea for me at the moment."

Ishvet spouts out, "Yeah, no drinking and flying drunk; can't have you guys' breaking wings or necks now." He slurs almost as bad as Akita was.

Over the next hour, various guards assisted the rest of the team to their rooms, including their Lieutenant Olek. Most agreed that this team needed a night off to let loose after all that had happened over the last month. Too bad the dining room had to suffer so much.

CHAPTER 13
PREPPING TO LEAVE

The following day Akita awakes to Vicar, waiting on her couch. "Good morning, Vicar."

"Good morning, Akita. How does your head feel this morning? I have come with healing if you need it."

Akita smiles, "You know I have never been afflicted with hangovers, in the traditional sense, but I am a little fuzzy-headed. I need coffee."

Vicar offers an elbow and escorts Akita to the dining room for some much-needed coffee.

As they enter the room, Vicar asks, "Anyone need some hangover healing?" Olek raises a hand, barely getting it off the table. "You must not have found Shamash yet. Let me get some coffee, and I'll be right there, Olek."

Akita asks, "How did everyone get to their rooms last night? For that matter, how did I get to my room?"

Olek answers, "Before we got too sloshed, I asked the guards to help with that. As for you getting to your room, I believe your new friend," he says with a wink and a grimace from the hangover headache, "Wulf carried you with Gavin making sure he didn't miss a step and drop you. However, Greta was waiting for you in your room."

Akita looks at Olek, "I was right about you. Thanks for thinking ahead."

Vicar lays hands-on Olek's head, and the effect is immediate. Olek is clear-eyed and no longer lying his head on the table.

Akita remembers Ghod, "Vicar has anyone checked on Ghod? We need to get the gate and stairs in place today, so we can go find that cave tomorrow. But, of course, first, I need to go check on our two Wyverns in the courtyard."

She grabs her coffee and heads for the courtyard, not waiting for an answer. She is intent on talking to Drako and Ransom if they are up to it. But, as she steps through the door, she sees Ransom staring at her. The sadness is immense in her eyes, so Akita walks straight to Ransom, Akita places her coffee down on the ground and wrapping her arms around Ransom's snout as best she can.

Akita speaks out loud to her, "Ransom, I am glad to see you awake; you gave us quite a scare when Drako brought you into the courtyard." Akita moves to hug Warrior, too, as he did not leave Ransom's side all night.

Akita hears a quiet voice in her head, "Masters friends were good to me just like Drako said they would be. I am sorry I couldn't save my master; I tried so hard to dodge that big Black Dragon."

Akita is surprised and moves back to look Ransom in the eye, "Oh! I didn't know you had the ability to talk to us yet, Annut must have talked to you on your way here." Akita gives Ransom a more serious look, "However, young lady, don't you blame yourself, not even a little bit. You followed Rogue's instructions and did your best. Unfortunately, we think that the Dragon was being controlled by the Dark Wizards; it would have taken a team of us to stop the attack."

Ransom turns her head, looking at Akita, "I thought Dragons were on our side now, so when it attacked, I was confused. Master said Dark Wizards, but I didn't know they could control Dragons."

Akita responds, "Neither did we. The Dark Wizard that was here tried to get the ability to control Annut. He failed because we found her, and we stopped him. So, this presents us with yet another challenge to address."

Ransom growls, "I want to help. I want to avenge my master."

Akita smiles, "Somehow, I knew you would. Let's get your strength up first; you have been through a lot over the last few days." With that, she turns to Drako.

Walking over to Hunter first and giving him a big hug, she states, "Hunter and Warrior, my boys, thank you for watching over these two and keeping them warm while they were weak and tired." Then, turning to Drako now, she gives him a big hug too. "Drako, how are you feeling today?"

Drako looks to Akita, "I am thankful to all of you for saving Ransom. I am tired and sad but mostly angry. Like my sister, I want revenge. She and I will assist you in the demise of all the Dark Wizards across the land. My master was unusual, that we know, but he had been a good person for the last ten years. I will tell his sisters of our plan."

Akita is impressed but not shocked at their decision. "Well, Drako, let's get your health up and then discuss the possibilities."

Akita heads to the blacksmith shop. Outside she can see a huge gate that is completed and part of the spiral staircase sticking out the huge blacksmith shop doors. She finds Ghod at the other end of the stairs.

Akita waits for him to finish attaching a platform. Ghod turns to her, "Almost done, will need Hunter and Warrior soon. Will need several guards, as well to hold them in place and help with securing them to the ledge and wall."

Akita responds, "Well, I guess that answers all my questions for the moment. I'll go get the guards on a wagon and ready to head that way."

She walks out of the smiths' shop and amplifies her voice. "Olek, get ten guards and meet me at the wagons. Gavin, Wulf, Ordyn and anyone else, it would be helpful to be at the cave."

Everyone meets at the wagons full of meat and supplies. Akita sees Gavin coming towards her. "Gavin, we are going to need your help again today. We need you to manipulate the stone to attach the gate and stairs safely. Would you help us get this done today?"

Gavin chuckles, "Of course not, why would I do that?"

As Akita smiles, others who don't know him so well have shocked looks on their faces. How could he say "No" to Lady Blackwing? For goodness sakes why is she smiling at him?

Akita responds, "Good, I knew I could count on you." As she watches everyone's responses. "Let's get the wagons headed up and unloaded into the cave. Ghod is about done with the stairs, so Hunter and Warrior can fly them up to us."

Akita looks around for Mandrake. He is just coming out from the Keep. Waving him over to her "Mandrake, we will probably have to put twice as much ice in the cave to melt for the hatchlings. It may be a day or two before we get back from the cave."

Mandrake responds, "No problem I just went to reinforce the ice in the storage room if you know what I mean."

Akita nods. "Sham, Scotch and Danny, do you have all that we need?"

Sham answers, "Yes, Lady Blackwing. I believe we do and are ready to head up to the cave."

Akita is thinking out loud, "All we need is Ghod now so he can ride up in the wagons." As if on cue here comes the old grump now.

Ghod starts giving orders, "I need these guards here to help me move the stairs out of the blacksmith's shop so that the Wyverns can pick it up easily."

The guards start following Ghod back to the smith's shop. Warrior helps them by simply lifting the stairs off the ground so that the guards can push it out of the shop. Once it is out Warrior sets it down and heads for the gate. Ghod and the guards head back to the wagons to ride up to the cave.

As Ghod and the guards get into the wagons, Akita states, "Warrior and Hunter are taking the gate to the cave. Us, fliers, as we have been called will meet you up there." With that Warrior and Hunter go flying over with the gate. "Umm… Ordyn. Ghod may not like this, but we may need him there sooner than the wagons."

Ordyn chuckles, "One kidnapped grump coming up." He swoops down and grabs Ghod under the arms. "Oof, you are heavier than you look. Don't blame me it's Akita's idea."

Ghod retorts, "Of course it is. The indignity of it. I'll get even with her next time we have a barrel of ale."

Ordyn replies, "There is the ledge over there, at least it's not a long flight."

Ghod glares at Akita as Ordyn sets him down, and then looks at the gate. "Have him bring the gate up but let's hope we are enough to hold the gate in place while Gavin secures it and makes the opening fit the gate perfect."

Akita turns and nods at Warrior, telling Hunter to be ready on the ledge to brace it with a leg or even his head if need be once Warrior sets it down. "Move off to the side and against the wall until Warrior gets it set down. Then Hunter will help hold it in place while you work your magic, Gavin."

Warrior moves the gate in front of the opening, but he's too big to fit against the mountain wall and continues to hold it. Warrior sets it down at a slight angle, Hunter puts his head up against the gate and gently tilting it up straight as Warrior lets go.

Akita and Ghod look at its placement. It's almost where they want it but not quite. Ghod asks, "Hunter can you move it to the right until I say stop and then we will push it in against the wall."

Hunter starts to nod but then thinks better of it, and does a light Dragon growl, as he speaks to Ghod. "Yes, and I suppose that means to barely move for me, as Warrior just told me."

Ghod replies, "Yes, now just a little to the right. A little more. Ok, stop. That is really good, Hunter. Now move it closer to the cave wall, ever so slowly. A little more. Stop, good job. Now if you can hold it there until Gavin can secure the hinge plates, we should be ok."

Akita smiles at her boys, "Great job." She looks down the cave and sees a surprising site. The hatchlings are making their way down to the cavern door. "Oh! We have company coming to see the new gate." She can't help but notice a difference in their size today.

Akita cautions the hatchlings, "It would be best if you stay back away until Gavin has the gate secured. It would be dangerous if it fell in towards you."

Addrit asks Akita, "Why are you installing a gate? Are we not free to leave and our friends to visit?"

Akita smiles, "You have a while yet before you will be able to defend yourselves. Your friends will have a key to get in. Sham and Scotch will bring you food and new straw. We just have to keep you safe for a while. There are creatures and people who would do harm to you if they knew where you were or even that you had hatched."

Addrit replies, "Oh! They have food now?"

Akita laughs, "The food is on the way, should be here anytime, but the gate installation has to be completed before we can bring it in unless Annut comes and carries it around to you."

Everyone hears Annut, "They can wait, they only just finished the last batch Ordyn helped the men bring up yesterday. I am afraid that in a weeks' time they will be ready to fly down and catch their own meat."

Akita looks shocked, "Well I will have to get the men started building a pen to hold the cattle and sheep." She looks at Gavin who has molded the rock around the hinges and is now molding the cave entrance to fit the gate.

As Gavin finishes, Ghod points to the lock on the gate. "Gavin, can you pull the rock back so I can hide the other half of the locking mechanism in the stone? We just need to leave this edge clear, so the gate latches into this half."

Gavin nods and it looks like he just folds the stone back allowing Ghod to place the mechanism perfectly in place. Gavin then folds the stone back over and around the three sides. Ghod slides the gate into place and locks the gate. "Hunter you can back up now. Thank you for your help."

Ghod hands Akita and the people she designated a key and asks them to try it in the lock to be sure they all work.

On the final test, the gate is left open. The wagons have stopped at the bottom of the hill. Akita and the rest of the fliers bring up the meat and put it in the trough. Akita takes a minute to greet the three unhatched eggs, as has become her custom.

Akita goes out to the ledge, "Warrior and Hunter, please go bring us the stairs. Each one of you grab an end and fly together if need be. If it's not that long, Warrior grabs it in the middle and Hunter be there for support if he needs it."

As the two Wyverns fly off, Ghod leads Gavin to the spot on the ledge he was thinking to attach it to. "I want to wait until they return with it, but this is where I measured the length from for the stairs." Looking over the side, "Gentlemen, as I am not sure how much the Wyverns will be able to help with this one, I will need you to be ready to support the stairs until Gavin can secure it."

Gavin replies, "Once I secure it up top here, I will drop down and pull up any rock that is there to secure the bottom as well." Ghod nods in agreement.

Mandrake returns from the hatchling cave, "Akita, I had Wulf melt one ice block and I have stacked two larger ones to do a slower melt while we are gone. Those little brats in there were having fun knocking the blocks of ice down. So, I stacked them back up and created a bunch of ice cubes for them to play with. As they melt, they will have a slippery floor to play on."

Akita giggles, "Excellent. Just like children, they want to play. I am going to have to get Olek and the soldiers to start building a large pen up here. These hatchlings are growing fast. It's only been a few days and you can see a noticeable difference. We have no idea just how fast or slow these little guys are going to grow."

Olek walks up behind Akita at that moment, "I shall get it started because you are right. As I see it, we need to pen up most of this valley leading up here."

Akita nods, "Agreed. We will have to start setting up temporary contracts to buy livestock soon too." She looks down the valley and sees Warrior coming with the stairs.

Akita tells Warrior to set the stairs down on the ground in front of the cave. This will allow Ghod to coordinate standing it up properly.

Ghod looks down, "We need the top to be positioned right here where I am standing."

Akita nods, "I think if Hunter stands it on end that Warrior will be able to brace it in place with his wings. We can at least give it a try. The guards can help nudge it in any direction needed to make it stand straight. What do you think Ghod?"

Ghod agrees, "It is definitely worth a try." He points to the top end of the stairs where Hunter needs to grab it and stand it on the bottom end. "Hunter grab the stairs there and stand the stairs up till it's standing right here next to me."

Hunter nods and takes hold of the top of the stairs gently standing it up, by where Ghod was standing. Warrior takes it in both claws and wings holding it as straight as he could.

Ghod looks down at that base. "You three, stand facing Warrior and move the base to the right about half a foot." The guards do as Ghod says finding themselves facing Warrior's hind legs and big claws.

Ghod looks to Gavin, "It's straight so you can begin. I would lock part of that top stair into the rock as well."

Akita makes sure everyone is done in the cave, as she shuts the gate and locks it. "We would like to test Wulf's magic camouflage."

Wulf stands before the cave entrance waving his hands for a few moments and the gate begins to look like solid rock. Wulf has his key and moves to the lock to test that the key will go into the lock and work. As the lock clicks, he swings the gate open, and it maintains the camouflage. He closes the gate and starts knocking on the wall away from the lock.

Akita runs her hand over the wall until she finds the lock. The actual spot for the key is very small. "This is excellent. I will feel better leaving for a few days now, knowing that the hatchlings are protected and yet Sham can get in to feed them."

Gavin finishes securing the top of the stairs and heads to the ground. He puts his hands out using his skills to pull rock up around the base of the stairs to hold it in place.

Wulf meets him on the ground and looks up at the big structure. "Ghod left enough room to carry the bulky items and not get caught on the spiral. He thinks of everything."

As Gavin finishes securing the base, he turns and looks up at Warrior. "Go ahead and let go Warrior."

As Warrior releases the stairs, Wulf again adds the camouflage to the stairs, then walks to the opening in the stairs. He runs his hands around the solid rock to the opening and heads up the stairs.

When he reaches the top, he looks at Akita, "We will need some light in there, as it is pitch black."

Akita replies, "Well that was a bit weird seeing you step out of a rock floor. We will have Olek and Ghod come up with a way to add torches or something for light. In the meantime, Vicar can light it up so everyone can come and see how the lock works, as well as test your keys again."

Vicar sends a few light balls down to light the way. "Akita, isn't Quinn a warlock in training? Couldn't she help with the lighting when we are away."

Akita nods, "Very good idea and so can Shamash. In the meantime, Sham, Scotch and Ben, I leave you to it to make sure the hatchlings are ok for the night and lock up. The rest of us have to go get ready for tomorrow."

Ghod declares while looking at Akita and Ordyn, "I am going back in the wagon, as you don't need my services at the moment."

King Cirus kneels next to the Grand Master Dark Wizard King Carthon in the Cloud Giant Temple however he is still two and a half times as tall as King Carthon. The temple is dimly lit yet King Cirus' white sparkled skin reflects the flames from the lanterns. King Carthon looks diminutive next to the Cloud Giant King. Carthon is pretty much the size of King Cirus' shin bone.

Carthon is standing in front of his laboratory table with the ritual vessel levitating about six inches off of the tabletop. The vessel is slowly spinning and opening up to reveal the crystal sphere in the middle that contains the magic that was siphoned from Skrymir Darkwing. The sphere floats out of the elaborate lattice that it was housed in over to a golden rigging. The rigging consists of two hinged arms vertically mounted on a base plate. The two hinged arms taper to a second hinge where two identical calipers are affixed. The sphere fits between the two calipers and is held in place.

King Cirus leans in closer to observe the crystal sphere. It is glowing in a sky-blue light that pulsates at a slow rate. He can feel the magic radiating from it. It is powerful, but only a fraction of the power that he feels emanating from the amulet around his neck.

King Cirus turns to King Carthon, "Have you discovered anything useful yet?"

King Carthon exhales loudly, "It seems to be resisting my observations at the moment. I can tell that this is a piece of the power contained in the Frost Giant Amulet, but there is something more."

King Cirus can feel his jaw tighten, "Work faster Carthon. You know they will be back to collect their friend and I want all this done before that time. Inform me as soon as you know its secrets."

King Cirus stands up and walks out of the Cloud Giant Temple towards his enormous hut. The Black Dragon is still in the main courtyard and the Dark Wizard Leader Feron is standing beside it. Both of his hands are stretched out and glowing wisps of mist are rising from the palms of his hands. He seems to be in a meditative state, yet he is speaking aloud. The Dragon has lowered his head to the Dark Wizards level and is staring him directly in the face. The Dragon's head is enormous compared to Leader Feron. If it were to open its mouth, he could step right in with no problem. The Dragon's breath is so powerful compared to Leader Feron's stature that it blows and sucks his robes with each respiration.

King Cirus approaches and kneels down in front of the Dragon and next to Leader Feron. Leader Feron breaks his meditative state and looks up to King Cirus.

Leader Feron speaks in a slow respectful tone, "Yes, Sire?"

King Cirus puts his massive hand under the Black Dragon's jaw and lifts his head until he is face to face with him. Without looking at Leader Feron, "It is time that I speak to Thoraxian - the Shadow."

Leader Feron waves his hands and chants a short incantation that opens the mind of Thoraxian to King Cirus.

King Cirus closes his eyes and focuses his mind on the Black Dragon's mind, "Thoraxian are you in there?"

A deep gravelly voice answers back into the King's mind, "I hear you King Cirus-Titan Slayer. What do you want from me?"

King Cirus replies, "I want your help old friend. I need to know the secrets of the Amulets of Power that you Dragons made for us Giant Kings."

Thoraxian tries struggling against the magic that compels him to speak, "Grrrr! I will never tell you this! It is not for you to know. Hundreds of my brothers and sisters died for your kind and this is how you repay us?"

King Cirus grabs Thoraxian around the throat and applies moderate pressure, "Save me the sob story Thoraxian, you were not the only one to sacrifice family to destroy the Titans. That was a thousand years ago. I don't want to hurt you, but I need to know how they were created. I need to make more, or Dragons and Giants will be gone from this world forever."

Thoraxian can feel the pressure of King Cirus' hand squeezing his neck, "You will be the reason that the Dragons and Giants disappear from this world. Your lust for power has clouded your already cloudy mind. That's why there are only two races of Giants left and very few Dragons. You should have hidden or made peace like we did."

King Cirus is becoming impatient and starts to squeeze even harder, "Thoraxian you will not get a second chance to give me what I want. The Dark Wizards think that we need you, but I know how dangerous it is to have one of your kind around. If you don't give me what I want, I'll rip you to shreds right here in front of my home. Don't make me do that. All you have to do is tell me the type of magic that the Elder Dragons used to give the amulets their immense power."

Thoraxian gasps for breath as the King's hand grips tighter, "I guess there is no point in resisting you. Soon both of our kinds will be gone, and the lower races will inherit the world."

King Cirus loosens his grip on Thoraxian's throat, and the mighty Dragon inhales a deep breath.

The King tries focusing his mind even more on Thoraxian's mind. He doesn't want to miss a word of what Thoraxian is about to divulge to him.

Thoraxian pauses for a moment then sighs with a slight growl, "When the Titans descended upon our world and started to slaughter the Dragons and the five races of Giants, we were helpless. All that us Dragons had was our old magic. We knew that our best chance to survive would be to ally with the Giants. We would have to use our magic to help make each of your races stronger. As you know, the Dragons also have different races among us. We have Fire, Water, Stone, Ice, and Wind races. All our magic comes from our souls. In order for us to empower the amulets, we had to transfer the magic from our souls into it. This meant that Dragons had to sacrifice themselves for the greater good of both our kinds."

King Cirus interrupts, "You are telling me that there is a Dragon Soul inside my amulet?"

Thoraxian's voice becomes softer in the King's head, "Yes, but not just one. There are seven souls in each amulet."

King Cirus has a realization, and it makes his heartbeat faster in his chest and fear seeps into his mind, "All of this has been for nothing. There is no way I would be able to recreate the amulets. There are not enough Dragons in the world now, especially of each kind. I will have to find another way to protect my people."

King Cirus releases his grasp on Thoraxian and stands up. He looks down at Leader Feron, "You can take full control again. He has nothing more to tell me."

Leader Feron begins his incantation to resume total control over Thoraxian. Once he regains control, he commands the Dragon to sleep. Thoraxian lays on the ground and immediately falls asleep. Leader Feron then looks up to King Cirus, "Did we get what we needed Sire?"

King Cirus turns and walks away towards his hut. He passes Skrymir as he gets to the door. He looks down at Skrymir all caged up like an tiny animal. He has a flash of a thought to stomp him, cage, and all. He decides against it for now. Instead, he stops and stares at Skrymir for a moment. The King shakes his head, "All of this work to get you and extract that magic, and it will do me no good. Your friends will be coming for your again and I haven't decided if you'll be alive when they get here. You better hope they get here soon."

Skrymir looks up and out of his iron bar cage to King Cirus, "I am no threat to you now. So why don't you let me free?"

King Cirus chuckles, "Free? Ha! I still may have use for you. You may know how that piece of a Dragon's soul ended up inside you."

Skrymir has a surprised look on his face then tries to conceal it, "What do you mean?"

King Cirus furls his brow, "It doesn't matter anymore. For all my power I can't change what fate has in store for the my people."

King Cirus turns from the cage that Skrymir is trapped in and enters the hut. Skrymir watches him disappear into the darkness of the doorway. He then begins to think about what King Cirus said and what he witnessed when the Giant King was standing in front of the Black Dragon. He could see a physical change in King Cirus before he walked away from the Dragon. At the beginning, he seemed powerful and strong with his hand clenched around the Dragon's throat. Then after he released the Dragon, his shoulders seemed to slump and his posture slightly deflated. It appears that King Cirus did not get good news from the Dragon.

Skrymir moves to the edge of his cage. It is tall enough for him to stand in and about a six-foot square with a small cot. Once at the edge of the cage he stares intensely at the Black Dragon. He calls to it in his mind trying to make contact just as he has done with Annut -the Fast and his Roc Owls. He is straining so hard that he begins to sweat and almost passes out. Then he hears a faint voice become louder in his mind. He hears a deep gravelly voice speak, "Who is this?"

Skrymir replies in his mind, "I'm Skrymir Darkwing. I'm in the cage close to you. Can you break free of the mind control magic?"

Thoraxian strains mentally to Keep the connection to Skrymir, "I'm Thoraxian - the Shadow. I was almost free while the Giant King was interrogating me. If Leader Feron loosens the control over my mind so that I can speak to him, I will be able to break the spell."

Skrymir feels a wave of excitement come over himself as he realizes that there is hope for escape, "I'll get him to talk to you tonight. Just be ready to get us both out of here"

Skrymir loses the connection to Thoraxian and starts to feel faint from the straining. He makes his way to the cot and lays down to wait for the dead of night.

CHAPTER 14
UNANNOUNCED VISIT

Then the following morning Akita, Mandrake, Vicar, Ishvet, Ordyn, Greenbean, Fabby, Gavin, Wulf, and Vivian, begin to gather with the mounts to pack for the journey to the cave. They will all need to use flying mounts to cut days off the trek to the base of the Voskaola Mountains. Currently, they have six flying mounts; Akita's Wyverns, Warrior and Hunter, Mandrake and Vicars enchanted war horses, Apothecary and Judgment and lastly, Rogue's Wyverns, Ransom and Drako, if they are up to flying that far.

Akita finds Olek, "Olek I think we should take two soldiers with us to guard our supplies and the mounts while we are in the cave. They will have to ride on the Wyverns with Greenbean, Fabby, or myself. Please have them get their gear, extra sleeping blankets, and a tent for them. Have them meet us at the Wyverns in the courtyard."

Olek bows, "Yes, Lady Blackwing. Right away." He starts to walk away, and stops, "Aren't you going to say something?"

Akita throws up her arms, "No! I am so over it. Just call me whatever you want as long as you get the job done." With that, she heads for Ransom and Drako.

On the way, she runs into Grace. "Akita dear, I know you have plenty of people to go to this cave, so I am going to take my ship and crew home to restock. That way we are ready to head back to the Cloud Giant Island when you return."

Akita is in full agreement, "Yes, I was wondering about your ship and crew. Be sure to see Shamash for some gold because we have need of your services yet again. I want you to know how much I appreciate all of your help. I think we have a great working relationship and that our friendship has been strengthened through our journeys and with our teamwork."

Grace is trying to keep looking serious but is struggling, "Yes, I would have to agree with you on all of that. It has been enjoyable not being the feared Pirate Queen, and to be part of something important. Plus, having real friends has been great." With that, she heads for Shamash's office.

Akita comes face to face with Ransom and Drako. Hunter and Warrior are there too awaiting their saddles and packs. "Drako, Ransom, we could really use your help for the next few days. Not everyone has flying mounts, so if you would allow Gavin and Fab Ulous to be your riders for this cave exploration, I would greatly appreciate it."

Drako looks at Ransom for a moment, and then replies, "Akita, friend of Rogue, we will gladly come with you and assist. This is part of our pledge to you to destroy the Dark Wizards."

Akita bows her head slightly, "Thank you. I never want to take your help for granted. I will get saddles and we will have Wyvern size saddlebags for the supplies we need."

Everyone is startled when trumpets start sounding over the Keep. Akita thinks to herself, 'now what!' They all look to the Keep walls wondering what is going on. Suddenly, the double doors to the Keep side entrance come flying open and bang against the wall. Shamash comes running out of the Keep, pointing up to the sky with one hand and holding his pants up with the other while shouting, "The Griffins are coming, the Griffins are coming, the Griffins are coming!"

Akita shouts back to Shamash, "Calm down, we are all out here to see them." She can't help but chuckle at his excitement, he seems so discombobulated, which is so not like him.

Shamash states, "Well it has been years since we have been visited by the Earl of Stonia, Jarkon Elderwolf."

The Griffins have shiny mirrored silver armor that reflects the sunlight, a wolf coat of arms is emblazoned on the chest plate, a fitted helmet with small silver wings adorns the majestic birds' heads and shin plates cover the front legs down to the talons. The lead Griffin is carrying the Earl. Earl Jarkon is wearing the same silver armor, with the same wolf on his chest piece. His silver helmet has bright white feathers flowing over the top and down his neck. It almost looks as if shimmering angels are descending upon Blackwing Keep.

The small contingent of Griffins flies over the Keep and land just outside the gates. Vivian can see her father leading the group, along with two riderless Griffins and twenty-one mounted armored soldiers. Vivian and Akita head through the gates to greet the new arrivals. Vivian is out in front as Akita hangs back, allowing Vivian a chance to greet her father and the others.

The sight of the Armored Griffins with the armored soldiers is amazing. Akita can picture an army of Wyverns looking just as spectacular. As the Earl and Vivian walk up to her, Akita is thinking, 'Oh damn a night of formalities and Duchess this and Duchess that', wondering if they will be able to head to the cave soon or not.

Vivian steps up and introduces her father, "High Duchess Akita Blackwing of Blackwing Keep, I would like to introduce you to Earl Jarkon Elderwolf of Stonia." Then turning to her father, "Father this is the High Duchess of Blackwing Keep, Akita Blackwing, that Ghod asked me to come help in her fight against the Dark Wizards. Much has happened since I received that message."

Akita steps forward extending her hand and gives a slight nod, "It is a great pleasure to finally meet you Earl Jarkon Elderwolf. Your daughter has been a great help to us and has become a good friend."

The Earl shakes Akita's hand and then kisses the back of her hand. "It is good that Vivian has been able to assist you. Please call me Jarkon."

Akita smiles and slightly giggles, "Please call me Akita, as all the formalities seem to get in the way. Look how long it took her to introduce us."

Jarkon laughs as well. "We are all just soldiers in the war against evil. From the looks of things as I was flying in, you are preparing to go fight it somewhere soon"

Akita nods, "Yes, we are. Come, I will introduce you to the team." Akita amplifies her voice. "Sham and Scotch, please come help these gentlemen care for their mounts in the Roc Owl pen."

Jarkon looks at Akita, "Roc Owls? I know of Roc's but don't know of anyone that has been able to tame one."

Akita states, "Lord Darkwing has an aviary of Owls that are as big as Roc's. When he is here, we have a stable for Martyn. She is kept on the ocean side of the Keep away from the horses and Wyverns. My thought is there will be more room on that side of the Keep for twenty plus mounts."

The team gathers for introductions, in which Akita introduces Jarkon in the formal first and then everyone on the team. Akita then gives a brief summary of what they have been up against since the death of her uncle. She then explains how they are getting ready to search for a cave on the far side of the mountain that used to be a Dwarven fortress under the mountain.

Jarkon's eyes are wide, "You and your team have been through a lot. I realize you have not given all the details. How long will your trip take?"

Akita thinks for a moment, "We have packed for two full days. It depends on if we find the cave and how far into it, we can explore."

Jarkon looks around, "Akita, if you will allow my team and I, we will stay here and assist Shamash here at the Keep until you come back. Honestly, this team is remarkable to have handled all that you have without an army of hundreds. I am quite impressed."

Akita has no problem with them staying but needs to be sure the hatchings are not found.

Greenbean looks to Akita and Jarkon, "Akita you go to the cave with Mandrake, Vicar, Gavin, Ishvet, Wulf, Ordyn, and Vivian if she wants to continue with you. Fabby, Ghod, and I will stay and fill Jarkon in on our 'Adventures'. We can fill you in on our discussions when you return."

Jarkon nods, "That would be quite acceptable, however, before you go, I need to tell you what we found at the Dragon Temple. It is quite disturbing."

Akita remembers that Vivian was going to ask Jarkon to send soldiers to the Dragon Temple. This has now piqued her interest. "What did your soldiers find?" She gets Annut's attention, so Annut hears it too.

Jarkon notices everyone looking at him, "My men found that the Dragon Temple has been totally cleared of vegetation. Someone was searching for information or clues. Due to the fact we have been finding and arresting an unusual number of Dark Wizards lately, I would say it was them and they found what they were looking for."

All the team members look at each other and then to Akita, as she states "That is distressing. I wonder if the Dark Wizards at the Dragon Temple were able to gain control of a Black Dragon and send it after Rogue."

Jarkon looks to Akita, "Wow, word travels fast, as that is one of the reasons, I brought a team to Blackwing Keep."

Akita looks to Ransom, "The Black Dragon killed one of our friends and almost succeeded in killing Ransom there. Our Clerics did some magnificent healing work. Ransom, where were you when both of you were attacked?"

Ransom answers Akita, "We were headed this way over a forest west of masters house"

Akita states aloud to everyone, "If I understand Ransom, that would have put them southeast of the Dragon Temple."

Jarkon states, "Sorry for your loss. Go find whatever you think there is in this cave that might help. Your friends and I will see how best to align to fight this scourge of Dark Wizards and of course the Cloud Giant King."

Akita agrees, "Jarkon is right, we are wasting time here. Let's mount up and get to that cave."

Vivian looks to Ishvet, "I asked my father to bring Orien, for you. He was my brother, Kalen's Griffin. He was killed a few years ago fighting the Goblin King."

Ishvet looks over to Vivian then to Orien, "He is a beautiful creature. I would love to ride him. I believe Rani would want me to continue flying. Do you think he'll like me?"

Vivian looks up at Ishvet and smiles, then feels her face flush, "I'm sure he'll like you; I can't see why anybody wouldn't like you, you're so great and strong, um, um, I mean…you'll be just fine."

Ishvet feels a warm sensation on the back of his neck and a smile form on his face without him realizing it. He begins to speak, but stammers a bit,

"I… I… hope I don't have to wear all that shiny armor.

Vivian giggles, "No Ishvet, you won't have to wear the armor. You don't need it anyway; you have all that beautiful Dragon skin to protect you."

Orien walks up to Ishvet and looks at him and cocks his head to the right then starts speaking in a low slow voice, "Sir Ishvet you remind me of my Prince Kalen. I would be honored to fly you to your next destination."

Ishvet takes a step backward and gasps at the same time, "You… You… Can speak!

Vivian comes up beside Orien and puts her hand on his neck and starts giggling, "Yes, he can speak. Now you know why I thought it was so weird that Annut spoke to me in my head. Griffins are well educated at Elderwolf Keep."

Akita runs up to Ishvet laughing excitedly, "Did I just hear him speak aloud? How do we teach Hunter and Warrior to do this? I was just getting ready to ask Annut to teach them to speak the Dragon way. I guess that won't be necessary now."

Orien bows to Akita, "My Lady, it is a pleasure to meet you. I am sorry to say, that of all the creatures I have encountered, we are the only ones that can speak this way."

Akita bows back to Orien, "It is also a pleasure to meet you. It is a shame that I won't be able to hear my boys' voices this way. You take good care of Ishvet for me. Sorry to be in a hurry Orien, but we must leave if we want to make it to the cave before we lose the light."

She looks around to confirm that everyone is ready to depart, and has their coats and packs. Under her breath and making a mental count, "Okay Wulf is on Ransom with a soldier, Gavin is on Drako, Ordyn is on Hunter, Mandrake is on Judgement, Vicar is on Apothecary, Ishvet is on Orien, Vivian is on Zora, and I have a soldier with me on Warrior. We should be ready to go now."

Waving to Jarkon, Greenbean, Fabby and Shamash; she, the soldier and Warrior take off straight for the mountainside. Everyone else follows suit and launches into the air. The sight of three Wyverns, two enchanted War Horses, and two Armored Griffins flying over the valley toward the mountain amazes Akita as she looks back over her shoulder.

After a half hour of flight, Warrior starts to gain altitude to fly up the face of the mountain. The trees and valley start dropping away below them. The mountainside goes from dense forest to sparse trees to rock in no time. However, it is still a long trip to the top of the mountain that is completely covered in ice year-round.

Wulf flies up beside her on Ransom. Everyone is bundled up in fur-lined cloaks, enjoying the freedom of the flight. Before they knew it, they were cresting the top of the Voskaola Mountain. Everyone follows Akita down the icy landscape towards the bottom of the north side of the mountain. It's a sheer cliff face from where they are so it should be a quick descent and easy on the mounts.

As they fly down the mountain the clouds look like a quilt you could walk on, however on their course they will fly straight through the cloud layer. Warrior flies farther out away from the mountain to prevent them from flying into an unseen rock or outcropping of the mountain. As they drop through the clouds, they can see the base of the mountain. It's just an easy glide to the bottom now. Midway down, they spread out looking for any sign of a cave entrance. Akita also looks for a spot to set up camp. She is hoping the entrance is lower than the ice and rock they are currently flying over.

Akita notices the Griffins circling an area farther down the mountain and wonders if the eagle eyes of the Griffins have spotted something. Ordyn flies Hunter over to Ishvet and Vivian, hovers above them. Hunter uses wind gusts from flapping his wings to clear the dust, dirt, and debris away from the area. Hunter then pulls away, as the Griffins move in to remove some rather large boulders. As the boulders fall away a gaping hole is revealed in the side of the mountain. As she flies Warrior closer, she can see pieces of a broken path that once climbed its way to the cave entrance. This must be how Vivian and Ishvet located it. She then notices a huge flat area about one hundred yards from where they are circling.

Since they need to set up their camp, Akita, and Warrior spirals down to the area she spotted. She is glad the cave is below the ice pack and nearer to the base of the mountain. As she lands, Wulf lands next to her, as well as Mandrake and Vicar with their steeds. The soldiers slide off Ransom and Warrior, and they start scouting the area and collecting wood for a fire.

Akita starts digging in saddlebags, "Let's get these tents set up and our stuff stowed, so we can start dinner. I believe Ishvet and Vivian found the cave. We may need to move some of these boulders to have enough room, as well."

Wulf looks around the area, "These two boulders on the east side of our campsite and the one on the west side of our campsite, should be pushed down the hill. Then I believe we will have the space we need for mounts and tents."

Mandrake answers, "I fully agree with you, Wulf."

Ransom looks to Warrior and heads to the two boulders. They each place a foot on a boulder and push. Ransom's starts rolling first, while Warrior's seem to rock back towards him, and he needs to adjust his grip. Ransom seems to do a Wyvern laugh as Warrior needs two attempts to get his boulder moving. Warrior seems a bit miffed and heads straight to the third boulder before Ransom thinks about it, sending this one flying more than rolling down the hill. Warrior snorts and nods his head as if in triumph.

Akita looks at the Wyverns and states out loud, "Hey you two, anything that wakes up because of those boulders rolling down the side of the mountain, you get to take care of it."

Hunter, Drako, and the Griffins have now landed. Hunter states to Akita, "If anything is awakened, that means we get to play a bit and get our dinner. I don't see a problem with that."

Akita throws her hands up in exasperation, "Fine, just be sure it doesn't get near the camp."

Everyone starts to set up camp and get supplies together to begin dinner. Mandrake opens one of the large saddlebags on Judgement and finds Meh-Kola inside. Meh-Kola jumps out and yells, "Surprise!" This startles everyone at camp. As soon as they see it is her, they go back to what they are doing.

Mandrake shakes his head and smiles, "What are you doing here Meh-Kola? If you wanted to come all you had to do is say something."

Meh-Kola walks back and forth on Judgements back and purrs at Mandrake, "How would that have been any fun for One?"

Mandrake chuckles, "Yes you are right, it was fun seeing my brother jump in his robes. Okay, now you better go speak to Akita, she'll need to know how you can contribute to this endeavor."

Meh-Kola jumps down from Judgements back and blinks to where Akita is sitting by a new sparked fire, "Ta-Da!"

Akita was taking a drink of water when Meh-Kola pops into existence right beside her, the fright causes Akita to spray water all over the fire, "By the Gods Meh-Kola what was that? You scared me half to death."

Meh-Kola giggles, "Mandrake thought One should show you what One can do. You do know that One is a master thief amongst other things. One became the best, because of the abilities that One has. This is just an example. One can pass through doors and walls as long as One can see light on the other side. One is as quiet as a gentle breeze, and One has claws that can cut through almost anything."

Akita stares at Meh-Kola in disbelief as she tells Akita this while licking her paws and rubbing them on her face, "Well, that is going to come in useful… um …Meh-Kola can you stop preening for a minute. It's kind of distracting."

Meh-Kola stops mid lick and looks up at Akita, "Um… okay One didn't realize that you were so jealous that you cannot lick yourself." Then she starts giggling so hard that Akita realizes it was a joke and joins in on the laughter.

Akita stops laughing and smiles at Meh-Kola, "You are going to fit right in here. I just must ask one thing. Where do your loyalties lie?"

Meh-Kola tilts her head and furls her brow, "Two months ago One would have told you that Ones' loyalties laid with whoever paid the most gold, but after what One has seen and heard in the last few weeks, One knows that One must have true loyalty where Ones' true friends are concerned. One hopes that is enough for you and your friends?"

Akita pauses and thinks about what Meh-Kola has said and slowly nods her head in agreement, "Meh-Kola that is all you can *truly* be loyal to. Welcome to the team but, be warned you may become family if you stay around long enough."

Akita stands up and amplifies her voice just enough for everyone in the camp, "Everyone let's get our bellies full and get to sleep. We have a long day ahead of us and I want to set out at first light. Ordyn please take the first watch tonight."

The sun begins to set above the Cloud Giant Island and the Giants of the island return to their huts for the night. Enormous braziers are lit all around the courtyard in front of the Cloud Giant King's massive hut and Skrymir can feel the heat radiating from the one nearest to him. The light flickers against the iron bars of his cage and the scales of the Black Dragon that is about fifty feet in front of him. The Dragon, Thoraxian – the Shadow, is curled up facing Skrymir and seems to be oblivious to the activities around him.

A group of Dark Wizards approach the Cloud Giant Kings hut and then enter. The voice of King Cirus can be heard from Skrymirs position. He can also make out King Carthon's voice.

King Carthon hesitates then speaks clearly, "Sire are you sure that the Dragon is telling you the truth!? That can't be the end of our endeavor to recreate the Amulets of Power."

King Cirus grits his teeth and speaks through a tightened jaw, "Carthon! There was no lie in what he told me. He would have no reason to lie. Thoraxian knows that both of our races are doomed and there is nothing that can stop that now. Even my Amulet, as powerful as it is, cannot stop the changing of the world.

King Carthon steps forward one step and exclaims, "Sire! There must be a way. I can do many miraculous acts with my magic. Combined with yours we could create an army big enough to wipe the world clean of all the lesser races. Please, I implore you to not give up when we are this close."

King Cirus leans forward and rests his elbows on his knees and looks down at King Carthon and speaks with a sad tone of his voice, "It is done. I believed that the only way to preserve the Giants was to destroy the races that have sprung up at our heels. I thought that I could create more amulets so no one could stand against us. I was wrong. I will not lose any more of my people. We will leave this realm into another that only we know. That is the only place we will truly be able to live in peace."

King Carthon bows his head and starts to leave the hut but is stopped by King Cirus' words, "Carthon, take your men and return home to the mainland. You have One day. Leave Skrymir and the containment vessel with me."

King Carthon doesn't have the will to turn and look at King Cirus when he answers, "Yes Sire, we will do as you bid. Shall we take the Dragon?'

King Cirus lets out a barely audible "Yes"

King Carthon directs one of the other Wizards in the group, "Gather all the Wizards on the island and prepare to leave at dawn. Get my mount Hector ready for flight. Feron you will ride the Dragon back to the Dragon Temple. I'm leaving at once to return to my Keep."

Skrymir could hardly believe what he had just heard. Now it would be even more dire that he and Thoraxian escape tonight. As the Dark Wizards leave the hut, he calls to Leader Feron. Leader Feron comes over, "What do you want?"

Skrymir puts his head to the bars and speaks quietly to Leader Feron, "I heard the craziest thing earlier while you were in the Hut. The Dragon over there was talking with someone hiding in the bushes behind him. I saw his eye open, and he even said your name."

Leader Feron slowly turns his head to catch a view of the Dragon, "Preposterous, Dragons can't talk, and he is under my spell."

Skrymir clacks his tongue and shakes his head, "That's what he wants you to think. He's toying with you so that he can find a way to eat you."

Leader Feron moves his head closer to Skrymirs and whispers, "You really think so? I had a feeling that he was holding back secrets from me. I need to learn these before we leave this island."

Skrymir half smiles and makes his tone sound urgent, "You better get over there and question him before King Clouds decides to Keep him here."

Leader Feron hurries over to the Dragon. He looks up the road to the Cloud Giant Temple and can see that the others he was with are just reaching it. He gets to the Dragon's head and kicks it in the side of the jaw. The Dragon doesn't move or open an eye. He takes one step back and gets into position to start the incantation. The incantation reduces the control over the Dragon's mind, so that it can speak mind to mind. If the mind control spell isn't reduced, the Dragon would not be able to think or convey any thoughts. Feron will still have enough control of the Dragon in order to compel it to answer the questions he wants answered.

Skrymir watches from the cage to look for his opportunity to contact Thoraxian. He sees Thoraxian stand up as Leader Feron stands in front with his arms out, hands glowing, palms to the sky. Skrymir closes his eyes and concentrates on Thoraxian trying to make contact with him. He tries using all his strength and sweat starts to form on his brow. In his mind, he is screaming 'Thoraxian'.

Thoraxian answers Skrymir with a grumble that then forms into words, "I hear you Skrymir. I am almost free. Be ready for me to pull apart your cage and for you to quickly climb on my back."

Skrymir answers back with the last of his energy, "I will." Then he falls to his knees in the cage from exhaustion.

Skrymir watches from behind the bars while trying to recoup his strength. He sees the moment that Thoraxian breaks free from Leader Feron's hold upon him. Thoraxian's eyes become bright and his pupils' contract and focus on Leader Feron. Leader

Feron is still standing there with his arms wide open, and eyes tightly shut, muttering an incantation that is no longer working.

Suddenly Thoraxian opens his mouth, slides it over Leader Feron, snaps it shut, chews a couple of times, raises his head and swallows. He then moves towards Skrymirs cage as quietly as he can. He slides one claw into the bars on each side of the cage and pulls it apart with a sharp metallic crack. He then leans down and Skrymir climbs upon his neck. Thoraxian turns and extends his wings and starts flapping them to get into the air. He can hear distant yelling and see small pockets of light emerge from the darkness all around.

Skrymir and Thoraxian hear the voice of the Cloud Giant King ring out all around them as they gain altitude. Then they can feel the air working against them as they are being pulled back with it. Thoraxian flaps his wings faster and as hard as he can. King Cirus is yelling for them to get back here or else be destroyed. Gusts of wind hit Thoraxian, and he spins around to avoid being caught. He then dives back down to elude the King's wind magic and it works.

As he gets to the bottom of his dive, he uses his momentum to propel him faster. They reach the cloud barrier, but Thoraxian is prepared. He sprays a tight column of fire at the barrier and a hole large enough for him to fly through opens. He must Keep up the flame all the way to the other side. After a minute they are outside the barrier and can once again see the stars in the sky.

Thoraxian enters the mind of his little passenger, "Skrymir, which way are we going?"

Skrymir answers back, "Look for the coast then turn south, and we'll follow it all the way to Prayla."

CHAPTER 15
DARK DELVES

The next morning after a good night's rest, they awake to hot coffee made by Wulf with biscuits and cheese. Nothing fancy but it will get them on their way.

Akita looks at the team, "I do hope this is the cave entrance we are looking for. Let's go!"

Ishvet stares at Akita, "You have that little faith in Ordyn and I, let alone Vivian's knowledge?"

Akita giggles, "I have all the faith that you found the cave you believe we need. I just hope what we are looking for is truly in this cave."

Ishvet must agree with those thoughts. "What exactly are we hoping to find, again?"

Ordyn answers, "We are hoping to find a weapon to help us with the Cloud Giant King and I am hoping we will find the answer as to where the other Amulets of Power went."

Wulf looks to Mandrake and Vicar, "They aren't asking for much, just a needle in a haystack. Well, let's get going."

Vicar sends light balls through the entrance and enters first with Akita.

The lights float down the tunnel in front of them as they come to a large cavern. There are two tunnels off the other end of the cavern. Each tunnel looks as if it has a hand-carved arch with runes or some type of artwork. So far none of the tunnels are small, they could have easily brought the Wyverns and other mounts in with them. The cavern could hold all their entire camp and all the mounts if it wasn't for a large pool of water in the middle of the room that seems to have a slow whirlpool in the middle of it. The roof is jagged as if a huge hammer struck it from above, with a steady flow of water draining down from the middle.

Gavin and Wulf say at the same time, "The ice pack is melting?" Gavin continues, "There would have to be a heat source somewhere for this kind of drainage."

Wulf states, "Yes but we are further down the mountain than we thought we would be, so maybe that accounts for some of it."

Akita, Ordyn, Vivian, and Ishvet have moved on to the tunnel entrances to examine the markings.

Vivian points out a Dragon carving that is very damaged and the other Dwarven runes to Ishvet.

Akita and Ordyn see a hammer carving and runes, but most are destroyed by time or the Great Eruption.

Mandrake suggests "I don't think we should split up, as we don't know how big this tunnel system is."

Gavin replies, "I have been enchanting rocks along the way. They will glow for two days or more so we can find our way out. On the other hand, I do not believe we should split up either. I tend to stay to the right when exploring caves, eventually it will bring you back to where you started."

Ishvet chuckles, "That takes us down the Dragon tunnel, Akita's preference. If I know her, she's hoping for another clutch of Dragon eggs."

Akita thinking to herself and decides to be contrary. "If going right works, then going left in the opposite direction should work too." She marches into the left-hand tunnel.

Gavin laughs, "Well the Firestarter has decided to go left. You know that didn't have anything to do with Ishvets statement. No why would she do that?"

The team laughs as she straightens her shoulders and keeps going, with Vicar walking fast to keep up with her, to light the way.

They travel for a good fifteen minutes. The tunnel has a slight down slope to it and starts to snake right. This tunnel widens to a big cavern that is more of a common room. You can see where there was a place for cooking fires and stones around for sitting, however there are also many rocks that fell from the ceiling. There are doors on each wall of the room, some collapsed and some you can see debris on the other side. The saddest observation is that there are skeletons all over the room, all sizes and some in armor. Akita notes, "These people were caught off guard when the grounds started moving." Mandrake and Vicar check out some of the rooms, Meh-Kola stays with them. Gavin and Wulf start looking in the other rooms that aren't blocked.

Vivian states, "They didn't know what hit them. They had no warning and no time to run. Looks like no one left or stayed around to bury them."

They head through the next tunnel. Akita notices a small crack in the rock headed down the middle of the tunnel. The tunnel starts turning back to the left, which is not normal for Dwarven Caves. The Dwarven Caves Akita has been in and the ones she was taught about were giant sprawling cathedrals underground. Maybe this tribe was just getting settled.

Akita sees an opening up ahead and notices that the crack is now a little wider. As they get to the entrance to the next cavern, the air gets cold which is not unexpected in a cave under a mountain covered in ice, but they have been consistently moving downward.

As Vicar's light moves forward illuminating the cavern, they notice the crack cuts the room in half and is now big enough for them to fall through. What is most interesting to them is the sides are covered in ice. Vicar sends another light into the crevasse. It seems to open to another ice cavern far below. The crevasse runs right into the next tunnel, as well as continuing to widen.

Akita thinks to herself, 'This crack is big enough to fly a Wyvern or a Dragon through.'

A voice in the dark asks, "Who is there that has spoken to Dragons?"

Startled, Akita starts spinning around looking for where the voice came from. Quickly she realizes that it was in her head and must be a Dragon. She starts laughing at how funny she must look to everyone else while she was spinning in circles.

Akita answers the voice out loud, "I am a friend of Annut – the Fast. To whom am I speaking?" Akita signals to Gavin, Wulf, and Ordyn to follow her, as she flies slowly into the crevasse.

Ishvet whispers to the others, "The door to the right had a Dragon on it. She purposely went left, and I bet she found a Dragon anyway. Are you kidding me? The last time she started talking to the air, with others standing around, it was Annut talking to her."

Meh-Kola flies down the crevasse looking to see if the team can find a way to follow, but it looks too dangerous. She flies back to Mandrake, "If you can make icy steps for the wingless as you head down the crevasse, then all can follow."

Mandrake agrees, "I can do that. Vicar light it up for me please." As Vicar throws out an orb, Mandrake starts creating ice blocks as steps and descending to where the others flew.

As they reach the floor of the next cavern, they see an even bigger cavern just ahead of them.

Ishvet notices cold forges with old tools and a few skeletons lying around them. He walks over to one and notices a box of stones with runes or other markings on them. "Mandrake, come look at these stones. Do they look like the ones Ghod uses for enchanting?"

Mandrake states, "I really haven't paid much attention to the stones he uses. It might be worth taking them back with us, but who wants to carry them?"

Meh-Kola purrs, "One has a bag One can put them in until we get back to the Keep. They will feel like they weigh nothing to One. In this way, One can help today." She pulls out her bag and they start putting the stones in it. "Maybe One can get this Ghod to make One an enchanted dagger." Meh-Kola giggles, "Ghod make One something. That's kind of funny."

When they have all the stones the group proceeds through to the next Cavern to find Akita face to face with a White Dragon, with Gavin, Wulf, and Ordyn behind her. The Dragons' eyes are brilliant blue like an iced-over lake, scales are pure white, with pearl white horns and ridges. No one in the group can deny that this Dragon is stunning.

Akita turns to her friends, "This is Aphorea - the Brilliant. She does not know the names of the Dragons she has heard speaking and does not respond to them. So, I am not sure if Annut knows of her. I was just asking her how long she has been down here? As I am sure if King Windu knew about her, he would have tried to capture her."

Aphorea tilts her head and speaks to all their minds, "You mean that want-to-be, play King? I have been here longer than his great-great-grandfathers. I have listened in on conversations over the millennia, I just have never met these 'talkers', as I call them. I have had to stay in hiding, since the Titan Wars. Honestly, if your mind had not been touched by a Dragon and piqued my curiosity, you all would have been frozen in place before descending the crevasse. The only time I have left for more than an hour's hunt each week, was after the Great Eruption to allow the mountain to settle. I was saddened that the people who lived here were all but wiped out. Lastly, Akita is it, you exude an affinity for Dragons, so I am giving you a chance."

Ishvet whispers to the team, "She has an affinity, more like an obsession for Dragons and Wyverns." A few on the team giggle and others nod.

Aphorea looks at Akita with her big icy blue eye, "Would you please introduce your friends? As much as I know I should be leery of all of you, it has been over a millennium since I have talked to anyone or seen more than shadows at night while hunting."

Akita looks to her team and introduces all of them and each has a special greeting for the ancient majestic White Dragon.

Ordyn steps up and bows, "Why would you, in all your glory stay hidden for so long, as to not even have contact with the few other Dragons around?"

Aphorea replies, "Ah! You answered your own question. I do not know what you know of the Dragon Wars with the Giants, but there are so few of us left we must be careful. Where some Giants moved off to live in peace after the Titans were defeated, I hear whispers that others are not so content."

Vicar states, "Yes, the Frost Giants and the one Earth Giant Queen live on another continent and are friendly. With that said the Cloud Giants are what brought us exploring."

Aphorea turns to look directly at Vicar, "Are they still power-hungry, conniving, butchering menaces to the world? Someday, I would like… never mind, it can never be."

Ishvet finishes her sentence, "Someday, I will kill the Cloud Giant King Cirus, and in the very near future if all goes well here." His voice and tone radiate with bitterness. "We will also eradicate the Dark Wizards from all the lands, as well."

Mandrake puts a hand on Ishvet's shoulder. "Aphorea, we know you have no reason to trust us or tell us anything, let alone help us in our current mission. However, Ishvet and Ordyn found old tomes that alluded to the idea that there might be a relic or weapon in this cave to help us on our mission to rescue our friend from the Cloud Giants. We would be eternally grateful if you could share anything to help us. Our friend has been held captive for too long now."

Aphorea inquires, "Tell me about this friend of yours that means so much you all would risk your lives against the Cloud Giants to save him."

Akita tells about Darkwing's early life and the Lesser Frost Amulet of Power. Ishvet tells of their friendship and fights with the Dark Wizards. Mandrake starts talking about Darkwing the man, with Vicar finishing their part of the tale. Gavin tells Aphorea of the last month or so that he's known Darkwing, and of the strong friendship of the group. Finally, Vivian states she was unconscious when they went to fight Evad Chaos, and that is when Darkwing was kidnapped, so she never got a chance to meet him. With that said though she knows after working with this group and hearing the stories, she has no problem helping them rescue a good person.

Aphorea nods her proud White Dragon head, "I wish I could have had friends like you all this time. Let me think about this, becoming involved could have dire cosequences, and I will contact you with a decision that might help you."

Akita shows her obsession as Ishvet would put it, by walking right up to Aphorea and giving her a hug. "You don't have to be alone anymore and no one in this room will ever betray you. We have an agreement with Annut – The Fast, that extends to all Dragons, of friendship and protection."

Akita bows to Aphorea, and the group leaves this cavern retracing their steps.

Greenbean knocks on the door to Shamash's office and walks in. "Hey Shamash! How are you today?"

Shamash looks up, "Good day, Greenbean. I am doing fine. The Blackbrew twins will be happy, as the Seeking Shard finally arrived. I am having it set up in the study so people can use it in privacy."

Greenbean replies, "Oh that will come in very handy indeed. I was wondering if you had received any messages for the twins, as they were waiting to hear from the Frost Giants."

Shamash smacks his forehead, "The messenger just left, and she delivered two messages from Skip." He hands her the messages as he has others he needs to tend to.

Greenbean opens the first message.

Mandrake and Vicar,

Wulf Wari's affairs are being put in order. I have hired trusted friends to pack his things and we will get them on the next ship to Prayla. His banker is settling his accounts and preparing them for me to transport. Yes, you read that right I am transporting Wulf Wari's personal effects and funds as well as my own. Omoth is getting too dangerous for those that do not agree with the current ruler.

See you soon.

Skip Bass

Greenbean looks at Shamash, "We are going to have another guest at the Keep. Skip says it isn't safe there anymore, so he is personally bringing Wulf's, as well as his own belongings."

Shamash answers with a chuckle, "We are going to have to build onto the Keep at this rate."

Greenbean opens the second message from Skip.

Mandrake and Vicar,

I finally received a reply to Wulf Wari's personal message to King Iglis. However, not from the King, but from Princess Gianna. She regrets that her father has decided to stay out of this battle and has forbidden her to help in any way. She did suggest we try to find the other Amulets of Power, although she does not know where they would be due to the Dragons taking them. She wishes us luck and the Blessings of the Gods.

Skip Bass

Greenbean sighs, "Well the Frost Giant King has opted to stay away from this fight. His daughter Princess Gianna suggested we do exactly as we are doing, look for the lost Amulets of Power. She has no idea where to find them."

Shamash shakes his head, "Uncanny how we are choosing the right path with so little information. It is nice she suggested that is the way we should go, as I would hate to waste all this time to come up empty-handed."

Greenbean nods, "I will talk to Greta and Olek. See you at dinner with Jarkon." Shamash absentmindedly nods his head, once again buried in his messages and work.

As she heads through the courtyard, she sees Greta coming from the prisoners' quarters with a stack of blankets. At the same time, Olek walks out of the blacksmith shop. She waves them both over to her.

Greta greets Greenbean and Olek, "Lady Greenbean and Lieutenant Olek, I hope your day is going well. The Gods know we could use a few more of those."

Greenbean imitates Akita by stomping her foot, "I am Greenbean to you, always and forever, don't forget it." She starts laughing and Greta relaxes beginning to giggle too. "My day is looking good at the moment but Olek we are going to have to look at expanding the Keep soon and Greta we will have another guest soon."

Olek replies, "Are we going up or out, although up will be easier, however, we need to make sure the walls will handle another level. If we expand out, meaning extending the five-story walls out, we will have to move some stables and outbuildings, as well as another roof addition. Well, I will work on two plans to see what Akita wants when she returns. Greta, you have a good day." With that, he turns to go about his business.

Greenbean calls to him, "How hard would it be to move the barracks from inside the Keep to a separate building adjacent to the Keep? Then we could convert the old barracks to guest rooms."

Olek thinks a minute and answers, "That is an excellent idea. I will work on it and let you know." Then continues his original errand again.

Greta answers, "I will get the last room ready, as we just put the twins in separate rooms. When do we expect this new guest?"

Greenbean thinks a few minutes, "I will have to find out as I don't know how long it takes to sail from Omoth to Prayla. Of course, the perfect one to ask left this morning to restock her ship. I will let you know soon, but I imagine a couple of weeks at least."

Greenbean heads into the Keep meeting up with Fabby and Earl Jarkon.

CHAPTER 16
THE TEST

The soldiers had made a late lunch not knowing when the team would be coming out of the cave. Just as the two were done eating, they notice the team coming towards the camp.

Akita sits down by the fire. As the others gather, she states, "I cannot imagine purposely staying alone and quiet for that long. Especially knowing other Dragons were around and talking. Aphorea has taken her duty, whatever it has been very seriously."

As Ordyn sits down, he says, "We are lucky that she maintained her senses and didn't go crazy with all that isolation. However, she did state that she was here before the Great Eruption, and she was sad for those that perished here. So maybe she has only been totally alone for the last sixty-plus years. Maybe the Dwarves that lived here kept her existence secret and because she did have them around her, she didn't feel she need to talk to the other Dragons. Just a thought."

Mandrake states, "She is definitely trying to decide if she can trust us. If we are worthy of her help."

Vicar finishes, "Aphorea's question about Darkwing was not just about him and if he was worthy of being rescued, but if we are worthy of him, the realm and her help."

Meh-Kola then makes an interesting statement, "Aphorea, is an intelligent ancient creature. One is sure she has seen the light that shines on you as a group and may be generous with her help. She may even join us." As Meh-Kola preens and washes her face again while speaking.

Akita looks to Meh-Kola, "I hope you are right. Aphorea deserves to have a life with the Dragons again. With us, she could have that again. I am sure she understood my message to her about Annut."

Gavin looks at the group, "Akita is going to have to expand the Keep and the stables at this rate. I feel we must consider the Dragon hiding in or around the lake by Neg Grove too. He is hiding for his own safety and after hearing about the Black Dragon, I can see why. Now add this beautiful White Dragon that has been hidden for so long. Yeah, we have work to do."

Then Akita sits up straight as if listening for something. Most realize that Aphorea is talking to her. Akita looks at Wulf, "Aphorea would like me to return to her cavern, but she wants the newest member to join me, that would be you Wulf. Are you up for whatever test she has for us? I feel like she wants to test me but also you because the newest member of a group can be the weakest link, not that you are a weak link to us."

Wulf replies with a chuckle, "I fully understand you, as well as her request. Let's go. Anything I can do to help, and I will be protection for you, as no one should enter any cave alone."

Akita and Wulf head for the cave, leaving the rest by the fire. It doesn't take as long for the two of them to get to Aphorea because they can fly through the caverns now that it is their second time through the cave.

As they land in front of Aphorea, Wulf hears her voice, "Do not panic, Akita is fine, no matter what you see."

Wulf sees Akita rise in the air and start to fall, he catches her before she hits the ground and just holds her. He knows he should trust Aphorea, but he can't help but whisper to Akita words of encouragement hoping to maintain a connection while she is out.

Akita sees a bright white light and is pulled into a different reality. "Whoa. What is this?" She is speaking but it's as if in a bubble that no one can hear her. "Wait this is the day my family died." As she sees a little girl hiding behind a bush, holding her hands over her ears, quietly sobbing. For the first time, she sees her father and brothers trying to fight Annut by themselves.

Then just as fast, the scenery spins and she witnesses herself a little older and in the stables. "Oh! This is when Lightning gave birth to Nightmare, my pony. For a stallion he is and was the most calm, confident pony I had ever raised. He is still a proud stallion but has never been as difficult as most stallions can be."

The scene changes again to the day of her aunt's funeral. "I tried so hard to be strong for my uncle. I knew I was the only Duchess of Blackwing Keep now, so things were going to be expected of me. I wasn't sure if I was ready or not."

This time the scene change shows her when she found Hunter and Warrior. "This was a hard trip to make I had to lead them home over five miles by killing rabbits, birds, and squirrels, to feed them while they followed me. They were too big for me to carry one of them let alone the two of them."

The next scenes are the failed attempt to rescue Darkwing, her threatening King Windu, and Rani's Funeral. "Yes, we do not always succeed, but we don't quit either."

The last scene is of her standing in the Blackwing Keep courtyard watching Ransom and Drako fly in with Rogue dead on her back. "We have lost friends; however, we retain their memory and move forward to support our friends that are still with us."

Everything goes black and Akita finds herself laying on the floor with Wulf holding her head and shoulders in his lap.

Wulf whispers, "Welcome back. Are you ok?"

Akita nods, "I believe Aphorea, was searching through my memories. Most of them went by really fast, but she stopped at key points in my life. The last one was of Ransom, Drako, and Rogue."

Aphorea speaks to Akita and Wulf, "I am sorry I had to invade your memories like that, but it is very important I know you. Your memories told me what kind of child you were and what kind of leader you are. It showed me the loyalty of the team you have. Wulf didn't get tested like you. What he did by catching you and supporting your head the entire time we were viewing your memories told me about his character and the type of friend he is. He was worried about you, he kept checking that you were breathing, and he kept whispering words of encouragement to you in his attempt to help you get through whatever happened to make you collapse."

Aphorea moves her entire body over about five feet. Akita and Wulf figure she is just changing position to get comfortable again.

Aphorea speaks again, "The two of you have passed the test. Wulf because if he is the newest member and is that protective of you, then I know the rest of the team is more so or at the very least the same. I heard what the little Fenton said to you, and knowing her race as I do, you nor I have any reason to worry about her."

Akita is shocked and relieved that Aphorea was able to glean all of that from her memories and the very little interaction the Dragon has had with the rest of the team.

Akita states, "I am glad you have found my team and I as genuine. It has only been a few months that we came together, even though I have known everyone individually for years. I feel we have become a very good cohesive team whose individual talents complement each other. Our common goal at this time is saving Darkwing, destroying the Dark Wizards and their leader King Cirus."

Aphorea looks at Wulf and then at Akita, "I have a weapon that may help you in your fight against the darkness of this world. I have the Amulet of Power from the race of Magma Giants. It will enhance your innate fire abilities and allow you to control anything fire-based. The Amulets were created for the Giants to increase their power against the Titans that were destroying our world. Each one was created individually for each specific race of Giants, so it will only work for that specific race. Upon you, it will allow you to match the power of the Cloud Giant King but no more. I am entrusting it to you to cleanse the continent of evil. However, be warned that power causes a craving for power. The Sea Giant and Magma Giant Kings could not curb this power-lust and it ultimately destroyed their kind."

Aphorea reaches out a closed-clawed hand to Akita and Wulf. She opens it to reveal a small wooden box "I will give this Amulet to use as you see fit. Use it well. There is another condition that must be met, Wulf I know that you have deep feelings for Akita. You must pledge yourself to protect her no matter the consequences for ever more. At any cost, this Amulet cannot fall into enemy hands. If something should happen, take the Amulet to Annut – the Fast for safe keeping.”

Wulf nods to Aphorea and turns to Akita, “If you will allow me, High Duchess Lady Blackwing of Blackwing Keep, I will pledge to be your protector for eternity. As Aphorea so bluntly pointed out, there are feelings for you but no matter what happens between us personally, I will be a part of your life as protector.”

Akita shyly smiles, “I accept if Aphorea accepts, only because she is the one asking this of you.”

Aphorea grumbles a Dragon sigh, “Akita come take the Magma Amulet of Power. Put it on and never take it off even to sleep or bathe. Now with that, I will fly you to your campsite and say my goodbyes face to face, may I join you at your fire tonight?”

Akita starts giggling, “Of course you can, you are always welcome to join us anywhere we are.”

Akita opens the tiny box and pulls out a beautiful Amulet of Power and has Wulf clasp it around her neck. The chain is heavy gold with an ornate gold amulet to hold the gem. The gem it in looks like black rock that is on fire or that lava is running through it. She instantly feels a jolt of power flow through her and a warmth. She grabs the box that was holding the amulet to take it with her.

With that Aphorea stretches her leg out for them to climb up for the ride out of the cave. Akita, who is used to riding Annut climbs to Aphorea's neck and reaches down to give Wulf a hand if he needs it. Instead of climbing he just flies up and sits behind Akita.

Aphorea walks through the cave in a different direction than Akita and Wulf had come in through. After a few minutes, they see a large hole as Aphorea launches into the sky from the mountain. She flies out and around to the campsite. She lands to the side of the Wyverns and Griffins.

Wulf stops Akita from dismounting Aphorea for just a moment. "I meant what I said in there. However, normally I would go to your father or uncle and announce my intentions, but since I can't do that, I want you to know my intentions are true."

Akita nods, "Let's keep getting to know each other and moving forward like we have been. Life keeps throwing us into insanity but maybe we can find time in between for us."

Wulf nods and takes Akita's hand as they fly up and land by the campfire. Akita smiles flying confidently next to him.

As they reach the fire, she announces loudly that they are about to have a special visitor, "Aphorea is joining our fire tonight, so please make her welcome."

Akita starts the introductions, "When I say your name nod your head or make a noise so that she can see who is who. Aphorea – The Brilliant, please meet, Warrior," Warrior nods and rears up, "Hunter," Hunter nods and bows, "Drako," Drako nods, "Ransom," Ransom nods and rears like Warrior, "Zora the Griffin," Zora states "It's my pleasure", "Orien the Griffin," Orien states "Pleased to meet you", "Judgement," Judgment prances and nods, "and last but certainly not least, Apothecary," Apothecary nods and rears up. "They are our mounts, our friends, our partners in battle, and we love them very much. Aphorea – The Brilliant, welcome to our family. Aphorea is going to stay here with us, out in the open for the first time in a millennium."

Aphorea speaks to everyone, "It is nice to have your company for the night. It has been interesting and refreshing to meet you on this day. I will look forward to seeing you again someday when this realm is safe."

The soldier hands Akita and Wulf some stew as they sit down by the fire. Akita holds out the Amulet of Power for all to see.

Vivian blurts out, "Wait is that the Magma Amulet of Power?" She looks over at Aphorea.

Akita answers, "Yes, we, Wulf and I passed the test. Aphorea asked Wulf to make a pledge to protect me from now on. She also knows and appreciates the loyalty we all have for each other and Darkwing. Also, with me taking the Amulet of Power, she is now free to leave this cave if she should want to."

Ordyn states, "That just leveled the playing field against the Cloud Giant King. I take it we are headed back to the Keep in the morning so we can meet up with Grace."

Akita nods, "I think that is the best action to take. We need to get back to Darkwing as soon as possible. We will be lucky if he has not been tortured out of his mind or worse." Akita visibly shivers even though the Amulet is warming her, and she is eating hot stew.

The evening is quiet and soon everyone is headed to their tents. Akita looks over to the

Wyverns who are staring at Aphorea, and she is staring back.

Hunter looks over at Akita as he senses her gaze, "Aphorea is telling us about the Titan wars. It's like a bedtime story."

Akita answers, "She has been alone a long time. Enjoy the storytelling. Good night."

Akita goes to her tent and is shocked to see a second cot in it. As she turns to look around Ishvet, Mandrake and Vicar are quickly ducking into their tents. Wulf steps out of his tent and asks, "Where did my cot disappear to?"

Akita looks to Mandrake and Vicar's tent, then to Ishvet's and Ordyn's tent; she points to the tents and then opens her tent to show his bedding. Akita and Wulf can hear snickering coming from the other tents.

Wulf nods and states, "That's ok I have slept on the ground for years." As Akita waves him over to her tent.

Akita whispers to Wulf, "We are adults, let's just go to bed." Wulf nods.

She watches as Ishvet sneaks out and looks into Wulf's tent. He looks to Akita's tent and smiles.

Akita and Wulf get into their respective cots, cover up, and fall quickly asleep.

The following morning everyone wakes to find that Aphorea is gone from the campsite. Most of the group notices that Akita continuously stops and looks to the sky for any sign that Aphorea is coming back. After a light breakfast, the group and the soldiers break camp, load up the mounts, and head back over the Voskaola Mountains for Blackwing Keep.

CHAPTER 17
UNLIKELY RENDEZVOUS

As the sun is rising, Skrymir Darkwing and Thoraxian are flying into Blackwing Keep, startling the soldiers with a new and strange Dragon. The lookout on the west side of the Keep wall runs for their Lieutenant, as they spotted a large dark creature flying towards the Keep. The archers on the wall have bows drawn pointing at the Dragon as it starts to land. The courtyard starts to fill up with soldiers carrying pikes and swords. Then Skrymir spots Olek, Greenbean, and Fab Ulous standing in front of the soldiers. Darkwing jumps up so that he can be seen, waving his arms. The Dragon lowers his head so that Darkwing can walk down its neck to the ground and step off its huge head, right in front of his friends.

Olek yells to the soldiers, "Stand Down!!! Back to your duties!"

Greenbean runs and embraces Darkwing. "By the Gods how did you get away?" She looks at the Black Dragon. "Wait, where did you find a Black Dragon?"

Darkwing holds up a hand, "First can we get this Dragon something good to eat. He probably has a really bad taste in his mouth, as I imagine Dark Wizard is nasty. He has been severely deprived and mentally tortured for too long. Second, I NEED FOOD! Oh, and a bath. Then I will tell you everything. Where is Akita?"

Shamash comes running out of his office, holding up his pants again, as he trots up to the others. "Thank the Gods you are here and okay."

Darkwing looks to Shamash, "Well I am here but far from okay. I have no power at the moment, I have to get back to that island before the Cloud Giants leave. But again, I need a bath and food. Thoraxian here needs food and peaceful sleep. Then I will tell you all at the same time what has happened. But where is Akita?"

Greenbean takes Darkwing by the arm, "Fabby will make sure Thoraxian is fed. Akita is on the other side of the mountain looking for a relic or weapon to help in rescuing you. If I understand you now, we need to rescue your power?"

Darkwing sighs, "It's more complicated than that. I will be down after my bath."

Darkwing takes a long hot bath, dresses in fresh clothes, and heads for the dining room. As he heads through the Great Hall he hears and feels a heavy thump outside. He heads out to investigate.

Annut is in the courtyard, staring at Thoraxian. Darkwing calls out to Annut, "Sorry to interrupt. Good to see you Annut."

Annut replies, "Ah, Frostbite you are back but something is missing. Akita will be so glad to see you are safe, as she has been working hard to have a successful rescue this time. Thoraxian is a long-time friend and was filling me in on the current situation with the Cloud Giants, Dark Wizards, as well as your escape. I have informed him of the events here at the Keep. I think you need to talk to your friends first."

Darkwing answers, "Ok. I was actually just headed to see them when I heard you out here. I will leave you two to talk." He then turns and heads back into the Keep and to the dining room.

Quinn brings Darkwing lunch as he sits down with Greenbean, Fabby, and Earl Jarkon.

Greenbean formally introduces Earl Jarkon to Darkwing. "Darkwing this is the Earl of Stonia, Earl

Jarkon Elderwolf. Do you remember the Paladin that was bit by the Basilisk? Her name is Vivian, and this is her Father. He just arrived with a squad of armored Griffins to aid in the fight against the Dark Wizards."

Earl Jarkon nods, "So you are the one they were trying to rescue from the Cloud Giants. It says a lot about you that you were able to save yourself. Inner strength as well as physical strength are good qualities to have."

Darkwing replies, "Nice to meet you Earl Jarkon and thank you for the comments, but I didn't get out unscathed. How is Ishvet doing? I was watching when Rani was killed by King Clouds. I wanted so bad to freeze him where he stood."

Greenbean states, "It wasn't only Rani we lost. Concerning the Black Dragon, do you believe that the Dark Wizards can no longer control him?"

Darkwing nods, "He ate the Dark Wizard who was controlling him just before we left. In fact, that was the main reason he was able to get me out of a cage and fly away from King Clouds and his Dark Wizard minions. Why do you ask?"

Greenbean recounts the attack of the Black Dragon that killed Rogue and severely injured Ransom. She explains Drako's heroic actions in getting Rogue and his sister, Ransom, here for healing.

Darkwing looks at Greenbean and Fabby, "That would explain the seriousness of what I expect is a conversation going on between Annut and Thoraxian right now. However, we, or I should say, I need him, and we must go back as soon as Akita returns. King Clouds has my magic in a vessel, and he is planning on taking his people and my magic to another realm. Currently, I couldn't even freeze your big toe."

Fabby shakes his head, "Sorry to hear about your power, you must feel naked without it? I can't even imagine being without my power."

Darkwing agrees, "I am going to have to see what kind of weapon Ghod can make me on short notice so that I have something to fight with when we go back."

Ghod walks into the dining room at that moment, "So it is true, the Black Dragon brought the wayward one home. Did I hear you need a weapon?"

Greenbean looks at Ghod, "Yes, he is going to need a weapon with frostbite. I think that will confuse his old captures. However, Darkwing, what weapons are you proficient with? I have only witnessed you using magic."

Darkwing thinks a moment, "Well as a kid we were all taught a bow for hunting, and a staff for defense. We really didn't have any swords around, only knives for butchering our kills and axes for chopping wood. I guess I get to play hunter for a bit with a bow and staff. I was pretty good, but not like my grandfathers."

Ghod scratches his chin, "What would you think about battle-ax on a quarterstaff. It would be like a staff with a sharp biting blade, longer than a typical Dwarven Battle Axe and I can enchant it with cold magic, that way you have it for when you get your powers back as well. Let me see what I can come up with before Akita returns. First, I eat."

Greenbean suggests, "When you get a chance you might want to go to the study and let your people at your Keep know you are back and safe. Shamash just had a Seeking Shard placed in there. Akita told me that Martyn and Mylar are really upset, so maybe Stan can calm them a bit."

Darkwing replies, "Ah, moving up in the world of messaging are we. Good. But I will have to make sure Stan doesn't let them fly here, at least not yet. The trip back to the island is going to be dangerous, with King Clouds, the only good thing will be, he ordered the Dark Wizards off his island. With that said, I have disturbing news for Ishvet that I will tell him first so he can try to process it before we proceed."

Earl Jarkon states, "If he has ordered the Dark Wizards off his island, we need to keep watch on the Dragon Temple and that area for activity. That temple has been cleared out of all the vegetation and I can tell you it wasn't that way several months ago when I flew over it. When I was last there the vegetation covered the entire temple so that you wouldn't know it was there. My General tells me that it's in plain view now."

Greenbean asks, "What is in the Dragon Temple? Or has it been stripped of artifacts over the centuries?"

Earl Jarkon replies, "Yes, the relics and artifacts are gone. I don't know if the Dragons moved them when they went into hiding or if they have been stolen. However, there are glyphs on the walls and artwork that seems to tell a story of before the Titan wars."

Fabby states, "We might want to visit there at some point. There might be clues as to how the Dark Wizards managed to gain control of Thoraxian. We know that Evad Chaos had other nefarious ways he was going to try to control Annut."

Darkwing chuckles, "Well, Leader Faron, will never be able to tell us now. When next he sees the light of day, he will be fertilizing the vegetation. However, I have no clue how many of the other Dark Wizards know the spell of how to gain control of a Dragon."

Annut speaks to those at the table, "I am taking Thoraxian to my cave to hide him. We will return when Akita arrives."

Greenbean acknowledges Annut, "That is probably safest. Since we have no idea of the whereabouts of the Dark Wizards, we can't risk any of you being ensnared again."

Thoraxian states, "If they try again, they will have to kill me. I am not letting that happen again. I owe my freedom and life to Darkwing. I thank the Gods he knew the Dragon Way to talk. I regret what they made me do to your friend and the young Wyvern." With that you can hear the two Dragons take off from the Keep.

Earl Jarkon sighs, "That's going to take some time for me to get used to. The Griffins talk to us normally, but if you would have told me yesterday that Dragons had the ability to communicate telepathically, well, I would have laughed in your face. With that said, I think it is a huge benefit to be able to talk to them."

As Darkwing finishes eating Annut speaks to him only, "Excuse yourself from the table and find Sham. Have him bring you to the eggs, please. Tell him to just uses horses for this trip. Oh, and tell him you will need a bag of snacks."

Darkwing looks around the table and states, "Well, Lady and Gentlemen, I will return later as I have to go see a man about a horse." With that he strides out of the dining room and out to the stables. He understood that Earl Jarkon does not know about the eggs. He figures Greenbean and Fabby understood his message.

Darkwing finds Sham, "I was told to ask you to take me to the secret cave on horseback with a bag of snacks."

Sham claps his hands, "Oh yes, give Scotch and I just a minute. The wagon is full but Scotch and Ben can bring that up behind us."

Darkwing is confused, "Ok then. I will just wait right here."

About five minutes later Sham returns with two horses and a bag. "Lord Darkwing, I saddled Akita's horse Nightmare for you. Shall we go?"

Darkwing climbs in the saddle waiting for Sham. Sham climbs in the saddle of one of the stable horses and takes off at a full gallop out of the Keep and up the hill, with Darkwing right behind him. Darkwing is wondering what the hurry is, but Sham is showing no signs of slowing as Darkwing comes up beside him. Nightmare seems to be enjoying the long run.

As they reach the back of Annut's cave, Darkwing notices the addition. "I was wondering and still am, how we are getting up there. I see someone has been hard at work up here, with fencing going in and where did this rock structure come from."

Sham dismounts and ties the horses to a nearby tree. "Follow me, Lord Darkwing." Shams walks up to the backside of the rock and disappears into the rock wall. Darkwing decides to follow as instructed and finds a dimly lit spiral staircase.

Darkwing exclaims, "Wow, this is interesting." As he walks out through the top to a familiar rock wall. He watches Sham walk up to the walk and insert a key releasing a hidden gate to open. "You guys have been busy."

Sham simply states, "We needed the ability for non-flyers to get into the cave. So, Ghod and Wulf came up with this."

As the gate opens, Darkwing is shocked. Three Dragons the size of ponies are waiting for them just inside. A Dragon that is primarily yellow and orange starts spinning around and then trots down the tunnel with a Black Dragon and a Red Dragon following.

Sham states, "The Yellow one has chosen Wulf, the Black one has chosen Olek and the Red one has chosen Greenbean. I suggest we follow them; they are very excited."

As they reach the cavern Darkwing notices three eggs have not hatched. He walks through touching them and greeting them. When he puts his hand on the last egg, he hears a little voice say, "Frostbite is back" and he hears a loud crack, causing him to jump a little. He then notices two black horns poking out of the top of the egg.

Sham sets the bag down next to Darkwing and shews the other three away from it. "Your food is coming up right behind me in the wagon. You can wait a little bit longer."

Darkwing looks down the other tunnel to see Thoraxian watching him. Thoraxian states, "I have never witnessed this before. Annut says I am the father of at least two. I assume one of them is the little black one there next to you."

Darkwing hears another crunch and sees a tail pop out the back of the egg. He starts chuckling because it is a sight, he never thought he would see, horns and tail sticking out of an egg. Then there is the sound of thumping against the shell.

Darkwing finds himself cheering on the little Dragon. "Come on, if you're going to be my Dragon friend you need to be stronger than that, bust that shell or stay inside."

Darkwing's taunting gave the little Dragon the extra push he needed to bust another crack. The front of the egg breaks away leaving the legs and belly showing. The baby rolls forward standing on all four legs, but still cannot see anything. He side-steps into the cavern wall attempting to break away the rest of the shell. After the third hit the last of the shell breaks and falls away. Standing in front of Darkwing is a little Grey Dragon with black horns and ridges.

Darkwing looks at the Dragon, "See you did it, little fella."

The Dragon looks up to him, "My name is not Fella, my name is Granite, and I chose you. I was so upset when you disappeared. I waited for you to come back to hatch."

Sham looks to Darkwing, "If it is talking to you and has told you its name, it has chosen you. You might want to feed him the snack in the bag while I go, look for Scotch and Ben."

Darkwing laughs, "Yes, Granite chose me. I can tell this is going to be an interesting relationship." Darkwing opens the bag to allow Granite to feed.

Thoraxian is doing that odd Dragon smile, "I think I know which two are my son's. I am going to back out so Annut can greet her new baby."

Darkwing helps Sham, Scotch and Ben bring up the meat and water for the Dragons and then sits down with Granite for a while. Granite lays with his head in Darkwing's lap and they have a nice conversation.

Eventually, Sham comes in and informs Darkwing the sun will be setting soon and that they need to leave.

Darkwing says, "Good night, Granite. I will come see you tomorrow." He looks at the others, "Right now we are keeping you a secret from a visitor at the Keep, but when Akita and the others return, I am sure they will come to see you."

Darkwing then turns to follow Sham out of the cavern.

When they get back to the Keep, Darkwing heads back to his room. Soon there is a knock on the door, where he finds Greenbean and Fabby. "I was wondering how long before you two showed up. I hoped you got my hint that Annut had called me to the cave."

Greenbean and Fabby enter the room and sit at the little table by the window. Greenbean looks at Darkwing, "From the looks of it and given how long you were gone, I suppose the egg that said it was waiting for you to return, hatched."

Darkwing smiles, "Yes, Granite broke out of his shell today. That was the funniest thing I have ever seen, horns and then tail, then he kept slamming into a wall to break the rest of the shell. He's a grey with black horns and ridges. Apparently, Thoraxian is the father of Granite and the other black hatchling. I think he was close to tears, watching one of his sons hatch today. He told me he had never witnessed a hatching of Dragon eggs."

Greenbean replies, "The other black hatchling with the golden horns and ridges is Addrit, the red and orange hatchling with yellow gold horns and ridges is Shemera, and the dark red with some orange hatchling with gold horns and ridges is Choren. Addrit chose Olek, Shemera chose me, and Choren chose Wulf. So, we figure Wulf will be around for a long time."

Fabby asks, "Did Annut say when the other two will hatch?"

Darkwing replies, "I didn't even think to ask. I was a bit overwhelmed with the loss of my power, I can't go home without being dressed like a bear, and then to find that Granite had been waiting for me to hatch. Yeah, I am a bit absent-minded thinking of all that has happened."

Fabby states, "Too bad you weren't here for the drunk fest. We had dinner to discuss everything the other night and Ishvet had had enough, so he had them bring out a barrel of ale. Let me tell you these magic users drunk is hilarious. Mandrake fell on his own ice trap twice. Gavin kept making objects and people disappear and reappear to mess with people's minds. Wulf kept doing illusions to the point Greenbean here pulled her sword to fight something she couldn't see. Even Meh-Kola got Ghod really good with his mug of ale that kept moving on him."

Darkwing frowns, "Meh-Kola? Who is that?"

Greenbean answers, "Meh-Kola is a Fenton. I guess the best way to describe her is a cat with

Dragon wings and tail. Meh-Kola actually knew Rogue and was in the same guild. She's also a friend of Mandrake and Vicar, she is from Omoth. She is an interesting character."

Fabby suggests, "Let's go meet Earl Jarkon for dinner and then get some sleep. I imagine the next few days we are going to be running hard and heavy."

Darkwing says, "I will meet you there in a little bit, I would like to freshen up."

CHAPTER 18
REUNITED

The following morning after breakfast Darkwing follows Ghod to the blacksmith shop.

Ghod states, "I gave this a lot of thought. I remembered Ishvet's blade that you enchanted for him. So, this is a sturdy halberd, with a twist. I put an axe on it with a sharp spike on the back. The staff is made of hickory, and you can split a hair on the axe blade. It is enchanted so that when it strikes, the ice burns through the target and causes instant frostbite to the area it hits. Take it and do some practice swings to check the balance of it."

Darkwing takes the staff and hefts it. He stands back and starts to swing the halberd like he would a fighting staff. "Oh! This is nice. How you got it so well balanced I will never know. It's like swinging a light stick." Darkwing strikes a log with the axe blade and the log splits in half and freezes on both sides. "Now that is nice. I can see how it will confuse King Clouds when he thinks I'm powerless."

Ghod chuckles, "Well then we will confuse him more." Ghod hands Darkwing an elaborate bow and two quivers of arrows. "First I need to see if you can string the bow as I have made it so that only a strong man can string it."

Darkwing puts down the halberd and takes the bow. The string is on the bow but loose. Darkwing sets the string in the bottom notch of the bow, then bracing the bottom of the bow on his leg he bends the top of the bow down trying to pull the other end of the string into the upper notch. His first attempt at stringing it was a struggle, so he repositioned it and tried again. "I haven't strung a bow in over sixty-plus years, but after repositioning, it wasn't that hard for me. I can see how some would not be able to string it." He draws back on the string to feel its resistance.

Ghod states, "I study each of you long before I ever have to make you a weapon. I watch how you carry yourselves and how you move, basically all your mannerisms."

Darkwing says, "Well whatever you do it works." He then takes an arrow and nocks it. The arrow takes on a strange blue misty hue. Darkwing looks at Ghod, "I take it this is enchanted the same way as the halberd and that only myself or someone looking really close will see this blue mist."

Ghod nods, "An arrow through a vital organ, neck or head will instantly freeze the area, and if it doesn't cause instant death, just give it a few minutes for the freeze to spread. Of course, another shot in the same area will finish the job. I remembered the story of your grandfather shooting two arrows at once, so I assumed you could do the same."

Darkwing thinks a minute, "I was taught to shoot two and even three at once, however, it's been sixty-plus years or longer since I have used a bow. Back in those days, I was behind a plow more often than not." Darkwing sees another log and takes aim. The tip of the arrow sticks into the bark and the ice starts to spread over all of the log. Retrieving that arrow, he tries two this time and hits another log with the same effect but the ice moves faster over a larger area. "Ghod, you have outdone yourself. Let me know what I owe you and I will bring it to you at lunch."

Ghod shakes his head, "Normally I would have a high price on these, but you are a friend and you have had an injustice done to you. These are my gifts to help you survive getting your magic back. King Clouds deserves all that is about to hit him."

Darkwing looks at Ghod, "Are you sure? I feel I should give you something for these."

Ghod laughs, "You know what I would like? Once you get your powers back, I would like some of those never melting ice cubes, because if I bring a cold drink in this hot blacksmith shop, my drink is hot in minutes."

Darkwing nods, "My friend, I will make you a crate of them when I get my powers back, because the heat in here, compared to their small size, might actually melt them. I will always replenish them for you."

Darkwing shakes Ghod's hand and takes his weapons with a couple extra quivers of regular arrows, to the training grounds. He needs to practice up, especially with the bow.

He starts out with one arrow at a time until he starts hitting bullseyes every time. He thinks to himself, "That's more like it." After retrieving the arrows, he resets himself and starts shooting two arrows at a time. One would hit the bullseye and the other would go above or below the bullseye. Thinking to himself, "Rusty but workable." He retrieves the arrows and starts shooting three at a time and the third arrow is usually far enough away from the other two to be useless in a fight. Thinking again, "Using the special arrows and only doing one or two at a time will cause significant damage."

Greenbean walks up with her blade, "I was watching you shoot. You are better than soldiers in this Keep. You hit the bullseye with at least one arrow every hit, most of these guys every third arrow goes high, right, or left. When this is over maybe you could give some special training so we could have some sharpshooters."

Darkwing looks to Greenbean, "If most of these guys have that issue, yes, I will have to make sure that happens just in case we are ever attacked here. We will also need sharpshooters from flying mounts, so they better be able to hit the bullseye every time."

Greenbean points to the halberd, "How long since you have handled a staff or two-handed weapon?"

Darkwing chuckles, "Since before the Great Eruption. With that, Ghod has it very well balanced. It was like swinging air in the blacksmith's shop."

Greenbean offers, "If you'd like let's practice some moves before lunch. See if we can work off the rustiness."

At that moment Earl Jarkon and his men walk into the training area. "Greenbean, would you allow us to watch and join you? I have heard of your reputation from reliable sources and would like my men to witness a master."

Greenbean smiles, "Of course, spread out here in front of me. We will start with some warmup stances and swings."

At that, the next three plus hours are weapons practice. Greenbean takes note of the skills of the Earls men. She thinks, "I need these guys to work with the soldiers of the Keep. It would be a good experience for them all." As for Darkwing she feels he is not as rusty as he thinks, his muscle memory is working very well.

As they head back to the Keep for lunch, Earl Jarkon states, "Greenbean, you have such fluid and strong strikes. It is like watching a deadly dance. I would gladly employ your services for a short time at my Keep if you would train more of my men."

Greenbean responds, "Earl Jarkon, once all this is done, I would be honored to come to your Keep and help train your men. Right now, Akita needs all the help she can get. This menace keeps getting bigger, every time we think we can stop and rest, something else pops up."

Earl Jarkon replies, "Oh absolutely, I plan on offering our services to Lady Blackwing to help destroy the Dark Wizards. She has a strong team and a good grasp of what needs to be done, as well as who can do it. That kind of life experience takes years to build, however, your team is exceptional in what you do."

As they walk through the courtyard gusts of wind start blowing the dust around. They look up to see Akita and her team flying over to land outside the main gates.

Darkwing turns to head for the gates. The team sees him standing in the middle of the entrance with his new weapons. Greenbean and Earl Jarkon walk up behind him. Fabby and Shamash walk up as well.

Akita flies over to Darkwing, off Warriors back, and wraps him in a huge hug. "I don't know how you did it, but I am so glad you did. Are you ok?"

The stable hands lead the mounts away to care for them and feed them. Darkwing waits for the others to gather.

Darkwing looks Akita in the eyes, "Akita my friend, they took my powers. We have to go back before King Clouds takes his people to another realm. However, there is more to tell, so let's go sit in the dining room and I will explain it all."

Mandrake laughs, "I am so glad you are back, and I love the nickname for the Cloud Giant King."

Everyone welcomes Darkwing back as they head to the dining room, except one. Vivian walks up to Darkwing and stares into his eyes. "Darkwing, I never got to meet you before the kidnapping. I was there at the first attempt to rescue you. I am Earl Jarkon's daughter, and I will be there to help you get your powers back."

Darkwing nods his head, "Thank you very much." He motions for her to lead and they both head to the dining room.

Vivian walks with Darkwing into the dining room. Darkwing waits until everyone has a plate of food, and the servants leave the room.

Darkwing begins, "So, after you left, I was taken to the temple and tied down. I was kept in what I would call a wakeful dream state. They wanted me exhausted but they wanted me to experience what they were doing to me."

Darkwing pauses and looks at Ishvet, "The next part is not going to be easy to hear. King Carthon III of Astya is the Grand Master Dark Wizard. He stood at my feet proclaiming to be the most powerful Dark Wizard on the continent. He then proceeded to remove my powers and put them in a vessel for him to study." Darkwing again pauses watching Ishvet closely. Ishvet's hands clenched into a fist and his brow started to furl plus he was starting to glow blue. "Ishvet we will help you with this situation, but let me finish the story, you are turning blue."

Vicar walks up behind Ishvet and puts a hand on his shoulder. He concentrates on calming Ishvet until he is no longer glowing blue.

Darkwing continues, "Before they extracted my magic, the Black Dragon flew in under the control of a Dark Wizard named, Leader Feron. He had the missing piece for the ritual. As they performed this ritual on me, I heard a voice call to me saying that we would be reunited. Somehow the magic was speaking to me. After they were done with me, I was put in a cage next to King Clouds hut. I was able to witness him have a conversation with the Dragon. I observed that Leader Feron had to loosen his control of the Dragon so it could speak to the King. It took all my strength, but I was able to make contact with Thoraxian at that time. After King Clouds spoke to Thoraxian, everything changed. I overheard him tell King Carthon that they would not be able to recreate the magic the Dragons used to make the Amulets of Power because there were not enough Dragons left in the world. King Clouds has decided to abandon this realm and has ordered the Dark Wizards to leave the island. That's when I was able to trick Leader Feron into lowering his control of Thoraxian. I convinced him that the Dragon was already breaking free, so he needed to check on him. As soon as he reduced the amount of control, Thoraxian broke free and ate him. We narrowly escaped the island. King Clouds still plans to take my magic with him when the Cloud Giants move to the other realm, so we must act fast."

Ishvet starts speaking through gritted teeth, "I can't believe that he has hidden this from me. I have met with him many times in my life and even asked for his help in tracking down the Dark Wizards. This whole time he was their freaking leader. I swear to Bahamut, I will kill him."

Akita stands and leans over the table resting her weight on the palms of her hands. She looks Ishvet directly in the eyes, "You better believe that I will be by your side to help you destroy him. Aphorea didn't give me this Magma Amulet for nothing."

Darkwing's mouth slightly opens, and he takes a gasp of air, "Um, excuse me. Did you just say Magma Amulet?" he slightly pauses and continues, "Yes I'll be there with you too Ishvet, but first Akita has some explaining to do, then we must get my magic back before we track down your father."

Akita sighs, "So Ishvet and Ordyn buried themselves in the library after our first attempt to rescue you, Darkwing, and found some old tomes about a cave that is on the far side of the Voskaola Mountain below your Keep. We decided to go check it out to see if there was anything that could help us rescue you. With the maps and Vivian's help, we found the cave. It seems to have been abandoned since the Great Eruption. We started our descent into the cave, we found the ruins of a Dwarven city, as well as skeletons with the armor still intact. We came to one cavern that had the beginnings of a crevasse that was covered in ice, which is unusual that deep into a cave. As we dropped down through the opening, we found Aphorea – The Brilliant, a White Ice Dragon.

We explained to her what we were doing there and that her help would be greatly appreciated, and then she told us that she needed to think about the consequences if she was to become involved. She asked us to leave her to her thoughts, so we went back to camp to wait. After a short time, she requested that Wulf and I meet her again in the cave. She entered my mind and went through all of my memories to see if we were worthy and deserving of her gift. We passed the test but before she would give us the gift, Wulf had to pledge to protect me, basically, forever. That was a bit awkward, but Wulf made his pledge. It was at that point she relinquished the Magma Amulet of Power."

Thoraxian speaks to the team, "Aphorea is still alive? I fought by her side in the Titan Wars."

Warrior calls to Akita, "Something is wrong with Ransom, we need you here."

Akita states, "Ransom must have sensed Thoraxian speaking to us, I have to get to her now."

The fliers follow Akita out of the Keep to the stables, while the others hurry to catch up. When Akita spots Ransom, she is cowering in a heap with her head under a wing and shaking violently.

Akita goes straight to her and climbs under her wing to hold her head. "Ransom hon, it's ok, I know what has happened, will you let me tell you?" Akita feels a slight nod of Ransom's head. Akita explains to Ransom the story and assures her that Annut has Thoraxian with her.

Gavin has a hand on Ransom's side to calm her, Wulf and Ordyn do the same as a show of support. Soon everyone is there to comfort Ransom as best they can, with Vicar assisting Gavin in the calming.

Akita reaches out to Annut, and in a few minutes a new voice speaks to all in the Keep including the mounts. "I am Thoraxian – the Shadow, I deeply regret the actions the Dark Wizards made me take. Drako you are a brave and strong brother to Ransom, and Ransom is strong and was loyal to Rogue. I am glad that Ransom is here with us today, I know that to say 'I am sorry' is not enough for Ransom, but I promise this will never happen again and I will protect you all fiercely or die trying. Ransom they can never take control of me again, as I now know how to counter it. As of right now I want to make amends, get revenge for what was done to me and Darkwing still needs me to help him get his power back."

There is a pause, then everyone hears Annut, "Most do not understand a Dragons Promise. I will vouch for Thoraxian, because to break a Dragon's Promise requires a life in exile or death. He now has a few reasons to live and fight for our cause."

Akita says to Ransom, "Thoraxian was under the Dark Wizards' power, he had no idea what he was doing and could not stop it. He was not himself for a time."

Akita looks to the group, "We need to know if Grace is back or headed this way. We need to leave immediately. I am going to go check at Prayla and if need be Salthall for Grace. I will return as soon as I can." Akita lifts off and sees Wulf following her. She thinks to herself, 'The new normal, I have a shadow,' as she heads for Prayla.

Annut speaks to Akita, "There is no need to fly to Prayla, as Grace and her ship are below my cave. She says she heard of the Black Dragon sitting and never left, as she wanted to be sure Blackwing Keep was ok. She is going back to Prayla for supplies and will wait for us there."

Akita lands again, and looks at the team, "Well, Grace will be at Prayla awaiting our arrival to leave. She just spoke with Annut."

Earl Jarkon speaks up, "With all that has been said here today, I want to help you with the Dark Wizard infestation, so I will go back to Stonia and cleans the Dragon Temple of its inhabitants. I will also triple patrols arresting or irradicating all that we find in the area, as some will not allow themselves to be arrested."

Akita responds, "That sounds like a perfect plan that might give us a head start on finding King Carthon. My uncle once spoke of a Pact between our Keeps, and I would like you to know that I am here to honor that. Any assistance that you need from Blackwing Keep will be given freely. If we are going to prevail over the Dark Wizards, we will have to reforge the alliances with all the Keeps of Alahora."

Darkwing states, "I, Skrymir Darkwing will include Darkwing Keep in the alliance."

Earl Jarkon retrieves his men from the barrack's and shortly they hear the Griffins take flight.

Akita states, "Grab your weapons and what supplies you need. We are not taking any mounts this time. We will leave for Prayla within the hour."

CHAPTER 19
RETRIEVING MAGIC

As everyone is gathered in the courtyard to leave for Prayla, Akita asks, "Warrior, Hunter, Ransom, and Drako would you do us a favor and fly some of us down to the docks? Ordyn, Gavin, Wulf, Meh-Kola, and I will fly down on our own."

The Wyverns answer by landing next to the gate outside the Keep.

Akita smiles, "Your rides to the docks have arrived. If everyone is ready, let's go."

As they are flying down to the docks, Akita and Darkwing sense a familiar feeling in their minds and look at each other.

Thoraxian reaches out to Darkwing and Akita, "Annut says I cannot join you and risk being injured or taken again. Bring the magic back with you and I can help you restore your magic. May the Gods be with you."

As Thoraxian finishes his message, Akita and Darkwing nod to each other.

Prayla is accustomed to the Wyverns that Akita has, and it always causes as stir when they land, but with two new ones the town is gathering to get a look at the large creatures that have been their heroes.

The team is headed for the ship when five-year-old boy walks out away from his mother towards Ransom. His mother is trying to catch him but is reluctant to get near Ransom. Ransom stops and looks at the boy.

Wulf flies down and picks up the boy, much to the mother's relief. He flies the boy closer to Ransom, and she allows the boy to pat her nose. His mother who is all tensed up again relaxes once she hears her son giggling. Ransom does a low purring growl, nods to the boy and mother, as she backs up to fly back to the Keep with the others.

Wulf turns to the mother and hands the child to her as he lands. "Ma'am they won't hurt your children, only attackers. You never have to fear grabbing your child, the Wyverns know and understand." With that Wulf joins the rest on the ship.

Wulf lands next to Akita, "That boy will be the talk of Prayla for a month, but the fear will be much less. I feel it is good for the people of this region to understand and not fear them since they will be assisting us in protecting the realm. The town is used to Hunter and Warrior, but you're adding more Wyverns, Dragons and now Griffins to the mix, so I am going to promote goodwill."

The team nods, as everything has changed in the last couple of months, and most in the region don't even know it.

Akita looks to Grace, "Well my friend are we ready to sail to the final battle?"

Grace notices the amulet around Akita's neck, "If that is the secret weapon, let's go. You are going to have to fill me in on what has been going on." Grace starts shouting orders to her crew, and the ship starts backing away from the dock.

Grace and crew clear the dock and point the ship out to sea. "We don't have to go to Port Tristan this time, so I am taking us straight to the Island. What I find interesting is the sail that is supposed to take us to the island isn't glowing, it isn't doing anything. At least I know the way now, but still. Mandrake and Wulf are you going to be our wind power again?"

Wulf and Mandrake move to the back of the ship with Fabby and Vicar standing next to them. As before, Mandrake creates a vortex of cold air and

Wulf creates a vortex of hot air. They gradually move their hands together and a larger vortex forms in front of them. The outward force is substantial, but not enough to move the ship as much as they would like.

When the vortex is stable, Vicar and Fabby place a hand on each of their friends and buff their magic output. The generated vortices get bigger, and the ship gradually builds up speed. Ordyn holds the helm while Grace runs around the ship checking for stress on the ship from the speed. She deems everything good, so she signals the team to get prepared.

Coming back up to Ordyn and Akita at the Helm, she states, "We should be there in four to five hours. Now, who wants to fill me in while I keep us on track to the Cloud Giant Island."

Akita starts by recounting her experience with Aphorea - the Brilliant and obtaining the Magma Amulet. Then she explains how Darkwing escaped the Cloud Giant Island, how he met Thoraxian – the Shadow, and the conversation that he overheard between King Cirus and King Carthon. She then explains that Earl Jarkon is headed back to Stonia to run the Dark Wizards out of the Dragon Temple. By the time Akita is done, it is time for Mandrake and Wulf to take a break and reenergize. The ship has enough momentum to continue at full speed for at least another hour or more.

Akita calls out to the team to gather in front of the helm on the lower deck, "Okay everyone, the last time we were in this situation we didn't fare well. I don't want a repeat of that this time. I have this amulet to help us and now we also have a better understanding of what we will face from the Giants as far as their abilities. We need to form a game plan; I will not lose anyone on this trip!"

Vivian speaks up first, "I have been training to keep my shield up for longer. I believe that with Fabby buffing me, I could encompass the whole team." She looks over to Fabby and he nods in agreement.

Ishvet steps forward one step with his head looking down, "It will be hard to return to the place where Rani was killed. I just want you to know that I have been training hard with Ordyn and I have honed my Blue Streak ability. I now understand it and I can use it with control and not as a reaction. Once I get going my whole body becomes a blade that nothing can stop." Ishvet looks up to the sky, "Thank you, Mother."

Akita smiles at all of them, "My goodness, it's amazing how much everyone has grown since we all met at Blackwing Keep just two months ago. I don't want this to sound weird, but I feel more like a proud mother rather than a leader."

Wulf interrupts with a tone of sarcasm, "No, that doesn't sound weird at all Akita. It's just that most of us are older than you." Then everyone starts laughing.

Darkwing speaks next, "That was good Wulf. However, back to our plan. We don't even know at this point if the Giants are still on the Island. They are going to a different realm presumably through some type of portal. If they are still on the Island, we need to find some way of keeping them there until we can get my magic back. Anyone has any ideas?"

Meh-Kola flies up from the ground to eye level with the team, "One knows about portals and how to block them. That is how One blinks from any place to the other. One creates a small portal. If they have a portal open on the Island, One will be able to sense it. One will take Wulf and he can put an invisible wall in front of it. One thinks Greenbean knows the kind of wall to which One speaks." Meh-Kola purr laughs and Wulf smiles.

Akita agrees with Meh-Kola, "That will keep King Clouds here in this realm long enough for us to find and retrieve Darkwing's power."

Vicar states, "Didn't Grace say the sail wasn't working today?"

Mandrake finishes, "If the sail is not guiding us, more than likely it won't open the cloud barrier. How are we going to get past the cloud barrier?"

Akita lifts the Amulet of Power and looks at it. "I think this will be a test of my abilities with the Magma Amulet of Power. I will see if I can open a hole for the ship to pass through."

Greenbean looks to the team, "When we land, we are going to have to find King Clouds fast and hope he is not near that portal. It will be easier to deal with him if he cannot even attempt to walk through the portal away from us, blocked or not. If he finds it blocked, he will try to attack the blockers."

Akita has an idea, "Mandrake, I know you can enchant your horses to fly, but can you enchant yours and Vicar's wings with the ice make them to fly? Have you ever considered that or tried it?"

Mandrake laughs and Vicar scowls, "Oh, Mandrake tried it once when we were young. He thought it would be funny to make my wings flap and I wasn't aware he did it. He enchanted them with the magic ice, and they started flapping superfast. I couldn't control them and I flew into a tree and broke my arm."

Everyone is laughing because after Mandrake's ice slide from the night they were drinking they can see him pulling pranks like this often. Mandrake isn't as mild-mannered as they used to think.

Mandrake responds, "Okay, okay. Yes, I can do that for short periods of time. I don't think Vicar will fly into a tree again because this time he will know it's happening."

Akita finally stops laughing, "I only ask because Greenbean is correct. We will have to locate King Clouds fast. That is easier if I carry Vivian, Ordyn carries Darkwing, and Gavin Carries Greenbean. I remember Ordyn saying how heavy Mandrake, Vicar, and Ishvet can be so the idea hit me of Mandrake enchanting the three of you with wings for as far as he can. Then one of you can carry Fabby. Meh-Kola and Wulf can still take off to find the portal and block it. We know it isn't very far to the King's hut and the temple is just up the hill from that. We won't know where the portal is placed in the area. Flying will let us see more of the area quickly versus running around the huts and temple."

Mandrake replies, "That would be an excellent advantage. We can try it here on deck to practice, but if someone flies off the ship one of you will have to retrieve them." He looks at his scowling brother Vicar and starts chuckling.

Ishvet states, "I am up for it, but I can now use my Blue Streak to go where I need to. I can cover the whole Island in minutes. So, give Fabby wings, and we will be set."

Vicar reluctantly answers, "I have to agree with the team but know this brother, you mess with me, and I will get revenge."

Mandrake stands closer to Fabby and Vicar. The team encircles them, just in case they need to catch one of the three, keeping them from flying off the ship. Within a few minutes wings form on Fabby, Vicar and Mandrake's backs. Vicar is cautious but Fabby starts flying around the ship with Ordyn following. Mandrake also feels freer to fly around the ship. Gavin follows Mandrake. Vicar finally starts to fly around the ship with Wulf and Akita following him.

Fabby yells, "This is awesome." As he flies up into the sails, making several trips around the ship and then back down to the group. "This will be a great advantage for the team."

Mandrake slowly lands by the group again, "I hadn't tried this on myself because well Vicar is always with me and had forbid me to use it on him ever again, but that was great."

Vicar flies around the ship a couple of times, and out over the railings to test his ability to get back to where he wanted to be. As he lands with the group, "Ok, we can do this. It is much better knowing the wings are there, than being caught off guard."

Akita nods, "Great. Now is there anything else we can think of that might catch us off guard? Anything we might need to anticipate before we get there?"

Darkwing answers, "Some things you can't plan for, it's up to chance and the decisions made in the heat of battle. I think we are all good at countering anything thrown at us individually and backing each other up. With that said as soon as we spot King Clouds and the portal, we need to land quickly before he can throw any winds at us. Remember he almost pulled Thoraxian, a full-sized Dragon and myself back to the ground. I am pretty sure he will try to blow us away, fast, and hard."

Wulf agrees, "Yes, most of us fly low, with one of us doing the spotting from higher up. That will minimize the time to land and the time he has to hit us hard."

Ordyn looks to Darkwing, "Buddy, I will set you down behind us. You have no magic, and you don't have the special abilities of a Greatsword Fighter either. Your arrows will do their job from a distance. I am pretty sure he will target you because you represent his failure in this realm. It would do us no good to get your vessel of power and have you dead."

They notice the ship has slowed down significantly, so Mandrake, Wulf, Fabby, and Vicar move to the back of the ship to start the winds again.

Grace states loudly, "Probably another hour or so and we will see the cloud barrier. The cook has made some lunch for everyone. I suggest you eat and get your strength up. Someone might have to hand feed our wind team though." She giggles at their expressions. "Well, you need your strength too and you're not going to be able to feed yourselves one-handed and keep the wind up."

Fabby assures Grace, "We will take care of it, don't you worry."

Akita goes to the bow of the ship to think. She knows it's going to be a short time before the cloud barrier is visible. She notices dolphins swimming in front of the ship as they move forward. They are speeding through the water and jumping forward as if leading the ship on its way. Akita takes it as a good omen, from the old sailing stories she has read and heard in her life.

Akita got lost in thought until she notices the dolphins splitting off and leaving. She looks up and the cloud barrier is looming in front of them. Looking over her shoulder, she sees that the sails are still not glowing or doing anything that would signify that they would open the cloud barrier for them again.

The Magma Amulet of Power is tingling on her chest. She feels like she needs to wait till the ship is closer before trying to open an entry point, but she also knows she doesn't want the ship too close because she is not familiar with using the amulet. The closer they get the stronger the pull from the Amulet of Power.

Wulf comes up behind her, "You, ok? You seem tense."

Akita looks at him, "Brace me, I am going to stand on the railing, as I don't know what to expect when I try this." With that, she steps up on the bottom rung of the railing with her shins against the top railing.

Akita holds the amulet in her left hand and reaches out to the cloud barrier with her right hand.

She starts concentrating and produces a column of fire in front of her. She pushes all her power into the flames until she thinks that she is almost spent. As she begins to give up, a voice starts to speak to her inside her head. It sounds like more than one voice speaking in unison. It tells her to let go and feel the fire. She takes a deep breath, clears her mind, reaches back out to the column of fire traveling to the barrier.

Wulf maintains a grasp on her, but Akita has started to glow as if outlined in fire. Akita can feel the essence of the fire she produced, and she can feel it grow in her mind. When the flame column hits the barrier, it begins to expand just as she sees it in her mind. She imagines it consuming the barrier. The fire spreads from where it hit and begins to burn away the barrier.

The team comes up to watch, but no one says anything, and the clerics do not buff Akita, because the power they are seeing is overwhelming.

The voice is back in Akita's mind telling her to control the fire. She reaches out again and imagines the flame to surround the whole Island. As the magic of the barrier is broken it sends a wave of heat and steam outwards. It comes towards the ship, but Akita is still in control and splits the wave in half so that no harm comes to the ship.

Akita steps down from the railing, "Well that was something. I heard the amulet speak to me and I could feel the fire and heat like it was alive. All I had to do was imagine it doing something and it obeyed. Now I understand how King Clouds controls the wind."

Mandrake readies himself to enchant Fabby and Vicar again because they will need to fly fast. The fire will be seen all around the Island and tip off the Cloud Giants. They won't be able to wait for the ship to anchor.

Everyone grabs their weapons and runs back to the bow. Akita turns and looks at Grace, who nods, knowing to meet them at the docks because this team is leaving now.

Meh-Kola senses the portal in the middle of the courtyard. She tells Wulf, "Hold One's tail." In less than the blink of an eye, Wulf finds himself on the beach, but only for a second. Meh-Kola blinks them again to the portal and he incases the portal into an invisible barrier.

Mandrake enchants himself, Vicar, and Fabby. The other flyers grab the others under the arms and fly to the Island. As they skim over the beach, they head towards the main compound to find nothing there. Ishvet uses his ability to skim over the water and up the hill to the temple. He sees the Cloud Giant King and two other Giants standing outside the temple. He uses his ability again and is on the beach as the others fly over. He yells to Akita and points towards the temple.

Vicar, Fabby, and Mandrake land just inside the tree line near King Clouds. Gavin, Akita and Ordyn set down Darkwing, Vivian and Greenbean landing within sight of King Clouds. They join on the path headed to the Giants, moving to block his path to the portal.

King Cirus spots them, "I figured that you would be back for Skrymir's stolen magic before we left this realm for good. You are either brave or stupid."

Akita amplifies her voice, "You have something that doesn't belong to you. Hand it over and we leave once we ensure you are gone." She sees a blue glowing light in the King's hand.

King Cirus shakes his head and chuckles, "I sense that you also have something that doesn't belong to you. While I'm sure it would be an interesting story of how you came to be in possession of something that belongs to my people, I don't have time for it. I will take it from your dead body, and it will go with me to the Cloud Realm."

Akita grits her teeth and leans forward aggressively, "You can try!"

Dark black clouds form over the Island, and the wind picks up. Thunder booms so loud that the whole Island seems to shake. Lightning streaks through the clouds causing the Island to light up momentarily as bright as midday. King Cirus motions to his guards to attack.

The guard starts heading towards the group and Darkwing unleashes two arrows right at the Giant's face, they hit their mark and freeze his eyes. The guard screams in pain and creates a wind around his body to repel any other arrow attacks. Gavin unleashes a rain of arrows that all are blown away. The guard directs lightning to the ground in front of him as he moves blindly forward. Vivian throws up her shield of light protecting them from the lightning strikes. Mandrake throws ice down around the Giants' feet and they watch the guard fall on his face pushing Darkwing's ice arrows further into his brain. They can visibly see the Giant's head freeze and in minutes he is no longer moving.

King Cirus cannot believe his guard was so easily defeated. Motioning the other guard forward, "You got in a lucky shot there Skrymir. You will not get that chance again. Squash those pests. One step and you can kill most of them."

The guard then puts up his shield and holds up his pike, heading towards Akita's team. The Giant instantly puts up a vortex of wind around himself to repel the arrows away from him. Gavin waits for the shield to come down, he adjusts so that when he shoots the arrow the wind from the vortex will carry it harder and faster into the giant's neck. Using a larger long arrow, he hits his target. At the same time Wulf throws a fireball in the guard's face, that turns the wind into a fire tornado and explodes. Between the two hits, the guard is gravely wounded. He covers his face and neck with his shield. Gavin then runs up on him, dodging the lightning strikes, hacking at his ankles. Gavin slices leave him bleeding and his Achilles tendon shredded.

As he dashes back out, the guard hits his knees swinging his pike and barely missing him. The guard throws his arm out sending a gust of wind at the group, blowing them back. Akita tumbles and rolls with the wind. Mandrake and Vicar slide backward on their feet. Gavin's wings catch the wind, and he is carried several yards backward. Fabby rolls to the side to dodge the wind, with the guards' shield down Fabby starts throwing javelins of light into his face and eyes. Akita sees that this Giant is hard to kill. She throws a fireball at the Giant and imagines it turning into a whisp then funneling right into his mouth. The fireball does just as she has imagined. The Giant grasps at his throat as the fire burns down his esophagus, the fire grows inside him, and the heat intensifies. In a flash, the Giant turns to ash and the wind scatters him across the Island.

King Cirus growls and lightning starts bombarding the team. The wind picks up and dust and debris reduce their visibility. However, Ishvet sees King Cirus place the vessel into a pouch on his belt.

Vivian yells to the team, "Everyone get under my shield now! Vicar I'm going to need you!"

The team huddles around Vivian and her shield goes up just as a bolt of lightning hits. Vicar grabs Vivian and buffs her shield. The shield expands and glows brighter. Several more bolts of lightning hit the shield and spiderweb down to the ground. Suddenly the lightning stops, and the wind dies down.

The team hears a loud yell. They look up at King Clouds to see bleeding claw marks appear sporadically all over his face. Some are near his eyes, others on his neck, and one long mark across his forehead. A little flash of grey and black keeps appearing for seconds and then disappearing again leaving more and more scratches on the Kings face.

Mandrake throws several ice shards in succession at his neck and chest, not wanting to accidently hit Meh-Kola.

Akita states, "We need that vessel before he drops it from our attacks."

Ishvet states to Akita, "I saw him put it in that pouch on his belt."

King Cirus bats Meh-Kola away and starts a tornado of wind towards the team. They scatter and Gavin makes a run and leap flying towards the pouch. King Cirus sees him from the corner of his eye and backhands him, sending Gavin flying out over the ocean. Gavin catches himself but has a way to fly before getting back into the battle.

Akita yells to the team to move back. The wind becomes so ferocious that the team is sliding and tumbling down the hill towards the Giant portal. When the wind stops the whole team is beside the portal and King Cirus is walking towards it.

King Cirus scoffs, "You really think that you can keep me from leaving? I see your barrier and it won't stop me."

Akita jumps in front of the portal, "It might not but I will!"

Akita reaches out her hands and a wall of flame rises from the ground. However, it is not an ordinary flame it is molten lava. It rises past the height of King Cirus and starts encircling Akita and the portal.

King Cirus gets as close as he can to the lava wall and reaches out his hands. An intense column of wind starts pushing into the lava wall. He inches closer and closer until the wind punches through.

Akita turns her attention away from the lava wall and produces a column of fire directed at the column of wind that King Cirus is producing. Each is putting their full strength into their spells. King Cirus is pushing Akita back away from the portal and he is moving closer to it.

Wulf sees that Akita is slipping back and moves in behind her to fortify her position. They are both still slipping. The others in the team see this and gather behind Wulf to reinforce him. Akita stops moving and the Cloud Giant King can go no further.

King Cirus growls and grunts using all his might against Akita's flame. Where the flame and wind meet in the middle a strange glow starts to appear. The two powers are equal and are starting to cancel each other out. Just as King Cirus realizes what is happening, both columns of power explode sending King Cirus on his back and pushing the team to the ground.

Everyone is dazed by the explosion. Their heads are foggy, ears are ringing, and their vision is blurred. As their eyes clear they can see that the huts around them have been blown apart. Akita and Ishvet are the first to stand back up and they can see that King Cirus is also getting up.

King Cirus clutches his amulet, "What have you done?"

Akita grabs her amulet and can feel the cracks running through and she can no longer feel the power within. She shutters and a fear sets in. As she begins to speak, she sees a flash of blue light streak past.

Ishvet sees his opportunity and uses his ability on the Giant King. The force of his ability knocks the Cloud Giant King through the portal and the portal closes. Ishvet reappears next to Akita, "Um, I didn't mean to do that."

Akita looks at him with a look of disbelief, "What do you mean, you didn't mean to do that? What were you trying to do? Now he's gone and Darkwing's magic with him. Of all the hot-headed Dragonkin things to do!"

Ishvet lowers his head, "I'm sorry Duchess, I meant to streak right through him." He then looks up and a smile forms on his Dragonkin face, "Instead I just knocked him into the portal" He pauses a second then lifts up his hand, "But I did get this before he flew through it."

Everyone is now back on their feet and surrounding Ishvet and Akita. They are looking back and forth at each other wondering what the heck just happened. Then out of nowhere Akita starts laughing at the top of her lungs. Then Ishvet starts in and all the others around him.

Akita stops laughing and puts a hand on Ishvet's cheek, "I don't know if I should be laughing or crying. There are so many strong emotions right now."

Ishvet doesn't say anything, but a tear falls from his eye onto Akita's hand. Wulf steps up to Akita, puts his arms around her, and turns her into his chest. Akita buries her head and sobs.

Akita finishes getting her emotions out all over Wulf's tunic and raises her head, "Okay what are all of you looking at? Darkwing has his magic so let's get back to the Keep and get it back in him."

Ishvet hands Darkwing the pouch, "Now don't go losing this again."

Darkwing smiles, "Well, I don't really have to worry about that anymore since you just knocked King Clouds to oblivion."

Everyone chuckles as they walk down to the docks to meet up with Grace.

CHAPTER 20
BACK AT THE KEEP

A waning moon shines bright in the heavens above surrounded by millions of stars. The cloudless night is reflected in the smooth waters of the ocean as Grace O'Malley's ship glides across the surface towards Prayla. It's a peaceful night with a good breeze. The exhausted team members are sitting around relaxing on the upper deck. Darkwing is clutching the pouch with the vessel inside. He is anxious to return to Blackwing Keep and have his power restored. As they get closer to Prayla, Akita can see the lights of the Inn and the lights of the Tavern along the docks. These buildings were rebuilt after the Leviathan attack, it is heartwarming to see them thriving again.

As the ship pulls up to the dock, Akita calls out to the Wyverns to meet them in Prayla to take people back to the Keep.

As the gangway is lowered, the messenger Alican comes running up to Grace. "Lady Grace O'Malley, I have an important message for you." Alican hands Grace the sealed tube. The young messenger shyly states, "I have always wanted to meet you and you are exactly what I pictured." Akita hands the girl a gold coin, and Alican turns promptly and runs off the ship.

Grace laughs, "She wanted to meet me, but didn't wait for a response. She must have felt embarrassed."

Akita smiles, "I know Alican, she's watching for you to see if you need her to take a response. It's just her and her mother, and that little one works hard to help her mom who cleans the mayor's house."

Grace opens the message and reads. "Well, there won't be a return message, but I need to leave for my Keep. Something needs my attention. If you need me, send me a message."

Akita nods, "If you need us let me know, as we will be there for you. I want to thank you for your help with this whole incident with Darkwing. We couldn't have done it without the loss of more lives if you hadn't been here for us."

Grace looks at Akita, "If you repeat this to anyone, I will deny it, but thank you for allowing me to help with a righteous cause and giving me some dignity back. I know we aren't done with these Dark Wizards, and I will let you know when I am available again."

Grace notices everyone standing around her. As each one leaves the ship, they either shake her hand or hug her with a word of thanks. When it comes to Darkwing, he gives Grace a hug and a kiss on the forehead. "Thank you for helping my friends in their efforts to save me. If you ever need anything you message me." With that he leaves the ship. Grace waves to the team and starts yelling orders to her crew.

The Wyverns land near the docks and wait for the team. Akita, Wulf, and Ordyn help the non-flyers pack the Wyverns. Meh-Kola decides to ride back in Ransom's saddlebag. As soon as everyone is ready, they all take off for the short flight to the Keep.

Akita reaches out to Annut, "We are back, and we were successful. It is late and we are all tired so we will see you and Thoraxian in the morning."

Annut answers, "I am glad that all of you are safe. A great price was paid today. Someone is at the Keep to see you."

As the team flies into the Keep, Akita comes to a dead stop mid-air and hovers. "Aphorea!" Akita flies straight to the White Dragon awaiting her in the courtyard. "I am so glad you're here, but I am afraid I know why you left the safety of your cave."

Akita lands and bows to the most ancient Dragon, Aphorea – The Brilliant.

Aphorea addresses Akita, "I wanted to see you when you returned to the Keep. Every Dragon on this world felt the destruction of the Cloud Amulet of Power and the Magma Amulet of Power. I reached out to Annut and Thoraxian the moment I felt the wave of power radiate from the Island."

Akita looks at Aphorea, "I feel like you entrusted me with this awesome power, and I let you down."

Aphorea shushes Akita, "I will say it was not an outcome any of us were expecting, but so you know, it was actually a blessing. As Dragons, we could not bring ourselves to destroy our kin in the amulets. We knew you would not destroy them, but I cannot say that we knew they would cancel each other out. In your mighty fight against the power-hungry Cloud

Giant King, you caused a conjunction in the power of the amulets. With both amulets being equal in power, it caused them to destroy each other. This freed the ones who sacrificed themselves and enabled them to move on to the next plane.

Akita looks stunned, "Are you telling me that there were Dragon souls in the amulets? Is that why I heard many voices speaking as one when I started to use it?"

Aphorea nods, "Yes, Akita. That was their sacrifice. To empower the amulets with their abilities. This is another reason we fought to get the amulets away from the abusive Giants. I knew this would weigh heavy on your conscious, so I wanted to see you tonight. You must understand that you inadvertently did a service for those Dragons."

Akita looks at Aphorea, "Thank you for telling me. I sobbed when I realized what had happened, and I was worried about what you three would think of me."

Aphorea states, "You go rest, I am going to go see my old friend Thoraxian and meet Annut. I will be here tomorrow for the ritual."

Akita nods and hugs Aphorea's snout.

The next morning there is a knock at Akita's door. As she opens it Wulf walks in with a tray of food and coffee.

Wulf says, "Good morning. I brought your breakfast to you because you are going to want to dress and eat immediately. Someone is here to see you."

Akita sits back down at her dressing table to finish her hair, "Who is here to see me? Is Darkwing up and ready for whatever it is we have to do to put his power back into him?"

Wulf laughs, "Yes, Darkwing is up and ready. As for the other let it be a surprise." Wulf helps himself to a breakfast roll and coffee.

Akita eats a breakfast roll and drinks half a cup of coffee, then refills it, "Ready?" She stands up looking at Wulf expectantly.

Wulf refills his coffee cup, and they leave the room to fly down the stairs to the courtyard. As they reach the great hall, Akita sees two familiar faces.

Standing in the great hall are Rogue's sisters, Midge and Roguette. Midge is Rogue's half-sister, a Halfling Hunter and Roguette is his true sister who followed in his footsteps.

Flying up and landing in front of them, Akita gives each of them a hug, as the three wipe away tears. Akita looks each of them, "We waited for you to arrive. I am so sorry that this has happened."

Roguette looks to Akita, "Greenbean filled us in on what happened. We understand what you have been up against."

Akita looks down, "My thought was to bury him here with our honored dead unless you wish to take him home."

Midge answers, "Rogue would want to be here near you. He was very fond of you, and always ran to help you when you asked."

Akita nods, "Would you mind if we have the service tomorrow. It will be a day for Rogue, instead of sharing it with the ritual for Darkwing."

Roguette replies, "That will be just fine. You have been a true friend to our brother."

Akita bows her head, "Thank you. Join us in the courtyard. Greenbean can introduce you to the team."

Wulf and Akita head through the Keep door. Akita looks up and comes to an abrupt stop. Standing in the courtyard facing the Keep entrance are Annut, Thoraxian, and Aphorea. Akita is stunned at the site of the three Dragons in the courtyard.

Akita joins the team all standing in front of the Dragons. "Good morning my friends. This is truly a special sight that most of us would never have dreamed of a couple of months ago."

Thoraxian answers, "Indeed." Aphorea and Annut nod. "Akita, I need your strongest Wizard, I believe that is Mandrake. I must teach him how to pronounce the words of the incantation. The Dragon language must be spoken aloud for it to work properly. The preparations for the ritual will take most of the day. I overheard your conversation with your friends. You might want to go ahead with Rogue's funeral today, while I am off with Mandrake."

Akita turns to Mandrake, "Looks like you have been chosen as the strongest Wizard for the honor of learning a new language and helping with the ritual."

Mandrake chuckles, "Don't you mean the only Wizard until Darkwing has his powers back. However, it will be an honor to participate in the ritual for Darkwing and to get to work with Thoraxian."

Akita turns to the others, "Let me go talk to the cooks and with Ghod. Wulf would you take Midge and Roguette to see Ransom and Drako, please?"

Wulf answers, "It will be my pleasure. Follow me, ladies."

After making sure the kitchen would prepare a special dinner, Akita heads to the blacksmith shop.

Ghod is examining the stones with the engraved runes and glyphs on them. He glances at Akita, "Our little friend Meh-Kola brought me a gift from that cave you found the White Dragon in. These are quite rare and will be very useful towards the weapons made for the Keep."

Akita looks at the stones, "I am glad they picked them up for you. I know Mandrake was hoping they would help you, none of us knew for sure." She looks around the shop. "I was wondering if you had made the marker for Rogue's grave yet. His sisters arrived today, and circumstances have it that we should do the funeral today. I know it's short notice."

Ghod nods and sets the runes down. "I knew we would get to it once Darkwing had his power. We can't leave Rogue on ice forever. Just a second." He walks to the corner of the room and grabs what looks like a long pole in the dark corner. As he walks back, Akita sees his creation in the light of the forge fire. "Just like I did for Rani, I tried to design something to honor Rogue."

Akita is impressed with his skills yet again. The marker has two daggers crossed at the tips, with a Wyvern perched above that crossing. Another Wyvern with its wings spread wide, each wingtip touching the hilts of the daggers and its mouth is open as if it is roaring in defiance. Hanging around the neck of the flying Wyvern is a chain with a single drop of metal like a teardrop.

Akita shakes her head, "I don't know where you found the time to make that, but it is stunning. The teardrop is appropriate, and only a few will understand it. I thank you for your service to the Keep and for being a friend. I am going to make an announcement for everyone to meet us on the hill."

She finds Olek at the Keep entrance, "Olek, can you have a few guards prepare to bring Rogue to the cemetery?"

Olek answers, "While you were away, we made a wood coffin for him, and I have two guards at the door awaiting your orders."

Akita amplifies her voice, "For those that wish to pay their last respects to our friend Rogue, please start making your way to the cemetery. Annut, Aphorea, Wyverns, Griffins, Horses and Foxes are welcome to join as well."

Akita tells the guards to wait fifteen minutes or so before bringing Rogue to the cemetery. As she starts her own walk out of the Keep, Roguette and Midge join her. They look up as the Dragons and Wyverns fly over, followed by the Griffins. The horses, Apothecary and Judgement soon trot by them and out of the Keep.

Roguette states, "Wow, I didn't expect that. I mean I knew Ransom and Drako would join but not the others."

Akita chuckles, "Wait till you get closer because if I am not mistaken, they will have their own way of honoring Rogue."

Ghod catches up with Akita with the marker wrapped and balanced on his shoulder.

As they walk out and up the slight hill, even Akita is taken aback by the sight before her. One of the Dragons has a deep hole already dug. The mounts have lined up with Annut and Aphorea in the middle, two Wyverns on each side, then the two Griffins lying regally in font of Annut and Aphorea.

Blitz has found a place between the two Griffins. Apothecary and Judgement on the ends. Some of the Keep workers have gathered nearby, and the soldiers have a full regiment, with swords drawn in a salute and General Ambrose out in front. Of course, right next to the grave site is Greenbean, Fab Ulous, Ishvet, Vivian, Gavin, Ordyn, Meh-Kola, Shamash, Ixenvorlux, Wulf and Darkwing. Roguette and Midge join the group. Vicar steps up next to Akita on her right side and Ghod comes to a stop on her left.

Akita turns to look for the guards carrying Rogue to his final resting spot.

As the soldiers come up beside the grave, Gavin uses his roots to make a net to hold the coffin. Draped over the coffin is a tapestry Rogue's sisters brought, depicting the Wyverns he loved so much.

Ghod steps up and with a mighty heave plants the marker at the head of the grave, leaving it covered.

Akita steps up as everyone gathers closer. "We are gathered here to lay to rest our Friend, a Scoundrel, a Protector of this realm, a Rogue extraordinaire, a Brother, and a man of Mystery. The man we knew was a fierce fighter, and a true friend, always there when you needed him. The man others knew was one of the best in his class. We had the honor of his presence in his chosen retirement profession as a good and honorable man. May he rest in peace knowing he was loved."

Akita reaches up and pulls the cover from the marker. Roguette starts to cry, and Midge comforts her. Midge looks to Ghod, "Thank you, that is truly beautiful and embraces our brother for all he was."

Vicar steps up, "Life is not written before we live it, and fate is not predetermined. We each make our own choices in life. Some may be good, and some may have unintended consequences. Rogue carved out his own path in life. Some may have judged it to be the wrong path, yet others may have judged it to align with their own. Neither matter, because it was the life Rogue chose to live. Rogue came to a point in his life where he reflected on his past deeds and judged them unworthy. He chose to live the remainder of his life in a way that he could judge to be better. Meeting these people that surround him now, made it worth it to him to walk a path of redemption. Rogue gave his life so that others may live. He is loved, he is forgiven, he is avenged, and he is redeemed. We now intern his body to the ground from which it was given. May his spirit be now at rest and obscured from the judgment of the living."

Everyone around has a tear in their eye at the very least. Akita is trying to stay strong but is losing that fight, with Roguette, Midge Vivian and Greenbean visibly crying. Wulf comes, puts an arm around her shoulders. Even some of the soldiers are wiping tears from their eyes.

Behind them Drako and Ransom roar, as they rise up, flapping their wings. Apothecary and Judgment simply preform a horses' bow. The Griffins stand and bow with their wings spread out behind them. Annut and Aphorea, bow their heads. As Aphorea raises her head, she begins singing a sorrowful song of honor, that everyone can hear in their minds. Hunter and Warrior take to the sky and fly a pattern of a heart barely missing each other in flight. As they land, they put one wing over their friends Ransom and Drako.

When the song ends, Roguette and Midge are amazed and so touched, that they sob uncontrollably.

Akita respects the moment of silence, then straightens herself, and wipes her eyes, "A special dinner is being served in about two hours, everyone is welcome to join."

Gavin uses the roots to lower the coffin slowly, as Drako walks up to cover the grave. People start heading back to the Keep.

Vicar hands the sisters, Rogue's dagger, and tobacco pouch then walks away with Ordyn.

Mandrake joins the team and the sisters at the head table for dinner. "Darkwing, this is truly a unique language that must be spoken for the ritual. I think it would take me years to learn the entire language, good thing I don't need to do that, or you would be powerless for a long time." Mandrake chuckles.

Darkwing bows his head, "If you want to learn the language, be my guest, but after the ritual, please. When I was captive not having my magic was horrible, but now I do feel completely naked."

Mandrake smiles, "Don't you worry any. I am meeting Thoraxian after dinner to keep going. Honestly, the only reason he is letting me eat and maybe sleep later is I need my strength for the ritual. He is determined to help get this fixed."

Midge is sitting quietly at the table. She takes her mug and taps her plate with her knife. "Excuse me. I would like to say Thank you to you all. I know my brother and had always figured he would just disappear one day. I never dreamed he would have found friends and a righteous cause, nor that he would have saved any lives other than his own butt. What you all did for him and waiting for us to get here means the world to me. I just wanted to say that."

Roguette looks at Midge, "Quit being so sappy. However, you took the words right out of my mouth. Thank you."

Akita looks at the team. "It's time to eat, drink and share memories. We all want to be rested up over the next few days. We deserve it, but then we will start concentrating on the destruction of the Dark Wizards in Darkforest because none of us, our friends, nor family will be safe until they are gone."

Ishvet states, "I agree, we need to destroy them, but we need a week off to recharge, investigate and study my father's Keep. Cliffshade Keep is good-sized, but unfortunately, I was not raised there so I know nothing about it."

Ordyn holds his mug up, "Here, here. I fully agree with you. Then we run recon too, around the area."

Gavin chimes in, "Well if we are going to take a week off, I have a Wyvern mother and eggs to check on."

Greenbean winks at a few of the others, "We have some other important things to tend to as well."

Akita announces, "I am going to go take a hot bath and go to bed. We have been going non-stop. I need some me-time."

Wulf states, "I will walk you to your room, as I am going to retire to my room as well."

Ishvet, Darkwing, and Ordyn all nod, "Sure you are." They state in unison, laughing.

CHAPTER 21
RESTORATION AND REFLECTION

Darkwing was up early in the morning to watch the sunrise from his room in the Keep. He had already been down to the kitchen to get a big mug of coffee. He savored this moment in the day when the dark of night is slowly melted away by the morning sun's first rays of light. It's so peaceful and serene, he could almost forget the events of the past few months and being without his magic. He forgot how coffee felt without his magic, he would never let it cool down before because his ice abilities did it for him. Now it's almost too hot to drink. He thinks to himself, "It's the little things that I miss the most." He chuckles softly to himself while staring at the horizon watching it shift from light pinks to reds, then to oranges. He muses, "It's going to be a good day."

Thoraxian lands in the courtyard and is met by Ghod and Mandrake. They are going over the plans for the altar that needs to be built to focus Mandrake's magic on the vessel and ultimately restore it to Darkwing. Thoraxian gives the details to both, "The main pedestal needs to be three-feet off the ground and the top of the altar needs to be in the shape of an "X" with restraints at each end of the "X". I know Darkwing won't like it, but it's going to be painful for a moment and we can't have him moving around. Ghod, do you think you can make this in a few hours?"

Ghod scratches his imaginary beard under his mask and visualizes the altar that needs to be built, "Sounds easy enough, it's very straight forward. I can have it done in less than two hours."

Mandrake chuckles, "I told you he could build anything you wanted."

Thoraxian nods and speaks to both their minds, "Mandrake it's time to practice your pronunciation again. If you say one word wrong, you could incinerate Darkwing into a pile of ash. Ghod I will check in with you in one and a half hours to inspect the altar."

Mandrake turns and heads for the Keep to go to the library and work on his pronunciation of the incantation. Ghod goes back to his shop to get the materials together for the altar and Thoraxian takes flight to return to Annut's Cave.

After Thoraxian lands, he decides to contact Darkwing and let him know exactly what he is in for during the ritual, "Darkwing, are you prepared for today?"

Darkwing answers back in his mind, "I am as ready as I'm ever going to be. It was a hell of an experience having it ripped out of me, I can only imagine what it's going to feel like having to shove back into me."

Thoraxian continues, "It is not going to be pleasant I can assure you. Mandrake must be very precise with his pronunciation of the Dragon words, or you could burn up from the inside out. I just want you to know the risks."

Darkwing takes a deep breath and clears his throat, "I have had this magic for so long that it feels like a piece of me is missing. I can't stand how I feel without it. If I had the choice, I wouldn't live the rest of my days without it. I will endure the temporary pain to feel whole again."

Thoraxian slightly chuckles, "I don't mean to laugh Darkwing, it's just that I never cease to be amazed by the race of Men. You on one hand can be so brave and noble, reaching out to lift others up and make sacrifices to help your friends. On the other hand, you have Men like King Carthon that only desire power and will do anything malicious to gain more of it. I see it in all the new races in this world. All your friends work to make this world better. They fight for justice and peace. That's what the Dragons have embodied for millennia. Us Dragons are almost extinct in this world, and it makes my journey to the beyond much easier knowing that all of you will be carrying on that ideal."

Darkwing sniffles a little bit, "Thoraxian I believe in what you call the 'new races". I see way more good in this world than evil. Evad Chaos, Leader Feron, and King Carthon are not representatives of the majority of the people that live in this world. They are the exceptions."

Thoraxian smiles even though Darkwing cannot see it, "Little one you give me hope. I hope I am around long enough to see you and your friends make a real change in this world. However, at this time, be ready to meet in the courtyard in little more than an hour and we will begin the ritual."

Darkwing sits at his table by the window in his room for a moment and watches as the skies turn to bright blue and the lazy pillowy clouds float by to unknown destinations. Then it dawns on him that he needs to message Stan and have his buddies fly down to Blackwing Keep immediately.

Darkwing jumps up from his stool and runs to the library to send a message through the Seeking Shard. When he enters the library, he sees Mandrake poring over parchments making notes and talking to himself, "Oh, sorry to interrupt Mandrake, I just need to send a quick message and then I'll leave you to your studies."

Mandrake looks up in surprise, "Oh it's no bother. I have it memorized now. Thoraxian is a good teacher. Yes, yes, go ahead and send your message. I'll be headed out in a moment to the courtyard for Ghod to finish the altar."

Darkwing says the spell to send the message to Stan and relays his wish for Martyn and Mylar to fly as quickly as possible to Blackwing Keep. Now he just has to wait until everything is ready. He wants to speak to Akita beforehand to see what her plan is with people spectating what may be an utterly painful experience for him.

Akita is sitting at the head table in the dining room when Darkwing enters. She is eating breakfast and speaking with Wulf and Vicar about how touching Rogue's funeral was. She senses Darkwing and invites him to the table, "Darkwing come, get some breakfast with us before your big day starts."

Darkwing goes and sits at the table but tells Quinn that he'll only have coffee for right now. He looks at Vicar and Wulf then Akita, "I best not eat before the ritual. Thoraxian says that the process is going to be painful for me. It will be one thing for my friends to see me writhe in pain and holler out, but it would even be worse if I vomit all over myself too."

Akita looks to both Wulf and Vicar for any indication of what she should say, "I think I understand Darkwing. If you would rather not have anyone there when the ritual happens, I will make it so. It's the least I could do for you."

Vicar shakes his head in agreement, "Akita, he has been through enough with the Cloud Giants. We don't need to be there during the ritual. We can wait for him right here and when he's strong enough, we will still be here for him."

Akita stands up, "It's decided then. I will let everyone know that they all need to be inside the Keep during the ritual or it could interfere with it. Darkwing we will be right here for you sending positive energy."

Darkwing gets up, grabs one more swig of his coffee and heads out to the courtyard. Akita enlists Annut's help in sending her message to everyone at Blackwing Keep to stay inside during the ritual.

Ghod is putting the finishing touches on the altar as Darkwing shows up. Darkwing gets a chill from looking at it. It looks just like the one he was strapped to in the Cloud Giant Temple. He is starting to get nervous now. He swallows hard and then takes a deep breath, "Ghod I have to tell you, this is not the prettiest thing you have ever made."

Ghod chuckles and stands up after adjusting some bolts underneath, "It may not be pretty, but the Black Dragon assures me that it will get the job done."

Thoraxian lands with a thud next to both of them and Mandrake can be seen walking up from the Keep doors. It's close to mid-morning and dew is still on the grass and the heat of the noon sun isn't quite upon them. Ghod looks to the sky, "It's going to be a hot one today. I don't envy you laying on this thing in the sun. you might as well be on a frying pan."

Thoraxian enters all three of their minds, "Oh he won't have to worry about that, once Mandrake begins the incantation, the sky will fill with storm clouds. The lightning in the air is crucial to this going smoothly."

Ghod bows slightly, "With that gentleman, I will leave you to your wizardry." He turns and walks back to his blacksmith shop.

Darkwing reaches into the pouch attached to his belt and pulls out the vessel. It is still glowing blue. He hands it to Mandrake. Mandrake motions for Darkwing to climb onto the altar and to place his feet and wrists in the straps. Darkwing climbs on the altar and does as Mandrake instructed.

Mandrake straps Darkwing down at all four points then takes his place between Darkwing's feet. He then starts reciting the first part of the incantation. Black ominous clouds start to form above, and the low rumbling of thunder fills the air. As Mandrake repeats the first part again, lightning crackles in the clouds. The flashes of light reveal the slightly worried expression on Darkwing's face.

Thoraxian speaks to Darkwing's mind, "Darkwing try to relax as much as you can. The next part of the incantation will put you in a dream state. You will still feel pain, but your mind will be protected."

Mandrake holds the vessel over Darkwing's body, then levitates it from his hand to about four inches above Darkwing's chest. He begins reciting the second phase of the incantation. First, Darkwing's vision gets blurry then a buzzing sound starts in his head. His body begins to feel heavy. Mandrake repeats the incantation, and the vessel begins to spin above Darkwing's chest. The blue glow intensifies, and the intricate metal casing opens like an upside-down lily blossom.

After a few moments, the small spherical stone slowly falls below the vessel and stops two inches above Darkwing's chest. Mandrake recites the third and final part of the incantation and tiny streams of lightning shoot out of the glowing blue stone into Darkwing's chest. Darkwing cries out from the pain as he is repeatedly struck. Mandrake repeats the incantation and speaks the loudest he has spoken so far. His voice begins to sound like thunder, deep and invasive.

Darkwing cries out even louder as the lightning from the stone rips into his flesh. Faster and faster the lightning strikes him then abruptly stops. The spherical stone shatters into dust and a blue ball of energy replaces it. The ball flies into Darkwing and his body convulses for half a minute. His skin turns a light blue color and Mandrake can see Darkwing's breath as if it is a cold winter's morning. Mandrake repeats the last phrase of the incantation and

Darkwing's skin returns to normal, and Mandrake can no longer see Darkwing's respiration.

Mandrake waits for a few more moments to see if the joining is going to stay. Darkwing went unconscious at some point at the end of the ritual and the vessel fell to the ground when the stone shattered. Mandrake feels confident that all went well but he will have to wait until Darkwing regains consciousness to know for sure.

Thoraxian speaks to Mandrake, "You did a great job Mandrake. I could hear the spirit of the Ice Dragon as it reentered Darkwing's body. It said that it was home."

Mandrake breathes a little deeper and relaxes his shoulders slightly, "That was intense! At one point I felt the thunderstorm go through me."

A weakened voice replies, "Well you could have kept that lightning to yourself, those bad boys hurt. You can stop worrying though, I'm intact and I can feel my powers better than ever. Thank you both so much. Now if you wouldn't mind, do you think you could unstrap me?"

Mandrake jumps and starts unstrapping Darkwing from the altar. Darkwing slides off the side and Mandrake supports him. Mandrake puts an arm around him and walks him to the Keep doors.

When they get there, Darkwing turns and reaches out to Thoraxian.

Thoraxian nods his proud Dragon head then looks at the altar. He takes in a deep breath and exhales a stream of fire onto the altar, melting it into a pool of molting iron. Thoraxian then speaks to all in Blackwing Keep, "Skrymir Darkwing is now whole again, may he ever be frosty!" Then he flies off to Annut's cave for a midday nap.

The storm clouds begin to dissipate, and two black figures backed by the sun are headed for the Keep. Darkwing hasn't even taken a step inside the doorway when he starts hearing Martyn yelling at him. Feeling strength coming back to him, he pulls away from Mandrake and walks out to the courtyard to meet Martyn and Mylar.

After hearing Thoraxian, the team decides to go out to the courtyard to meet up with Darkwing and see what state he is in. Akita comes out of the Keep doors first and runs into Mandrake. They both stand there and watch as the two big Roc Owls land and run over to Darkwing and give their version of a hug, Darkwing is lost in wings. A tear falls down Akita's face and she makes her way to the reunion. The rest of the team files through the Keep door and gathers around the Roc Owls and Darkwing. Some are clapping and laughing, and some have tears in their eyes. They are feeling as whole as Darkwing is in this moment. Evil has been thwarted and their friend has his powers back.

Ghod comes up from the blacksmith shop and pushes through the crowd that has gathered. In his hand is a large pitcher of tea. He gets to Darkwing and reaches out with the pitcher in hand, "I'll take those ice cubes now."

A week has passed since Darkwing received his power back. Darkwing flies home for a couple of days to make sure his staff had supplies and to reassure the rest of the Owls in his aviary that he is okay.

Midge and Roguette left the day after to go put Rogues affairs in order. They must notify other family members they were unable to contact on short notice.

Aphorea - the Brilliant returned to her cave in the Voskaola Mountains because it is still not safe for the Dragons. Before she left, she promises to visit again, as she was happy to spend time with others.

Greenbean, Wulf, Olek, and Darkwing have spent a lot of time with their hatchlings. The hatchlings' growth has everyone amazed. The carpenters of the Keep have been working hard to complete the corral for the hatchling feeding area. Shamash has planned for livestock to be brought up to the valley.

Gavin has spent time with Alura and her eggs. The Wyverns have a much shorter incubation time. It is only a matter of months before they will see her hatchlings.

On the fourth day, Mandrake and Vicar receive word from Prayla that the ship is coming in from Omoth. The next morning Skip arrives at the Blackwing Keep gates with a wagon full of Wulf's belongings and his own. The twins are happy to see their friend, but also curious about what is happening in Omoth that would make him leave. After taking Skip to his quarters and stowing Wulf's belongings in his room, the four men meet Meh-Kola in the dining room for an Omoth reunion and talk of home.

Ishvet and Vivian have been off flying for long periods of time on their Griffins, Orien and Zora. Without saying so out loud they have become a couple, and now Akita and Wulf can tease Ishvet and Vivian, just as he has done to them.

Greenbean and Fabby took a small trip to Salthall to check on her inn. She has to admit that Akita was right about having someone to run the inn that is not addicted to the Greenbean coffee. The shop was in a sad state when they returned. She hires a manager to handle her affairs, as she will be busy for a time hunting Dark Wizards with the team.

Ordyn has been working with Ghod on a new design for a long sword. Ordyn has an idea for a lighter-weight blade that can be swung faster so that the Greatsword fighters can get in and out of a fight faster and do massive damage. He knows that the Dark Wizards will use all types of magic, which adds a new dimension to fighting. They have also been working with Lieutenant Olek to develop a new fighting style for the Blackwing Keep army that uses warding rings to protect the soldiers from many offensive magic spells.

Akita and Wulf have kept themselves busy with affairs of the Keep. They manage to escape for alone time or dine in her room. When they do escape the Keep for flights, they take Ransom and Warrior, who seem to have developed a close friendship as well.

Thoraxian – the Shadow has decided to stay close to Blackwing Keep. He and Annut have been working on a cave next to hers and have already dug out quite a big area for him to make his home in. Since the destruction of the Magma and Cloud Amulets was felt by all Dragons, Annut and Thoraxian have made contact with several that are in hiding across Alahora. They haven't shared many details with Akita and the team out of respect for those Dragons' security.

About six days after Darkwing's ritual, Shamash received a message from Earl Jarkon detailing the securing of the Dragon Temple from the Dark Wizards. He stated that most were killed in the fight and that he had the survivors locked in his dungeon. He asked that Vivian and Ishvet be sent immediately to Elderwolf Keep, to question the Dark Wizards.

Vivian and Ishvet pack supplies, including two truth rings, and say their goodbyes to everyone before leaving Blackwing Keep. They take off from the Keep courtyard and head for Elderwolf Keep in the region of Stonia. Vivian is excited to be going home. Ishvet hopes that questioning the Dark Wizards from the Dragon Temple will lead to the whereabouts of his father.

CHAPTER 22
CLIFFSHADE KEEP

King Carthon lands his Owl Roc, Hetzer, on the grand balcony of Cliffshade Keep. Several Dark Wizards are waiting on the balcony for the King to dismount and resume his rule over the lands of Astya. Currently his Steward Volaern Nightleaf, a ruthless Dark Elf, has ruled in his stead. King Carthon has been away for months serving the Cloud Giant King, King Cirus, in his endeavor to gain control of the continent and uncover the secrets of the Amulets of Power.

Now the Cloud Giant King Cirus retreats to the Cloud Realm leaving King Carthon in charge and the Dark Wizards will have to protect their own. King Carthon sees this as his opportunity to show his true power. He has been obscuring the true amount of power that he possesses. He waited for his chance to betray the Cloud Giant King, but that opportunity never came. The secrets of the Amulets of Power were discovered but are unable to be recreated.

King Carthon dismounts, straightens his robes, and looks over his followers, "Tell me you have good news about my special project. I just spent a week traveling across Alahora to get home."

Volaern steps forward and smiles, "Yes, my lord. We have the subject in your laboratory. The subject is in a state of half-life. Leader Feron brought her to us before he flew to the Island, and we have been preparing the chamber to your specifications ever since."

King Carthon laughs and smiles, "That fool went and got himself eaten by that Black Dragon right before we were to leave the Island. Good riddance, I have enough imbeciles around me as it is. As to my special project, did you have any problems finding the ingredients I need?"

A short wild-haired Dark Wizard steps forward and slightly bows, "My lord, my brother had everything that we needed and had it shipped to us shortly before the Duchess murdered him in cold blood. My Lord please allow me to avenge my brother and destroy Blackwing Keep."

King Carthon glares at the short Wizard and speaks in a harsh tone at first, "I have told you that you will have your chance Aevid Chaos. Know this, your brother Evad was reckless and ignorant. He brought his death upon himself by assassinating the Duke. The Duchess is no pushover. She has power and a whole team behind her, including my son."

Aevid begins to speak, but King Carthon puts up a hand and stops him, "Volaern, see to the preparations for the next phase. I am weary from my long journey across Alalohra. I had to evade a whole platoon of Earl Elderwolf's armored Griffins just to make it here unseen. They have already taken the temple from the looks of it. I will be in my chambers, and I am not to be disturbed until morning"

All the Dark Wizards and Volaern bow and move aside for King Carthon to go into the Keep. King Carthon makes his way to his chambers and locks the door behind him. He walks into the bedroom area and removes his outer cloak, then his dress tunic. He places his hand upon his chest and feels the lump beneath his undershirt. He speaks to the lump, "There is no reason to obscure you now, is there?"

King Carthon closes his eyes and crosses his arms; he begins a reversal spell directed upon himself and a powerful spell of concealment is lifted revealing a pulsating aqua blue light emanating from the lump. He reaches under his shirt and pulls the lump out then lets it fall. The glow starts to fill the room and the amulet is out in the open. King Carthon looks down and picks up the amulet in the palm of his right hand, "There you are, blue as the ocean, deep as the night sky. Soon I will release all of your might upon the world, and they will cower and pledge themselves to us by the legions."

He stares at the Amulet of Power for a few more moments hearing the voice of the sea in his head. He now knows that the amulet was created by ancient Soul Magic of the Dragons and that the souls inside this Sea Amulet are the ones that have been speaking to him. He muses to himself that King Cirus would have killed him if he had known that the Sea Amulet of Power was beside him that whole time underneath my shirt. This makes King Carthon chuckle and shiver at the same time. After having his moment, he sees that his bath is drawn and ready for him. He climbs down the steps into the sunken tub that is at least six men wide on all four sides and three-foot deep in the middle.

As he steps in, the water slithers up his legs and then his body, drawn to the amulet. Once he sits, he takes his pointer finger and swirls it on the surface in a clockwise motion. All the water in the tub begins to swirl around in the same motion. King Carthon relaxes in the whirlpool tub until his finger and toes become pruned. Then he retires to the bedroom for a comfortable night's sleep in his own bed.

The next morning the servants wake him to a large breakfast of cured ham, bacon, sausage, poached eggs, and toast with a tall goblet of fresh cow's milk. He barely finishes his breakfast when Volaern comes into the chamber to give a morning update. Volaern looks tired and distraught from not sleeping the night before,

"My Lord you were correct. I just received word that the temple was besieged by Earl Elderwolf's forces. Almost all the Wizards and staff were killed. The ones that remain alive have been taken back to Elderwolf Keep for questioning. Luckily no one in the temple knows your plans or your whereabouts, but it's only a matter of time before they come here seeking you out."

King Carthon sits back in his chair and rubs his beard, thinking of his plans and the events that have transpired in the last few days, "Everything is about to change for them, and they do not even know it. Was all the research from the temple moved to my laboratory last week like I asked?"

Volaern promptly states, "Yes, my Lord. Your acolytes have been pouring over all of it since the crates arrived. They have pieced together the ancient language that you will need to unlock the power of the Dark Gods. The chamber was completed overnight and the woman that was found beside Evad Chaos' destroyed lair is secured inside."

King Carthon's eyes light up as a sinister grin forms upon his face, "Won't they be surprised when they see their friend again. Evad relayed all the names and descriptions of Duchess Blackwing's team to me shortly before the day he died. This woman's name was Jessa Redmayne. She was some magicless Fighter from Neg Grove. Apparently from the information that I received recently she was presumed dead and left to the sea in the beginning moments of the assault on Evad's lair. One of my Wizards found her barely clinging to life on a small rock quite far down the coast. He had enough wits about himself to preserve her and bring her to me. She has been in a coma ever since he found her and will only wake after she has been transformed."

Volaern snickers and wrings his hands as King Carthon speaks of his upcoming plans, "My Lord shall I go to the laboratory and assist you for the first phase?"

King Carthon stands and shakes his head no, "That won't be necessary at this point. I have all the help I will need." King Carthon pulls out the Sea Amulet and shows it to Volaern.

Volaern gasps and slightly leans back, "MY LORD! Is that the Sea Amulet of Power that you have spoken about? Why did you not tell me that you had it?"

King Carthon scoffs, "I could not reveal this to even my closest advisor, I could not risk that even a whisper of a rumor would reach King Cirus' ears. I have had this amulet for twenty years ever since my soulmate Ashonia gave it to me. She was its guardian. However, she was taken from me in more ways than one. Our lives were never meant to be a fairytale. I vowed to keep it hidden away for the sake of our son Ishvet, but it kept calling to me and I could not resist its magnificence. Now that Cirus is leaving this world, I will be the most powerful Wizard on the continent. Now go and head off any leads that could draw my Son or Duchess Blackwing to the Keep. I have work to do below."

Volaern scurries out of the King's chambers and King Carthon gets dressed and goes to the large library of the Keep. In the corner of the very back of the library is a set of shelves that conceal an entrance to a long winding set of stairs that descend into the bowels of the earth below the Keep that sits on the edge of a cliff. As King Carthon reaches the bottom of the stairs a doorway opens to a gigantic six-story cavern that is as big as a farmer's field. Several rooms are lined up against the sides of the great cavern and within are collected relics and stores of exotic ingredients.

About halfway into the cavern is an enormous glass and iron chamber the shape of a large cauldron. However, this chamber is open on top and has scaffolding winding around it all the way to the top. Several Wizards are pushing barrels up the scaffolding and emptying their contents into the chamber. It is almost completely full. In the middle on the surface of the greenish liquid is a small raft with Jessa Redmayne laying upon it.

King Carthon approaches a Master Wizard and is handed a scroll with an ancient language written upon it, Kind Carthon looks over the characters and closes his eyes thinking about the correct pronunciations of this long dead language. He opens his eyes and nods in acknowledgment to the Master Wizard and the Master Wizards walks away.

King Carthon walks up the scaffolding to the top of the chamber and speaks loud enough for all the Wizards and staff inside the cavern to hear him, "We are about to begin the first phase of the transformation. Lower the Wyverns into the chamber."

Above the chamber is a pulley system and attached to it are two hoists. Hooked to the hoists are large nets with the bodies of two Wyverns inside. The nets are lowered and released, and the bodies of the Wyverns fall into the green liquid. King Carthon reaches out his right arm in the direction of Jessa Redmayne and controls the green liquid around her unconscious body. It starts to swirl, and her body is pulled beneath the surface.

He then grabs the Sea Amulet with his right hand and holds the scroll with his left. He begins to recite the incantation in a loud commanding voice. The amulet begins to glow intensely, and the glow starts to surround King Carthon. After he is done reading the incantation he drops the scroll, falls to his knees, and thrusts his hands in the green liquid. The liquid begins swirling just as his bathwater had but on a much larger scale. A whirlpool forms inside the chamber and incrementally picks up speed. The blue glow that had enveloped King Carthon slides from him into the swirling green Liquid.

King Carthon picks up the scrolls then stands back up and recites the rest of the incantation causing the liquid in the chamber to turn purple and become iridescent. The bodies of the Wyverns and Jessa come together at the center of the whirlpool and begin to melt into a single blob of flesh and scale. Once they are completely joined into an unrecognizable lump, they sink to the bottom of the purple liquid. The whirlpool effect stops and the shimmering purple liquid bubbles as if it is boiling hot.

King Carthon walks back down the scaffolding to his Wizards and staff, "It is a success! Now we must wait for her to grow. Soon she will be a weapon that no one can stand against. I will wield her wrath as the Dark Gods did the Titans. When the process is complete, she will be a Titan reborn, thirty feet tall, have four arms, have control of the elements of ice and fire, and an impenetrable natural armor hair that is as tough as Wyvern scales. Nothing will be able to stop her. That is why the first place that I will send her will be Blackwing Keep!"

To be continued...

ABOUT THE AUTHORS

Theo and I met playing Xbox a little more than eight years ago. We have played several different games together. I'm a Dragon fanatic and love the fantasy worlds created in the books that I have read for years. Theo is a cat lover and very creative. He keeps us laughing and entertained when we party chat. I wanted to write a book and create our own world using the characters we developed in the video games we played and the characters that our friends made. Over two years' time we pieced together our ideas into what is now our first book, Blackwing Keep: Dark Wizards Demise. I could not have gotten this far without my friend and Coauthor Theo Moon. Now that we have that foundation, we were able to complete our second book in less than four months. We are excited to bring you the second book in the "Pact of the Keeps Series" Darkwing Keep: Return of the Cloud Giants.

CHARACTER DESCRIPTIONS

PRIMARY CHARACTERS

AKITA BLACKWING

**Description**: Demonan Female, age 42 in human years (Young for a Demonan), 6ft 2in height, she has a lean muscular build, long dark brunette hair, copper flecked red skin, ears are slightly pointed, she has fiery golden eyes, two deep red horns that start at the forehead and sweep back above her ears then come to a vertical point. She has two wings attached to just above her shoulder blades, the top of her wings rise to slightly above her head and the tips of her wings end at the nape of her knees, they are similar in color to the rest of her body and resemble large bat wings. She has a 4ft tail starting at her tailbone and ending with an arrowhead shape at the tip, fully controllable.

**Status**: Akita Blackwing is the last living heir of the Blackwing Family, after her Uncle the High

Duke Edmond Blackwing died, Akita became High Duchess of Blackwing Keep. She is a strong Fire and Fear Warlock, with some poison spells. Her fear spells intimidate enemies into thinking they are in major danger from much bigger forces than they actually see in front of them. The fire spells are, fire balls, fire tornadoes, fire columns, fire bolts, and smoldering spells. She has many curse spells that inflict pain and syphon the life essence of the foe. She has raised two Wyverns from pups that she found in her travels, they are named Hunter and Warrior. They are her main mounts.

Fab Ulous

Description: Human Male, age 35, 5ft 9in height, short curly blond hair, lean build. Nickname is Fabby, given to him by Akita. He has an unusual sense of style, wearing bright colors, the shirts have frilly necklines and pants are usually tight. His boots are the finest leather and knee-high.

Status: Traveling companion of Greenbean. Unique Cleric who heals and deals damage. His spells include calming, deep healing, as well as javelin of light that sears as it penetrates the foe, burning light, and a blinding light.

GAVIN BROKINHORN

Description: Demonan Male, age 35 in human years (Young for a Demonan), 6ft 3in height, dark red skin with slight metallic bronze sheen. His horns sweep back and curl to the front. He has deep yellow-colored eyes. The edges of his wings look a little tattered. He has a 4ft long tail that starts at his tailbone, it ends in a half arrow at the tip. Gavin is wearing the typical leather hunter's garb with a bow, quiver, and long dagger at his hip.

Status: Gavin grew up in Prayla on his mother and father's farm. He is a Hunter/Ranger, proficient with a Bow and Short Swords. He uses Earth Magic to manipulate plants, earth, and stone around him. He has the ability to befriend and aid the animals of the world. He is stealthy, being able to sneak through forests and Keeps, with a unique invisibility spell that he can use on himself and others. His best friend and traveling companion is a giant fox, named Blitz.

GHOD

Description: Half Orc Male, age 45, 5ft 11in height, his face is a mystery as he is always wearing a mask. He is extremely muscular from his years as a blacksmith. His skin is a light shade of green with dark green eyes. His upper and lower eye teeth are fangs that protrude over his lips.

Status: He is a Half Orc that was raised by Dwarves that found him as an infant in the forest. Growing up he perfected the Dwarven Blacksmithing talents, he is proficient as a Greatsword fighter. He makes his money specializing in Weapons and Armor smithing, with a special talent in enchanting any item with magic. He can be a nasty old grump but once you have earned his respect and friendship, he is a decent old grump.

GRACE O'MALLEY

Description: Human Female, age 40, 5ft 11in, fiery red hair, bright green eyes, lean build. She tends to wear frilly tops, tight leggings, with thigh-high boots and a pirate hat.

Status: She is known as the Pirate Queen of Alahora. She trained as a Rogue and Assassin. She is originally from Darkforest, but when the opportunity came to buy Aquara Keep from Akita's Uncle, she bought it. She has a pirates galleon called the Seahorse with a full crew for her Keep and ship. She has a reputation for being murderous and cruel, but how much is rumor or real, no one knows.

GREENBEAN

Description: Half Orc, age 45, 6ft height. She has long blonde hair she keeps up in a ponytail, bright blue eyes, with a lighter touch of green skin. She is muscular. She likes to dress in a plain tunic with a dark leather vest, pants, and thigh-high boots.

Status: Greenbean was born a Dwarf, at the age of 30, a Wizard she was fighting turned into a Half Orc, however she killed the Wizard before he could change her back, so she is stuck as a Half Orc. She is known as an exceptional Greatsword Fighter, fighting instructor, and a sword for hire. She owns a Café and Inn in Salthall, that specializes in an exotic coffee made from green coffee beans. This coffee is addicting to some, but it has energizing qualities. She is Akita's and Fab Ulous' best friend.

ISHVET BLUESCALE

Description: Half Human-Half Dragonkin Male, age 32, 6ft 5in height. He has deep blue scales with golden eyes, a tall toned muscular body, he has a medium-sized muzzle with sharp protruding teeth, his eye ridges are spiked with small horns, and he doesn't have any horns or ridges on the top of his head.

Status: Sir Ishvet Bluescale was Knighted by his Human father King Edmond Carthon III and has been traveling the country in search of the Dark Wizards that indirectly killed his mother, Ashonia. He is an exceptional Greatsword Fighter. He met Skrymir Darkwing in his pursuit of the Dark Wizards. Skrymir was able to enchant his Sword that is now known as Bitter Bite. He has joined forces with Akita Blackwing to destroy the Dark Wizards of Alahora. His best friend is his mount Rani, she is a Lamassu, which is pretty much a large flying Lion. He recently learned that his Mother was a Bahamut Dragonkin and that she passed on some type of power to him. He calls it the 'Blue Streak' ability; it causes him to glow blue and move at extreme speed while not able to be hurt.

MANDRAKE BLACKBREW

Description: Dragonkin Male, age 40, 6ft 5in height, with a bird of prey like sleek head, intelligent face, with red eyes, blue scaled with a light silver sheen. He is muscular with broad shoulders. He has four-and-a-half-foot-long Dragon-like wings that are mostly aesthetic and could possibly be used to fly if absolutely needed.

Status: Mandrake is from the continent of Omoth. He and his brother came to Alahora to find his parents' murderer. He is a Wizard of Ice magic, using icy bolts, ice walls, freezing rain, and ice floors, combined this with lightning magic and a little wind magic. He can also levitate items and animate ice sculptures. He has the ability to enchant horses with ice wings for flight. He is Vicar Blackbrew's twin brother. Both are in the service of Akita Blackwing as Advisors.

OLEK THROR

Description: Half Orc Male, age 35, 6ft 5in height, darker green skin with blue eyes and long strawberry blonde hair and a trimmed goatee. He is muscular. As with all Half Orc's his upper and lower eye teeth protrude over his lips.

Status: He is an officer in the Blackwing army. During an attack on Prayla, his skill as a leader was noticed by Akita, and His post in Prayla was moved to Blackwing Keep to groom him to take over for the aging General Ambrose. Currently, he is heading the division of soldiers fighting the Dark Wizards.

ORDYN BAISIN

Description: Bahamut Dragonkin Male, age 300, 8ft height, with a sleek horned head, deep violet eyes, metallic black scales, and black Dragon wings which were granted to him by Bahamut. He dwarfs the other Dragonkin's with his broad stature.

__Status__: Ordyn was a Human man who worked for the Kings and Queens of the realm. He was a devout follower of Bahamut until the day he died. Bahamut resurrected him as a Winged Dragonkin for his dedication in life. He went on to marry a female Dragonkin and have children. After his change, he went back to working for the Royal Family of Oscain. During one of his last assignments for royalty, he received a message that his family had been massacred. He is a Master Greatsword Fighter, whose main objective for the last one hundred years has been to hunt down Dark Wizards and Evil that killed his family. By chance, he has met Akita Blackwing and is now assisting with the demise of the Dark Wizards and their minions.

ROGUE

__Description__: Meso-Drow Elf Male, age 150 in human years, 6ft 2in height. He has dark skin, a black curly mane of hair, golden eyes and a tattooed face. He has a sleek muscular build, that allows him to sneak through small spaces and climb up out of site when needed.

Status: Rogue's real name is not known to anyone. He is a Rogue and Assassin in the Darkforest area of Astya. He has been retired for ten-plus years but enjoys aiding Akita in her many endeavors. He was successful in his old life as a master thief and stealthy assassin, but this could come back to haunt him. He has two sisters, Midge and Roguette who live with him on his farm, where he raises cattle and his two pets Wyverns Drako and Ransom.

SHAMASH

Description: Dragonkin Male, age 35, 6ft 9in height. He has a wide face with a short horn around his head and a beard of horns on his chin, red eyes, and grey scales. He is tall and muscular with broad shoulders. Shamash wears a tunic and pants with a traditional Clerics cloak.

Status: Shamash has been in the employ of Blackwing Keep for about ten years under Akita's uncle, High Duke Edmond Blackwing. He runs everything in the Keep that is not military. He remains a strong advisor to Akita now that she has taken over the rule of the Keep. He is a healing Cleric, with calming spells, light spells, and pain-relieving spells. He has a sister Ixenvorlux who is also a healing Cleric.

SKRYMIR DARKWING

Description: Human Male, age 102 (60 years spent in ice), 6ft height. Shoulder-length black hair, braided beard, and ice blue eyes. He has a muscular lean build.

Status: Lord Skrymir Darkwing was just a common farmer when the Cloud Giants came for the Frost Amulet that was a family heirloom given to his great-great-grandfather. After using the Frost Amulet against some Cloud Giants, he ran and hid in a cave, however because he could not remove the amulet and it froze him solid for over sixty years. When he was freed from the ice, he discovers that he had ice and Blue Fire magic. He can produce ice forms intuitively and can conjure Blue Flames that can heat and illuminate. The special type of ice that he makes is very hard to melt and some can regenerate. The flame will only consume materials if he wills it. Now he has a Keep atop the Voskaola Mountains, an aviary of Owl Roc's (Giant Owls), he has known Ishvet and Akita for many years. Darkwing is assisting them in the pursuit of the Dark Wizards.

VICAR BLACKBREW

Description: Dragonkin Male, age 40, 6ft 5in height, with a bird of prey like sleek head, intelligent faces, with red eyes, blue scaled with a light silver sheen. He is muscular with broad shoulders. He has four-and-a-half-foot-long Dragon-like wings that are mostly aesthetic and could possibly be used to fly if absolutely needed.

__Status__: Vicar is from the continent of Omoth. He and his brother came to Alahora to find his parents' murderer. He is a Cleric, who uses calming spells, deep healing, deep mending, removes pain, induces sleep, creates illuminating light and blinding light. He is known to preside over funerals and weddings. He is Mandrake Blackbrew's twin brother. Both are in the service of Akita Blackwing as Advisors.

VIVIAN ELDERWOLF

__Description__: Human Female, age 34, 5ft 6in height, long blond hair that she keeps up all the time. She has blue eyes and high cheekbones. Her body is very muscular compared to most women her age and height.

__Status__: Vivian is the daughter of Earl Jarkon Elderwolf, ruler of Stonia. She is a Pledged Paladin of great skill, trained by the famous Paladins of Oscain. She can produce shields of pure light, use light to damage targets, and sense Dark Magic. She uses a Mace and Shield fighting style. She wears full plate armor when fighting, otherwise she dresses in very loose comfortable clothing. She met Ghod several years ago and went with him on a mission to collect forging materials. He asked her to aid Akita Blackwing in her fight against the Dark Wizards. On her way to meet Akita, she was attacked by a Basilisk and almost died. Annut saved her life, and she was able to join the team.

WULF WARI

Description: Demonan Male, age 45 in human years (Young for a Demonan), 6ft 5in height. He has a lean muscular build, shoulder-length dark brunette hair, silver-flecked red skin, ears are slightly pointed, he has bright orange eyes, two deep red horns that start at the forehead and sweep back above his ears then curve down around his lower ear. He has two wings attached to just above his shoulder blades, the top of his wings rise to slightly above his head and the tips of his wings end at the nape of his knees, they are similar in color to the rest of his body and resemble large bat wings. he has a four-and-a-half-foot tail starting at his tailbone and ending with a hooked half arrow shape at the tip, fully controllable.

Status: Wulf Wari is a traveler from Omoth, who found himself held captive by Evad Chaos the

Dark Wizard. If the team had not rescued him, he would probably have died inside of the Leviathan. He came in search of a new pet and found so much more. He uses Illusion spells to confuse the enemy. He can use anything around him in a fight, mirror image, invisibility, a distraction spell, as well as fear, stun, and the fire spells.

SECONDARY CHARACTERS

AHHA

Description: Dwarven Male, age 130 (19 in human years), 5ft 1in height. Ahha has a red mop of hair with a red mustache and a red beard down to mid-chest. He has bright green eyes and a sleek muscular for a Dwarf. He is dressed in simple but serviceable armor head to toe. He carries a simple but well-made sword and blade.

Status: He is a traditional Pledged Paladin, who decided to set out with his friends on adventures. He wanted to spend some years seeing his world before settling down to a normal life within the clan.

IXENVORLUX —

Description: Dragonkin Female, age 30, 6ft 5in height. Her scales are a deep yellow with red eyes. Her head is like a cobra hood around a sleek face. She is lean and muscular. She prefers to dress in traditional Cleric robes.

Status: She is a healing Cleric, with calming spells, light spells, and pain-relieving spells. Her brother is Shamash, who is also a healing Cleric. She has traveled to Blackwing Keep assisting Shamash in the running of the keep and to be a healer for the Keep as Akita and team fight the Dark Wizards.

JESSA REDMANE

Description: Human Female, age 34, 5ft 10in height. A tall, muscular female, who is scantily clad in barely enough clothes to cover her body, with colorful tattoos on her sides and back. She has brown eyes, and shoulder-length red hair, with braids most days.

Status: Jessa was orphaned at a young age. She learned to hunt for herself, she would watch soldiers training and mimic their movements, teaching herself how to protect herself. She had a chance of meeting with Akita Blackwing while Akita was fighting some bandits. Akita was impressed with her story and told her that one day she would summon her to Blackwing Keep if she should want a position in the army. It would be after Akita finished her pilgrimage in Warlock training.

JUDAS SWIFT

Description: Halfling Male, age 30, 3ft 5in height. He has a red mop of hair, green eyes, and is lean in stature. He dresses like a Rogue, in a flat floppy hat, a tunic, a leather vest, leather pants, and knee-high boots.

Status: Judas is a Rogue employed as a special messenger and errand-runner for the High Duke Edmond and now Akita Blackwing. Halflings are known to be fast naturally but there is something special about Judas, as he can run a five-day trip in half the time.

KING WINDU

Description: Dwarf Male, age 150, 5ft height. He has dark brown eyes, with his onyx black hair and beard are meticulously groomed. He is quite overweight and wears a Sultan's desert robe with gold embroidery and green accents. Gold rings adorn each of his ten fingers, and an ornate jeweled broach hangs from a thick gold chain to the middle of his chest.

Status: King Windu was raised a Dwarven Fighter which is kind of rare for Dwarves. He struck out on his own at a young age and was curious about the world around him. He had studied artifacts growing up and decided to find them. As time went on, he gained wealth, loyal artifact hunters and over the years he found his way to Oceanfalls, where he decided to take over as King in a coup. He has successfully ruled for many years and is known to have a vault full of relics, artifacts and what he calls collectables. He sometimes employs Dark Wizards, Rogues, and Assassins to gain what he wants most.

MAGRATH BATTLEBREAKER

Description: Half Orc Female, age 40, 5ft 10in height. A tall, shapely female with long dark hair and bright green eyes. She wears leather tunic, leather vest, leather pants and thigh-high leather boots, with specially made silver gauntlets.

Status: She is a Greatsword Fighter, who is the last survivor of her battle group against a band of trolls. Her current husband, Ouch, saved her from certain death and they decided to travel and live great adventures rather than fight battles for the sake of battling. While adventuring, she and her husband met Akita Blackwing and took her up on adventurous employment.

MEH-KOLA

Description: Fenton Female, age unknown, she has a cat-like body mostly covered in short dark gray fur with vertical black stripes. She has a scaled region that starts at her neck and travels to the tip of her tail. Meh-Kola has two bat-like wings that are attached above the shoulder blades of her front legs. Her tail is covered in scales and resembles a Dragons tail with tiny horns running the length of it.

She has very sharp retractable claws on all four paws.

__Status__: Meh-Kola is from Omoth, little is known of her back story. She is an Assassin and Thief for hire. She has a very different way of speaking. She refers to herself as "One" which is the traditional Fenton way. She has a very special ability to "Blink" through seemingly solid objects. However, she must only see light on the other side of the obstacle that she is going through. Her razor-sharp claws can cut through almost any material. These abilities are uncommon for a Fenton. Meh-Kola met Vicar and Mandrake Blackbrew on the continent of Omoth many years ago and befriended them. She met Rogue through the Assassins Guild in Alahora. She has recently been invited to be a part of the team from Blackwing Keep that is pursuing the Dark Wizards.

MIDGE

__Description__: Halfling Female, age 40, 3ft 4in height. She has blonde hair and brown eyes and a slight build. She wears natural forest color clothing to better blend into the forest.

__Status__: She is a Hunter/Ranger, with earth magic, that is proficient with a bow and dagger. Her brother is Rogue, the man of mystery. When he goes out on a mission she often worries as to if she will see him again. They have a little sister named Roguette who has followed in Rogue's footsteps.

OUCH BATTLEBREAKER

Description: Dwarf Male, age 147, 4ft 11in height. He is a typical-looking dwarf, short and stocky. His dirty blonde beard hangs to the bottom edge of his chest, and mustache is wider than his face and turns upward at the ends.

Status: His name is Gozic Battlebreaker, but he earned the nickname ouch because in training he would always holler "Ouch" when he was hit. Ouch has a very quirky sense of humor. He was raised as a Pledged Paladin, but going against clan tradition, he trained himself to be a Devout Paladin like his mother, to be a healer. He met his wife, Magrath, as she collapsed after a battle, near death. Ouch saved her life on that fateful day, and they have never been apart since.

ROGUETTE

Description: Meso-Drow Elf Female, age 35 in human years (Young for Elves), 5ft 11in height. She has coppery brown eyes, long brunette hair kept in a ponytail, and slim build.

__Status__: She has followed in her brother's footsteps as a Rogue and Assassin. Not much is known about her, as she wants to be as mysterious as her brother.

QUINN DRAKZHUL

__Description__: Demonan Female, age 33, 5ft 10in height, with light red skin that has a copper glint, shoulder-length red hair, and brown eyes. She has a three-and-a-half-foot-long tail that tapers down to a barbed point. She is muscular. Her wings are like batwings that match her skin color and reach from the top of her head to behind her knees.

__Status__: Quinn grew up near Salthall. Her parents made her hide her Warlock abilities because she had no training and could not control them. She had heard of a Warlock in Salthall, named Void Roasten, but he would not train a youngling. He advised her to seek out Akita Blackwing for work and training, which she did. Now she works in the kitchens of Blackwing Keep, where she is free to proactively practice her spells and build her abilities up. Recently she has become smitten with Olek Thror.

Skip Bass

Description: Meso-Drow Elf Male, age 155 in human years, 6ft 4in height. He has bright green eyes, long white hair he keeps braided, dark tanned skin, and a lean build. He typically wears green or brown shirts and pants with brown leather boots, so he can hide in the forest better.

Status: Skip is a Hunter/Ranger, with dark magic and earth magic. He is a master with a bow and long dagger. He is from Omoth and old friends of Mandrake Blackbrew and Vicar Blackbrew. He built his home and forge on the edge of the forest near the Port City of Vaile. He has been assisting the Blackbrew twins in the hunt for an Assassin.

ADDITIONAL CHARACTERS

AMBROSE STAPLES

**Description**: Demonan Male, age 90 in human years (Retirement age for a Demonan), 5ft 11in height. His eyes are a silvery brown, his hair is grey, his skin is light red with a silver sheen, and wings to match. He wears the uniform of the Blackwing Keep military all the time.

**Status**: General Ambrose worked his way up the ranks in the Blackwing Keep army from a young age. Where Shamash was and is the right hand of the Keeps ruler, General Ambrose was and is the left hand of the Keeps ruler. He is reaching retirement age and although he was skeptical if Akita Blackwing would be able to fulfill her uncles' shoes, he is quite impressed with recent activities and battles.

BEN WEAVER

**Description**: Human Male, age 18, 5ft 8in height. He has bright blue eyes, dark black hair, and is barely shaving. He is well built for his age. He wears the uniform of the stable hands at Blackwing Keep.

Status: Ben is an orphan that lives with his blind grandfather. He is a street urchin in Salthall until the day he witnessed flying mounts fly over his hometown. His curiosity got the best of him, he had to go see them. The moment he saw them he knew he wanted to work at Blackwing Keep and was waiting to talk to Akita Blackwing first thing in the morning. She accepted him and even found a place for the old grandfather.

BLUE & ROSE BROKINHORN

Description: Demonan Male and Female, Retirement ages, 6ft and 5ft 9in height. Typical older Demonan couple.

Status: Blue and Rose have a good-sized farm just outside of Prayla, where they raise cattle and sheep, as well as some crops. Recently, Blue has been building special pens in hopes of raising Wyverns. Their son is Gavin Brokinhorn, who has recently been working with Akita Blackwing at the Keep.

DUKE EDMOND BLACKWING

Description: Demonan Male, Deceased.

Status: High Duke Edmond Blackwing and his wife lost their entire family, except for Akita to

Annut – the Fast. Her parents, siblings, and their children were all attacked as they headed back to Akita's Keep near Salthall for the summer. Akita had wandered off from the main group. Edmond and his wife then raised her as their own and the sole heir to Blackwing Keep.

DUTCH BLACK

Description: Human Male, age 25, 5ft 8in height. He has brown eyes, dishwater blonde hair, standard build. He wears tunics, pants, and slippers.

Status: Part owner of Mystical Messenger Service in Salthall. His partner is Snappy. Akita is one of their regular customers.

ELGIN BAILEY

Description: Human Male, age 50, 5ft 6in height. He has hazel eyes and greying hair, pudgy build.

Status: He is the owner of the Hungry Boar Tavern and Inn with his wife Lucille. They live in a set of rooms above the Inn, he manages the bar and patrons.

EVAD CHAOS

Description: Human Male, age 45, 4ft 10in height. He is short in stature, brown eyes, brown hair, and power hungry. He wears a cloak of the Dark Wizards and dresses in all black.

Status: He is a Leader of a Dark Wizard sect, under the Grand Master Dark Wizard. He has Goblin minions to defend his cave of treasure and potion ingredients. He has several lower Dark Wizards to do the lower tedious magic work. He has several bands of Bandits to do is killing and gather his ingredients. He is a creator of monsters, murder of Dragonkin and only one of many that are a menace to the realm.

GRETA RISAN

Description: Human Female, age 60, 5ft 5in height. She has bright green eyes, silver-grey hair, muscular form, dressed in long dress with a house apron most of the time.

Status: Greta is the Keeps House Matron. It is her responsibility to make sure the housekeepers and kitchen help keep the rooms clean and meals cooked. She has been an employee of Blackwing Keep since she was a young woman. When Akita came to live with her aunt and uncle, Greta took on the role of nanny.

KING EDMOND CARTHON III

Description: Half Sun Elf/ Half Human Male, age 50, 6ft height Dark Brown Hair, Blue eyes, manicured beard. Tall and lean, but quite muscular.

Status: King Carthon rules the region of Astya from Cliffshade Keep. His family has ruled the east coast region for hundreds of years. He is Ishvet Bluescale's Father. However, the King hasn't been present in Ishvet's life. The King is a well-known Wizard. It has been discovered that King Carthon may be tied to the Dark Wizards plaguing the lands of Alahora.

LEADER FERON

Description: Human Male, age 32, 5ft 8in height. He has brown eyes, stringy black hair, with a skinny build. He stays hidden in his Dark Wizards cloak.

Status: Leader Feron is a scholar from the town of Cliffside in Mina, and a self-proclaimed expert in Dragons. He is currently working for King Edmond Carthon on a special project.

LUCILLE BAILEY

Description: Human Female, age 48, 5ft 3in height. She keeps her hair up in a bun, and is in a dress and apron every day.

Status: Lucille is Elgin's wife, and she supervises the Hungry Boar Tavern and Inn rooms, keeps the kitchen stocked and cooks most of the meals. The couple lives in a set of rooms on the third floor of the Inn.

SCOTCH BROWN

Description: Human Male, age 25, 6ft 3in height. He is long and lanky, but strong. He has hazel eyes, short blonde hair that is always messed up, tanned skin from being in the sun a lot.

Status: Scotch is a stable hand that has been working at Blackwing Keep for a couple of years. At first, he thought it would be a job to get him through until he could save up to travel. Although he still wants to travel, the activities, excitement, and the awesome mounts he takes care of have made it hard for him to leave anytime soon.

SHAM RHAM

Description: Human Male, age 35, 6ft 4in height. He is tall and muscular. He has brown eyes, long strawberry blonde hair that is always pulled back or braided, he is also tan from working in the sun all the time.

Status: Sham is the lead stable hand that has been working at Blackwing Keep for over ten years. He makes sure all the mounts are fed, exercised, and cared for in every way. He has helped raise Akita's horse Nightmare, as well as Hunter and Warrior.

SNAPPY HOUND

Description: Half Wood Elf, age 24, 5ft 7in height. He is an average man, with shoulder-length black hair, brown eyes, and a bright smile. He looks more like his dad than his elven mom.

Status: Part owner of Mystical Messenger Service in Salthall. His partner is Dutch. He uses what little forest magic he has for various tasks and his natural ability with animals, with the Thunder Hawks. Akita is one of their regular customers.

DRAGONS OF ALAHORA

ANNUT — THE FAST: Female Fire Dragon, her scales are red, orange, red-orange, and dark red making her look like fire as she flies. Her horns and ridges are dark red. Recently spotted in the Prayla.

APHOREA — THE BRILLIANT: Ancient Female Ice Dragon, her scales are white. Her horns and ridges are like bright white pearls. Whereabouts unknown.

ASHONIA — THE SKY: Female Water Dragon, her scales are light blue like the sky reflected in water. Her horns and ridges are a darker shade of blue. Last seen in the region of Astya.

BUZZONTIR — THE SCARY: Male Cloud Dragon, his scales are dark grey to black. His horns and ridges are dark black with glowing cracks on the surface that mimic lightning streaking across a black sky. He has not been seen for hundreds of years.

JAXIAN — THE TSUNAMI: Ancient Male Water Dragon, his scales are a mixture of sea green, turquoise and light blues, like a clear ocean water, with turquoise horns and ridges. Vague reports put him in the area of Oscain near the southern coast.

RETHU — THE FIERCE: Male Fire Dragon, his scales are blue like the color of sapphire with blue, royal blue and dark blue scales, his horns and ridges are royal blue. Whereabouts Unknown.

RUKUR — THE BRIGHT: Ancient Male Stone Dragon, He is gold like precious metal, but his horns and ridges are like tarnished gold. Last sighting was 45 years ago in the region of Franken.

THORAXIAN — THE SHADOW: Ancient Male Fire Dragon, his scales are dark black with a silver sheen, his horns and ridges are onyx black and shiny. He was seen in the region of Craonia.

GLOSSARY OF RACES

RACES

o   Bahamut Reborn – Dragonkin biped Humanoid
    Dragon/Demonan Demon Humanoid

- Transformed by the God Bahamut

    - Can be any race before
      transformation

    - Was granted one special ability
      upon transformation

- Any Scale Colors

- May or may not have wings

- Rare to be Fire Breathers

- Any class

o   Dragonkin – biped Humanoid Dragon

- Any Scale Colors

- Do not have wings

- Rare to be Fire Breathers

- Any class

- o Demonan – Demon Humanoid
  - Various shades of Red Skin
  - Precious metal tints to their Skin
  - Leathery Dragon like wings
  - Long tapered tails
  - Any Class
- o Wood Elf
  - Tall Elves
  - Forest Magic
  - Typically, Rogues, Clerics, Hunter/Rangers, Warlocks, and Wizards
- o Sun Elf
  - Shorter Elves
  - Earth Magic
  - Typically, Rogues, Clerics, Hunter/Rangers, Warlocks, and Wizards
- o Meso-Drow Elf
  - Tall Dark Elves
  - Dark Magic
  - Typically, Rogues, Clerics, Hunter/Rangers, Warlocks, and Wizards

- o Half Elf/Half Human
    - Magic depends on which Elf the Parent is.
    - Strength depends on dominant characteristics from Parents.
    - Any Class
- o Human
    - Standard Humans
    - Rare to be Magic Users
    - Any Class
- o Dwarf
    - Short and Stocky
    - Long hair and long beards
        - Beard length will signify age and supposed wisdom.
    - Stone and Metal Experts
    - Rare to be Magic Users
    - Typically, Paladins, Fighters, Greatsword Fighters
- o Half-Orc
    - Half Human Orc.
    - Tall and muscular.

- - Protruding Upper and Lower Eye Teeth Fangs.
  - Typically, Fighters and Greatsword Fighters.
- o Fenton – Quadruped
  - Flying Cat
  - Long Hair or Short Hair
  - Soft, Supple Bat like wings
  - Magical
    - Blink, Invisibility, Stealth and more.

GLOSSARY OF CLASSES

- ➢ Warlock
  - o Dark Magic
    - ▪ Soul Energy Drain and Projected Fear
    - ▪ Illusions – Mirror Image, Invisibility
    - ▪ Fire – Smolder, Fire Ball, Fire Blast
    - ▪ Power Words – Stun and Kill
- ➢ Wizard
  - o Ice, Lightning, and Wind Magic
    - ▪ Freezing – Chill Touch, Ray of Frost, Wall of Ice
    - ▪ Storms – Control Weather, Meteor Swarm
    - ▪ Electric - Shocking, Lightning Strikes, Chain Lightning
    - ▪ Vortex Winds

- ➢ Cleric
  - o Healing, Power Buffing, Light Damage
    - ▪ Healing with Divinity Light
    - ▪ Searing Light Javelin Magic Spears
    - ▪ Power Buffing with Light
    - ▪ Illumination
    - ▪ Calming spells
- ➢ Hunter/Ranger
  - o Earth Magic/Fighter with Daggers and Bow
    - ▪ Magical and Non-Magical Arrow shots experts
    - ▪ Root Traps
    - ▪ Invisibility and Stealth
    - ▪ Manipulation of Earth and Stone
    - ▪ Special Bond to Animals
- ➢ Rogue/Assassin
  - o Chemistry, Fighting, Stealth
    - ▪ Shadow Cloaking
    - ▪ Dash Invisibility
    - ▪ Potion and Poison Crafting

- - Targeting Blades, Blade Flourish
- ➢ Paladin
  - o Pledged
    - - Light Magic to generate shields of Protection
    - - Empowers team members in close proximity during battle
    - - Detect/Dispel Evil, Good and Magic
    - - Fighter – Shield of Faith
  - o Devout
    - - Light Magic to Heal the Wounded
    - - Heals team members in close proximity during battle
    - - Detect/Dispel Evil and Good
    - - Fighter – Shield of Faith
- ➢ Greatsword Warrior
  - o Heavy weapons – two handed weapons
    - - No Shields
    - - Brute strength
    - - Inner Magic to empower their weapon abilities
      - • Only encompasses the individual

- ➢ Keeps and Territories
  - o Blackwing Keep – High Duchess Lady Akita Blackwing
    - Prayla- Prayla, Stagbreak, Salthall
  - o Darkwing Keep – Lord Skrymir Darkwing
    - Voskaola Mountain, Emberfrost, Deerbreach
  - o O'Malley Keep – Grace O'Malley Pirate Queen
  - o Cliffside Keep – King Edmond Carthon III
    - Astya - Mina, Darkforest, Myst Marsh
  - o Elderwolf Keep – Earl Jarkon Elderwolf
    - Stonia - Neg Grove, Riverhost, Dragon Rest
  - o Oceanfalls Keep – King Windu
    - Craonia – Oceanfalls City, Port Tristan